"Spirits In Our Midst"

Ghost Stories

"Spirits In Our Midst"

Ghost Stories

BJ Lawyer

ISBN Numbers:
Paperback: 978-1-7378975-5-2
Hardback: 978-1-7378975-6-9
E-Book: 978-1-7378975-7-6

Library of Congress Cataloging-in-Publication Data: Has been applied for.

Book Cover Design: Unique Graphic Art / Bradley Peterson /
                      Tucson, Arizona
                      br.peterson@gmail.com;
                      www.bradpetersonart.com

Editorial Services: Jennifer Murgia
                      Jennifermurgia8@gmail.com;
                      www.jennifermurgia.com

                      Janet M., jpmcurated,
                      owner at jpmcurated.com

Formatting: Kari Holloway
                      KH Formatting;
                      khformatting@gmail.com
                      Khformatting.com

Illustrations:
Cover Photo: Original "The Haunted Tower", Manoel
                      C. Lima; mood6063@verizon.net

Longwood:	Photo: Public Domain Image, Manoir Colimacon in France "Meditations" By Loren Grean
The Legend of Lake Blaine Road:	Photo: B.J. Lawyer, Author "The Shortest and Sweetest of Songs" George MacDonald (1824 – 1905)
Carl's New House:	Photo: B.J. Lawyer, Author "Demon" Alexander Sergeyevich Pushkin (1799 – 1837)
The Family:	Photo: B.J. Lawyer, Author "Do Not Stand at my Grave and Weep" By Clare Harner 1934
The Hanged Man's Wife:	Photo: Public Domain Image "The Night Is Darkening Round Me" Emily Bronte (1818 – 1848)
Mandy:	Arrigo Boito (1802 -1856) B.J. Lawyer, Photographer Kris E. Sirk
The Twins:	Photo: B.J. Lawyer, Author "A Jewish Family – In A Small Valley Opposite St. Goar, Upon the Rhine" William Wordsworth (1770 – 1850)
The Old Miner's Cemetery:	Photo by B.J. Lawyer, Author Location: Old Miner's Cemetery, Jerome Arizona "When I Am Dead My Dearest" Christina Rossetti (1830 – 1894)
Cold Hands:	Photo: Public Domain Image "All The World's A Stage" William Shakespeare (1564 – 1616)
The Second Path:	Photo: Public Domain Image "A Parsonage in Oxfordshire" William Wordsworth (1770 – 1850)
The Asbury Home:	Photo: Rodanthe, N.C. Photographer Unknown, Public Domain "One Sea-Side Grave" by Christina Rosetti 1853
Dudley's Remorse:	Photo: Public Domain Image Ernest Dowson "Vitae Summa Brevis" 1890s
What A Bargain:	Photo: Public Domain Image "How Doth the Little Crocodile" By Lewis Carroll (1832 – 1898)

The Voice in
The Freezer: Photo: B.J. Lawyer, Author
                          "The Velveteen Rabbit" Margery
                          Williams (1881 – 1944)

The Boy on
The Pier: Photo: Pok Rie, Malaysia; Public Domain
                            Image
                          "The End of the Pier" Nicole Callihan,
                          Nicole Callihan.com,
                          nicolewriting@gmail.com

Hot Tub Sally: Photo: Andrea Piacquadio;
                            www.pexels.com
                          "The Stolen Child" W.B. Yeats (1865 –
                          1939)

Bucky's Best: Photo: Public Domain Image
                          "The Old Astronomer To His Pupil"
                          Sarah Williams (1837 – 1838)

The Indian: "Sees Behind" by Kirby Sattler,
                          sattlerartprint.com 713-445-7033.
                          With permission.

Author Photo by Mallory-Dalton Glenn Sirk. In Loving
Memory of Kim Clark White

TABLE OF CONTENTS

DEDICATION

For Booleboo, my favorite ghost.

Edward Bailey Miller
1940 – 2015

"Voices of the night, echoed by the winds of time,
Can you not hear them?"

Barnabas Collins (1770 - ?)

LONGWOOD

CHAPTER ONE

I lived in Derwood, Maryland back in 1977, which is close to where this story took place. Back then, I was in tenth grade and trying to fit in. I always hung out with older kids and for the most part had good luck doing it. I never got into much trouble other than teachers finding weed in my locker every now and then or the occasional beer in my backpack. Lucky for me, I managed to talk my way out of a lot of stuff, most times. Unfortunately, in the autumn of 78' I wasn't so lucky.

There was this place in Brookeville, which was the next town a few miles over from my own, although the kids that lived there were still in our high school district. Anyway, as history has it this place was bought in 1935 by an attorney, who eventually turned it into the Longwood Preparatory School for Boys, which opened in 1947, but closed suddenly in 1951. The records were sketchy as to why it closed, but one could only guess. At which time the federal government picked it up and it became a civil defense training center until 1958. Talk has it there were many tests and exercises where personnel were taught how to deal with nuclear aftermath, and the challenges of the training were said to be extremely intense and often gruesome. It was never proven, although many of the old timers still swear to this day that there were many cruelty accusations regarding both man and beast during this time, which could have resulted in the facility's final shut down.

Since the complex was so large, the state decided it would be a perfect sanitarium for the poor and wayward. It remained a sanitarium for a few years until a fire broke out in one of the rooms, set by an eleven-year-old child who suffered from pyromania. A few people burned to death in their beds that night and others died of asphyxiation due to the locks on the doors. Locks were legal back then. Better a fire to end the escape of the crazy than have the crazy loose – or so it seems.

Since then, the grounds and buildings have been off limits and no mention of the sanitarium, or the Civil Defense Training Center has ever been in the newspapers to date. The events that took place at Longwood had always been treated with kid gloves and were very hush-hush. That alone throws red flags everywhere, which for the most part, people ignored.

For a long time, the doors and windows were boarded up to keep the neighborhood hoodlums out, but it didn't take too long for local kids to figure out that breaking in wouldn't be that difficult. Since the place was pretty isolated and not patrolled by police, as far as we knew, it was inevitable that someone was going to get in. The question was who was going to be the first to do it?

Chapter Two

One of the varsity cheerleaders, Isabelle Adams' parents had gone out of town one weekend to participate in some kind of real estate function. You guessed it; they were realtors. Anyway, for two whole days and nights Isabelle had the house all to herself. It didn't take long for her to spread the word about having a party, and by Wednesday of that week she had already collected enough money for some of our older, legal friends to buy us a keg of Bud, two huge bottles of Vodka, a fifth of Jack Daniels, and a shitload of assorted chips, salsa, and other munchies. Her party was officially the talk of the school and most everyone was planning to be there.

Unfortunately for Isabelle, and all of us, the cops broke up the party a little after ten p.m. As it turned out, two rival high schools had heard about the party and so many people showed up it quickly got out of hand. There were a couple of fights on her front lawn and unbeknownst to Isabelle, one of her immediate neighbors had just seeded his lawn. People kept creeping over the property boundary line and after repeated requests for people to stay off his lawn, to no avail, he finally called the cops. Looking back, I don't blame him at all for getting pissed.

So, people got together and decided to take the party to Longwood. Of course, they did. I mean, how perfect, right? Within a half an hour everything had been loaded into trunks of cars and pickup trucks and the party began its relocation to the new destination.

Everyone arrived and parked along the deeply rutted, partially graveled lane that led to the gates. They had been chained and padlocked to prevent any would-be trespassers from getting in. Too bad for them, because evidently no one thought that the trespassers would be young, fit teenagers who could easily climb and scale any iron gate known to mankind.

Once we maneuvered the party favors, especially the keg over the massive gates, we were home free. Within minutes we were all at the building's entrance doors and marveling at its gloomy, weather-beaten stonework. It was all very creepy to say the least and everyone loved every minute of it.

Looking back, if we had been older and not all about the party, we would have noticed the intricate and beautiful patterns in the masonry that someone obviously took a great deal of time and effort to create. But to all of us, it was just an incredibly ghastly looking place that we couldn't wait to explore, preferably high off our asses.

Chapter Three

The beautifully designed French entry doors where chained shut and boarded over, but after searching for another access we finally found a broken window at the kitchen entry on the second floor.

Mike Thompson, a senior and one of the football "elites" decided to make the climb up the wall. It looked like the stonework edging was barely wide enough to accommodate his feet, but he was more than happy to attempt the adventure.

We all watched, sphincters clenched, as he began his assent up the wall, praying that the old mortar wouldn't crumble beneath his weight. Most of the dudes were already buzzed and betting on when he'd fall back to Earth, while the girls mainly stared in fascination and couldn't believe he had the balls to attempt the climb in the first place. When you're young you never stop to think the worst things will ever happen to you. Instead, you think you can accomplish anything. The funny thing is that most of the time you can. It's only later in life you want to slap yourself in bewilderment that you made it out of that stage of your life alive with all limbs intact.

We all watched as he made the climb and before we knew it, he was inside and safe. Three minutes later the lobby windows opened; we entered the building and began setting up the night's extravaganza.

It didn't take long for everyone to look around and the couples began to quickly disappear to explore their own wonderlands. But for a lot of us, being in the main lobby was satisfying enough. The whole place was frightening, and we just wanted to enjoy the party without risking our necks.

All the gruesome stories about the place made the party a hell of a lot more fun and looking back it was the best party I can remember, until the shit hit the fan that is.

The place seemed to cast a spell on all of us. In hindsight, we didn't care about our parents' rules about getting home on time, or even any possible trouble we'd face if we were late getting home. Before long, several of us became mesmerized with walking around the facility and trying to imagine what the folks who were housed there could have gone through during the time they spent at Longwood.

We sat for a while on a bleacher in what had once been an auditorium or gymnasium. The hour was late at this point, and we were all just passing a bowl of weed back and forth, and I was looking towards where a basketball hoop once hung. Its framework was still mounted although the net had long since rotted. The backboard was slanted as time had stolen the strength for it to hang erect; the old preparatory school colors faded to almost nothing. I remembered hearing about a story where some high school kid, a few years before us, was wandering around the place on a bet one night. He wasn't alone as I think the story went, and as I heard it, he opened the door on the second floor and without a flashlight he walked into what he thought was a room. As it turned out, he was above the gymnasium and fell to his death and landed on the free throw line of the basketball court. Evidently at one time there may have been a small landing, possibly to adjust lighting or God knows what. I heard his friends all ran off in fear of getting in trouble and eventually they found his body a week later. The rats and the spiders and whatever else lived in the old place did a number on him and he was barely recognizable.

I always thought how awful that would be. I mean you trust your friends and you never think they'd fucking leave you in a place like that to rot to save their own skin. I guess it is what it is. Sitting there I just knew I'd never think of basketball the same again, and I never have.

CHAPTER FOUR

After we left the gym, we went deeper into the facility and beyond was what looked like the exam rooms. To our surprise the rooms still contained a lot of medical equipment. Perhaps it was all defective or outdated and not worthy of resale, but at any rate we found a lot of it repulsive. To our untrained eyes most of it looked like torture implements.

It didn't take long for the girls in our group to one: want to go home, and two: want to visit the bathroom, and that took us on another adventure.

As we were looking for the bathroom facilities, which we knew would be out of service, and most likely disgusting, we rounded a corner, and stopped dead as we saw a woman crossing the corridor, about ten paces ahead of us. She was sickly thin, and in our flashlight beams her flesh was a pale gray. She had stained, dirty gauze wrapped around her arm as if she had pulled loose from a peripherally inserted central catheter or PICC-line; the end of the gauze swaying alongside her as she took each step. She was dragging what looked like a stained sheet filled with something. She was enveloped in a white, sheer veil and only glanced at us with a sort of uninterested indifference. We wanted to run, but our adrenaline was high, and we were only able to stop and stare. The woman was somewhat bent over as the load she dragged seemed to be very heavy. We all looked at one another and knew that whatever was in that sheet had to be dead or worse. On a second look, whatever was under the sheet looked as if it was moving. It began undulating and contorting as if a million maggots had suddenly hatched under there, were hungry, and trying to escape.

A few of the girls began to cry and run in directions they thought would get them safely outside, but instead, only drove them deeper into the asylum. As they ran, those of us who stayed heard the wails of their panicked voices. At that point we weren't sure if the girls had been caught by some unseen entity or had taken a dead-end corridor and were trapped in the dark. The only thing we knew for sure was that their voices carried throughout the building and screams of pain and terror rang in our ears for months after that night.

The hallways began to shake, and years of dust and neglect filtered down into our eyes and we could barely see the correct route in which to escape.

At that moment we all knew it was time to leave. The stories were true and if we stayed it would not end well for any of us.

To our disbelief the previously locked and chained exit doors opened as we began to run out of the building. As we left, figures appeared in white hospital gowns along the corridors. It looked as if they wanted us to stay. But it also looked as if they were glad we were leaving.

The next night one of the girls was found wandering in the wooded area between Longwood and a nearby subdivision. Her feet were raw and bleeding. Her clothing was torn and saturated with urine and feces. We were told she had gone insane and refused to speak a single word of what happened that night. No one from school ever spoke with her again.

Another girl made it home at daybreak, crying and irrational. When asked about that night in Longwood she only shook her head and refused to speak of it.

Two of the girls were never found. Some people say they still run through the halls of Longwood, screaming as if they continue to search for an escape. Some say you can see them in the tower room on full moons.

I won't ever go back there.

I think that sometimes, the dead want some living company. Even if it's for a short time.

"Come home."

George MacDonald (1824 – 1905)

The Legend Of Lake Blaine Road

Chapter One

The road that leads to Lake Blaine in Auburn County, Maryland is long and rutted. It has no stop signs or warnings of curves or soft shoulders and those that travel it know it can be chancy. It is located on the edge of town and isn't a main route of travel for anyone other than those few who want to live off-grid or maybe want to shack up with a certain someone in an impartial, out of the way place.

At night there is a lot of wildlife that the weary traveler needs to be aware of, and in the winter, the road has no county maintenance so when you figure in the off-cambered angles beneath mountains of snow drifts, well, it's super easy to find yourself in a pickle pretty damn quick if you ain't careful. If you slide off the dirt, there isn't much of a shoulder between you and the steep hillsides, if you're lucky enough to have a shoulder at all at that crucial moment. You are either dead or stuck. In other words, it is a bad fucking road, and if you want to live, you have to pretty much go slow. And just to emphasize again, "slow" is the word that needs to be remembered here.

Of course, there are always those drivers that just don't seem to get it, and those that basically think they are too competent for their own good to follow honest advice. Either group usually wind up hurt in some way or another or, as I said before, dead.

My name is Clarence Abernathy Silus, and I've been around these parts for nearly eighty-nine years now. You can take my advice, or not. If you don't, I can pretty much guarantee I'll be on this Earth longer than you will. It's your choice. Yep. I can pretty much guarantee that.

Oh, did I mention that the drivers who have the good sense to drive safe and come back in one piece usually have some pretty wild stories about seeing a gal in a white gown walking along one specific stretch of Old Blaine? (That's what the locals call it – Old Blaine.) These particular stories are from those that have traveled the road during the night, and yes, they are always at night. Although, why anyone would want to drive that road in the dark is beyond me, but who am I to judge? I'm only stating the facts, yes sir, don't cha know.

It seems that the description of the gal in the white gown that people see isn't always quite clear. Well, at least the stories always seem to differ a little. Some swear she's wearin' a wedding dress; some say it's a gown, like a young girl would wear to a prom, or a fancy school dance. But most seem to agree that she's wearin' a night gown. The reason bein' is that no one notices any jewelry on the gal or even a fancy hairdo, and she's always barefoot. She's never said to be seen carryin' an evening bag, but most of all, they say she looks tired. Everyone agrees on that.

This story's been goin' round fer years and years. I think I was probably about ten when I first heard it, and I'll be going on the big nine-O next March, that is if the good Lord sees fit and the creeks don't rise. But over the years the details vary in many ways. Hell, the next time I hear it I wouldn't be surprised if the gal is holdin' one of those damn cell phones with one of them blue teeth gadgets stuck in her ear. Anyhoo, I just wanna tell ya the facts. The facts that seem to never change. In my book, these are the important truths, the ones you want to watch out fer if you ever travel that stretch of road. Who knows, this advice may keep yer ass alive, so give a listen.

CHAPTER TWO

First off, if you see her, never stop your car after dark. If you have a flat just keep a goin'. Better to have to buy a new rim than a chunk of ground in a graveyard. That's my opinion.

In good faith, I must admit that the gal has never been said to have killed or hurt anyone. But my way of thinkin', is that who really knows fer sure? All the car wrecks along that road, well a good part of em', happened at night. Who's to say she didn't take a part in makin'em happen? Either way, she is known on every account as wantin' to catch a ride. Those that give her a lift all agree that as soon as she enters yer vehicle there's an overwhelming sense of sadness and despair. Lookin' at this young girl makes you remember every sad thing that ever happened to you that you've tried to forget. They also say that as soon as she gets in and closes the door, the inside temperature drops so noticeably you can see every breath you blow out of yer head. People have been known to turn on the heater even in the throes of summer when the heat index is at its highest.

On one particular night in mid-winter . . . I remember it was winter cause this happened just after my birthday and to my very own Uncle Pete, he was comin' over to watch us while my folks went into Hailey's Mills. It was the next town over, and they were gonna pick up some medicine for my little brother, Norris. Our town didn't have a pharmacy yet and his cough was real bad ya see. Anyhoo, when Uncle Pete got to the house he was all shaken up and the first thing he did was sit down on my parent's lumpy old, worn-out couch and put his head between his knees. Now Uncle Pete wasn't a yella' boy, he had some nerve in him and showed it plenty, but not that night. That night he was outright scared and shakin'.

Chapter Three

He waited for my parents to leave cause he knew they were in a hurry to get outta the house and it had already been dark pert near two hours. You know how the sun goes down real early in the winter months . . . Anyhoo, he said he and a buddy just got back from Old Blaine and they barely made it outta there alive. I never asked him what the heck he was doin' out there in the first place, and he didn't tell me. Like I told ya earlier, I was just a young un' myself so I probably shoulda asked Uncle Pete more questions than I did, but I was just too young to know better. I think I was about twelve. Lookin' back, I was surprised he mentioned anything about that night to me at all at my young age. I reckon he was just scared too shitless to know better and had to tell somebody. Like I said, he was pretty shaken up.

It seems he and his friend were headin' back towards town when they saw the girl in the white dress. He said it was long and full and was so lengthy it dragged behind her like a wedding dress, but he knew it wasn't. She had something in her arms, and he couldn't make out exactly what it was although she carried it very carefully as if she was protectin' it.

Pete was sayin' that no matter how many times you hear stories about things to beware of, when you see a girl at night in a thin dress along a dark road, with no shoes, you stop and ask if she needs help. You don't think, you don't try to kick up reasons why you shouldn't, you just stop cause that's the proper thing to do. "So that's what we did," Pete said.

Uncle Pete put his head between his knees again, then sat up and rubbed his forehead.

He told me the gal saw them coming and retreated into the forest line. She hadn't attempted to wave them down or even ask for a ride. She just stood there, out of the way, as if she was almost hiding.

They slowed down and Uncle Pete hollered out his window, asking her if she was okay. When she stepped backward, he threw the car in park and asked her again. She slowly walked toward them, guarding what she carried and wrapping it in her dress, only staring at them.

"Do you have an address? We can drive you there. It's cold and you don't have a coat on," Uncle Pete said.

The girl only stared back and shook her head.

"Come on. Get in the backseat. We will take you wherever you need to go. You just need to get out of this cold weather. We can't leave you out here. It just ain't right"

Uncle Pete said she awkwardly climbed in the backseat, and he noticed she wasn't shivering or seemed cold at all. There were some work clothes back there and even an old quilt, but she didn't even ask if she could use them to warm up. She just sat there cradling whatever was in her arms. Staring down at it and humming some kind of weird tune.

Once she got in and they began to drive, they rolled the windows up and cranked the heat to full blast. It had gotten cold with the windows down and the doors open, but Uncle Pete and his friend noticed that the car wasn't warming up, not by a long shot. They each looked at each other as they remembered the stories about Lake Blaine Road and realized they should have known better than to let her inside the car.

Her humming grew louder and as Uncle Pete looked in the rear-view mirror, he couldn't find her. It was as if she wasn't back there at all, except for her humming that is. His friend kept talking to her, he obviously could see her, but she didn't reply. He asked her name and at first, they thought she wouldn't answer, but finally she said softly, "I can't remember my name. It's as though it doesn't matter anymore."

The car seemed to get colder as if the heater didn't work. Uncle Pete said his hands got so cold he could barely feel them. His friend said he lost the mobility in his feet. The only constant was the girl's humming.

As they drove, they began to hear sirens up ahead in the distance.

Uncle Pete was afraid to turn around. Afraid to see what was back there, if anything. When he did, he flipped the interior light on, and the girl almost disappeared completely. What he saw he said he will remember forever.

Nothing but large black eyes, framed with wild, unkept hair. Her white dress was dark around her middle. Uncle Pete noticed it almost immediately. He knew it wasn't part of the dress's pattern and knew it most likely had to be drying blood. Her skin was the palest ivory, almost like bone itself.

Uncle Pete saw the flashing lights coming at them; it was an emergency vehicle. He knew there had to be an accident just ahead of where they were. It must have happened only minutes before. Possibly someone just in front of them.

They pulled over as best they could on the narrow road and stopped. The girl in the white dress began to laugh.

Uncle Pete and his friend turned to see her holding something up in the air in front of her and slowly swinging it back and forth. It was motionless and dangling inches from the girl's pale face. She was smiling now, and that constant humming grew louder.

They each felt a stab of pity until they saw the blood. There was so much blood. It was coming from the object she held above her face, and it saturated her dress with droplets that quickly enlarged as they absorbed into the fabric.

At that moment they realized she was holding a baby. Not quite an infant, but maybe a six-month-old child. The head was barely attached to its neck and with each perverse tilt of the girl's arms, the baby's head lolled from one side to the other. They could see the fluids still draining from its body. The girl's dress was saturated in blood, but she didn't seem to notice. After all the baby looked just as dead as she.

Perhaps the girl was in shock, had been involved in the accident and had wandered down the road searching for help until they found her. Perhaps she was simply the girl in the white dress from the old ghost stories and happened along at the perfect timing of the accident to capture the child in the grip of its death.

Pete said that without warning, she opened the car door, gracefully got out of the car and without looking back walked into the darkness of the forest. The last thing they remembered as she disappeared was hearing that God-awful humming.

Uncle Pete was never the same after that night. How could you blame him? I remember him rocking back and forth on the couch repeating the same phrase over and over in a soft whimpering voice, "We should have known not to give her a ride . . . but it was soooo cold and soooo dark outside."

My warning remains, stay off Lake Blaine Road after dark. The next dead baby might be yours.

"...my times of hope were cast in shade.

And pleasure dimed by longing,
For it was then an evil genius
Began to pay me secret visits.
Our meetings were quite dolorous;
His smile, his glance mysterious,
His venom-filled and caustic sermons
Poured frozen poison in my soul.
With endless standering remarks
He tempted Providence;
He claimed that beauty's but a dream;
Felt scorn for inspiration;

He had no faith in love or freedom;
He looked on life with ridicule –
And in the whole of nature
He did not wish to praise a single thing."

Alexander Sergeyevich Pushkin (1799 – 1837) ~

CARL'S NEW HOUSE

CHAPTER ONE

For most people, spring is the most beautiful time of year there is. Nature is awakening after months of rest as life resumes its amazing cycle of rebirth. Although in 1969, for Jackie and Stephanie Felton, who had just relocated with their family to Mount Vernon Street in Prescott, Arizona, it was the beginning of a long journey of running away from things that lived in the dark.

It all began on a blustery and cloudy evening in March when their father, Carl Felton, came home from work one night and informed the family that his company had transferred him from rural Maryland to Arizona. He explained what an amazing opportunity it would be for everyone, and the money would be a great deal more than it had been at his current position. He told the girls they would finally be able to take the ballet and majorette lessons they had been wanting and talking non-stop about for two years! He was very excited about his advancement and relocating west, and their mother, Rita, also showed enthusiasm toward the new change in scenery and all the possibilities Arizona would provide.

The plan was for the girls to finish out the current school year and then they would pack up their belongings, rent a truck, and begin their new adventure in the Wild Wild West.

The big day finally came, and it was time for the girls to say good-bye to their life-long friends. Climbing out of the school bus on their last day of school and returning misty-eyed and emotionally wilted, they both entered the house to find the packing had already begun.

Stephanie and Jackie were two years apart in age, but Stephanie skipped the fourth grade, so they were only a year apart as far as grade levels went. This new school year, Stephanie would be entering the seventh grade and Jackie the eighth. Both happy they were at least able to finish their elementary school years in the same school. Out west they had middle-school instead of junior-high (which was what they were used to back east), so now they would be going to the same school together. Neither girl wanted to move, but they knew it was inevitable and knew it would have been harder to leave in later years as their friendships would only grow stronger as time went by. Although they were young, they were also practical.

Less than two weeks later, the moving truck came and began carting off boxes full of the family's worldly possessions. The girls could only watch as each box disappeared into the truck. Each of the boxes were marked with different colored dots. The red dots meant the box's contents belonged to Stephanie and the yellow dots meant the contents belonged to Jackie. The other colored dots meant kitchen stuff, bathroom stuff, garage stuff, etc. In truth, the girls couldn't have cared less about the dots or what color they were. The only thing of any importance that day was having to say good-bye to their friends and neither of the girls were happy about that.

Once the moving truck was loaded and ready to leave, they all walked through the house one last time as a family, reminisced a little, and said their good-byes to Maryland.

CHAPTER TWO

Six days later they arrived in Arizona. They could have made it in two and a half days if they drove straight through, but Rita and Carl were determined to turn this drastic and unexpected move into a nice family experience, and as it turned out, they did just that.

The first night they stopped at Loretta Lynn's Dude Ranch in Tennessee and spent a couple nights listening to the sounds of sheep and cows filling the air. Then they went north and visited the Blue Hole in New Mexico and enjoyed the water and desert views.

The best part about the trip was stopping in Winslow, Arizona to see the meteor crater. Rita loved the desert scenery and had been browsing the internet for weeks learning what she could about the crater. Carl loved the excitement and energy she had put into the journey, and it made him love her even more as he watched her face when she saw the big dent in the ground for the first time.

They reserved rooms at the La Posada Hotel where a friend of theirs, Charlie McKenney, had suggested they stay if they were ever in the area. Charlie had a wonderful review of both the hotel and the town. It had been a long time since Carl had spoken with Charlie and wished he had hung onto his phone number. It would have been nice to have been able to look him up. He knew he had moved there a few years back and Carl was looking forward to surprising him. Unfortunately, Charlie must have had an unlisted number because his name didn't come up in the directory search and when they stopped for lunch at Percy's Diner, which was supposedly the most popular restaurant in town, no one recognized his name.

When the family finally pulled into their new driveway, each of them got out of the car and could do nothing but look up and marvel at the three-story old Victorian home that soared before them. Rita was speechless. All she could do was gawk at the old house as her eyes filled with tears and her hands folded over her face. Carl always had the perfect knack for knowing exactly what she wanted, and this time wasn't any different. He held her in his arms, momentarily forgetting about the children, who had already scrambled out of the car and were exploring the yard. The home had been built in the early 1900's and was located on the most esteemed street in the area. It was one of the first Victorian homes in Prescott.

The realtor Carl had hired, Jenny Shook of Welocate Realty, did a hell of a job finding exactly what they were looking for. He had only heard excellent things about her and not knowing who else to call in the Prescott area, he dialed the phone and hoped for the best. Yep, as long as Rita was happy, that was all that mattered in Carl's eyes and as far as he was concerned it was a job well done.

Carl told his family that the town had quite an exciting history and as soon as they were unpacked and settled, he would take them on a city tour and fill them in on all the dramatic stories that surrounded Prescott. He thought the kids would love hearing both the history and folklore alike. But what Carl didn't see were the eye rolls from the girls and the fingers jammed in their throats as they pretended to gag behind him as they hid from his view in the back seat trying to hide their giggles.

Upon arriving at Mount Vernon Street, they found their belongings; still in boxes, but conveniently located in each room according to the colored dots their mom strategically planned. Jackie acknowledged to herself that the color scheme thing was a good idea that made things easier in the long run. Both Stephanie and Jackie loved their new house and couldn't believe they each had their own bedrooms. It was like heaven.

CHAPTER THREE

The first night was quiet and comfortable. After their long journey, everybody was exhausted but glad to have finally arrived. Carl was just happy that the old car made it without any breakdowns. It was nice to be able to finally put the traveling drama behind them and relax in their new home.

When the sun rose the next morning, and the light filtered in through the bedroom windows, everyone began to awake for the first time in Arizona.

The girls loved the huge bathroom they would be sharing, and the fact that the backyard was endless, made them think of dogs . . . They had never been able to have a dog before and this was the first thing they begged for at the breakfast table. Carl told them a dog would be a happy addition to their family and as soon as they were settled, they would call a few rescues and take a look-see at the ones at the shelter.

Stephanie was the last one out of bed that morning and when she jumped in the shower, she was thankful there was still plenty of hot water. As she finished drying off and grabbed the doorknob to let herself out, she realized she couldn't turn the knob. It wouldn't budge. She banged and banged on it, and it still wouldn't turn. She started to get angry and hollered for someone to come and let her out. No one came. She looked out the window and saw everyone out on the far side of the backyard setting up the volleyball net. There was no way anyone could hear her, and the warm hand of panic slowly began to creep up her neck.

She knew she wasn't in any danger but being trapped didn't make her feel any safer.

After a few minutes of sitting on the toilet waiting for someone to come inside, she decided to open the window. Kicking herself for not thinking of that first off, she bent up the locks on either side of the window and pushed up. It wouldn't budge either. She was afraid to try and jiggle it too much for fear of breaking the glass. She screamed and screamed to get someone's attention but still, no one looked up at the house.

As she sat waiting for rescue, she heard the ticking of the space heater. It had come on and the dial was on high. She tried to turn it off, but nothing happened. She grabbed the cord to yank it out of the wall, but it wouldn't pull out. The room was rapidly getting hot. It was late summer, and the outside temps were already high. Now she started to get scared.

It quickly began getting very hot in there and the air became thick. Her breaths were getting shorter and shorter. Her heart started racing and she found herself officially entering panic mode. All she could do was bang and scream in hopes someone would hear her and come let her out.

As her strength began to leave her, she laid on the floor. Finally, her mom opened the door and found her.

"Oh my God, Stephanie! Stephanie? What on earth are you doing on the floor, did you fall?"

"Mom!" Stephanie said breathlessly between sobs. "You guys were all outside and I couldn't get the door open! The knob wouldn't turn. I guess it got stuck or something and then you weren't in the house and couldn't hear me yell for you!"

"Oh honey, the door wasn't stuck, I came right in, easy peezy. Oh wow, it's crazy hot in here! Did you turn on the heater? Here, take my hand I'll help you up."

Crying, Stephanie reached up for her mom's hand and let her pull her up on her feet. "The heater came on full blast and I couldn't turn it off!"

Shrugging the situation aside, her mother said, "Well, it's off now. Come downstairs and have some breakfast."

Stephanie was still a little unsteady but did as her mother asked.

Within a few days the boxes had been unpacked and everything was arranged accordingly. The home was shaping up and everyone began to feel contented in their new space, although Stephanie never felt comfortable in the third-floor bathroom.

CHAPTER FOUR

On a crisp and clear Saturday morning Carl had started clearing out some of the backyard weeds and overgrown vegetation which was almost taller than he was. They had become an eyesore to him and most likely to his neighbors as well, although no one had mentioned it to him . . . yet. He realized he would need a sickle or some kind of clipper to get them all cut down easily, so he went into the basement to see if there was anything down there he might be able to use before hitting the local hardware store.

They had only been in the home a couple of weeks, and he hadn't had time to properly check out the cellar. He knew the movers had put quite a few boxes down there, but since he hadn't needed anything in them, he had no reason to go down until now.

He noticed right off that the light didn't work when he flipped the switch. He knew there was an overhead bulb in the center of the cellar, which hung from a wire about two feet long. That had to be the culprit.

Grabbing a new lightbulb from the hall closet, Carl then walked to the already quickly-filling junk drawer in the kitchen in hopes of finding a flashlight, which he did, and approached the long rickety staircase which led down into the old cellar. As he peered into the darkness, he shined the dim beam of the flashlight down the ancient stairs. He was rudely awakened as he realized that no matter how old a man was, and no matter how brave or big and strong he thinks he may be, entering a dark cellar of an old home that was at least a hundred years old would scare the shit out of anybody. Trying to forget every horror movie he ever saw; he slowly entered the cellar. He checked his weight on each step, not knowing if there would be a rotten board, and slowly made it to the dirt floor below.

Not thinking about bringing a stepladder, he was relieved to find he was easily able to reach the light bulb. He quickly replaced the old one as he held the flashlight in his mouth, while pushing thoughts of *The Night of the Living Dead* rushing him from the darkness behind, out of his mind. The light of life filled the room and Carl felt foolish that he had begun to let his thoughts of horror carry him away.

As he began sorting through a few boxes for what he needed outside, he noticed a small wooden door on the back wall of the cellar. Interesting. At first thought he guessed it might be an entry to an old coal chute. Back in the days when the house was built, wasn't that how most people heated their homes? It had to be. He walked over and turned the knob and the door easily pushed open. It creaked and moaned as he knew no one had probably opened the door in decades. The old-fashioned iron handle was dusty with probably years of unuse.

The room was empty except for a few old tools, one of which was a short ax. It was a lot like an ax someone would throw in competitions today. The business end was attached to the wooden handle by straps of leather. It was actually super convenient because it was exactly the type of tool he needed to chop down some of the larger weeds in the backyard. Both amazed and delighted that he didn't have to drive all the way into town and visit the hardware store, he snatched the ax up off the dirt floor and left the small room. As he turned towards the door to close it, there was a cool draft that blew outward, and he felt the breeze hit him in the face. It smelled of years past, old and dank. It wasn't a bad smell, only a smell of damp earth. He walked up the stairs and almost forgetting to shut the light off, he turned and flicked the switch and closed the cellar door.

Carl realized he had begun to really enjoy Arizona and as luck would have it, getting the hell off the East Coast made him happy. His life was already turning into an adventure that not many people were lucky enough to experience. It seemed the greater majority of folks lived in the same town they were raised in, or at the very most left their town only to move into the next one over. Carl had been one of them. At first he was unhappy, to say the least, about his company transferring him to Arizona. It might as well have been Hell. But the move brought he and Rita closer together as a couple, which he never would have thought possible as they were a perfect match to begin with. The sun rose and set for each of them upon the other. Yes, their life was blossoming and growing by leaps and bounds and Carl's heart was already content knowing his family was in the west. He was full of anticipation and eager to start their new lives.

CHAPTER FIVE

The girls and Rita were at the volleyball net swatting the ball back and forth and having a good time. Stephanie packed a mean serve and those on the other side of the net ducked every time they heard her slap the ball versus trying to counter. No one ever kept score, it was all about having fun, and winning or losing wasn't part of the family experience.

Carl was at the weeds along the property line. His mission that afternoon was to chop as many of the tallest ones down that he could and now that he had the little ax, he was ready to start hackin'.

The first few went down easily and as he raised the ax, he also happened to observe out of the corner of his eye, Stephanie spike the ball into Jackie's face, thereby hearing the "smack" as it made contact. He heard Jackie scream and knew she would have a black eye, or at the very least broken glasses. He also saw the sharp end of the hatchet fly off the handle and with the combined force of his swing and his mis-aimed thrust he felt most of his middle finger separate from the rest of his hand as he gripped the doomed weed. It didn't hurt at first. It happened so fast, but within seconds the searing, hot pain of the blow lit up his awareness and all he could do was yell his favorite word. "FUUUUCK!" Hearing this his family came running.

Jackie held her face thinking he was going to start yelling at Stephanie. Rita didn't know who to comfort first because she had seen what had happened to the both of them, and Stephanie was laughing. It wasn't that she was laughing due to her enjoyment in her family's misfortune, in fact she had no idea what had happened her dad at all. After all, she had been serving and concentrating on the game.

Once it was all sorted out, they were in the car and headed towards Prescott Community Hospital, which is now Yavapai Regional Medical Center as we know it today, the closest and only hospital nearby. Thankful it was a small town, they were in and out in two hours. Unfortunately for Carl no one had thought of grabbing his lost digit, and he left the hospital short a finger and with four stitches. Easy come, easy go.

That evening after dinner Carl was tired. His hand was throbbing and between his pain pill and the two Budweisers he drank, neither of which seemed to help, he sat in his favorite chair in front of the TV beginning to feel sorry for himself.

"How ya feelin' babe? Can I getcha anything?" Rita asked as she walked up behind him and slid an arm around his shoulder.

"Nope. I'm just tired. I should have been paying more attention. Christ, I can't believe I did that!"

"Well, you could have whacked off your whole hand so consider it a good day."

"Yeah, you're right. I guess I could have. How is it that you always find the good in things?" he asked her.

"Guess I'm lucky that way."

"No. I guess I'm lucky that way." He pulled her in for a kiss on the cheek.

"Did you tell the hospital people that the ax you were using was a million years old and rusty to boot?"

"Yep. They gave me a tetanus shot, which by the way, hurt more than axing off my damn finger."

She began to laugh. "How about another beer, tough guy?"

"Sounds good and make it a big one. Then it's bedtime for me. I'm gonna milk this battle wound all I can. You know that don't you?"

"I had a feelin'."

"Oh, and how's Jackie's face, by the way?"

Stephanie drifted into the room that very moment, flung herself on the couch and said, "I don't know, but it's killing me!"

"Hardy, har, har, you creeper!" Jackie blurted out as she entered right behind her.

"Oh gawd," Rita said. "You girls need to find some new lines. Now be nice."

Carl and Rita finished watching the news and they all went upstairs to bed.

Everyone in the home slept soundly that night, although downstairs in the basement, behind the old wooden door, things had begun moving.

CHAPTER SIX

The ax had only been a part of it. When Carl opened that old wooden door, he, without knowing it, had released a life-force that was older than time. It was more than an essence or spirit, it had evolved.

It first had entered the old house back when the home was being constructed. It was born before the Earth had cooled. It was older than air. It could not be contained. It could not be reckoned with. Those it touched withered and died and that was the way it had always been. The way it will always be, and now it was awake.

Chapter Seven

The next morning Carl went outside with a cup of coffee and looked for the ax. He found it right where he had left it, stuck in a tree stump. The first thing he noticed was that the handle had evidently never separated from the business end. It was still securely mounted by the leather straps as it had been the day before. However, he distinctly remembered seeing it airborne and watching as the old leather frayed apart. He saw it sever his finger and watched as the ax blade hit the ground. He knew he didn't imagine it. Shit, his finger was also on the stump, maggots crawling all over it already. How he wished he would have come out yesterday and picked it up. How gruesome was that? Although it was only a small digit from his body, it was still a piece of himself that he didn't need to see on a dirty stump with bugs crawling all over it. How did it get there in the first place? He had been clearing weeds and tall stalks. Now it looked as though it had been placed there purposely, as if his gruesomely axed off finger was on display in some twisted side show.

He wondered what the hell he should do. Pick it up and carry it to the trash? Bury it? Hell, even though he knew it was his, he didn't even want to touch it, much less look at it. The thought seemed revolting and looking at a piece of oneself with those thoughts, made him suddenly nauseous.

After shaking the maggots off as best he could, he wrapped the finger in a hanky from his pocket and ran into the kitchen. He held his finger under the running tap water from the sink, picking out the rest of the maggots who were able to dig into it deeper until it was washed clean. If Rita would have known, she would have been completely revulsed. Once the maggots were displaced, he wrapped the finger in a small plastic bag – quickly pressing out all the air and sealing it shut. Horrified, he threw it in the freezer, trying to bury it as best he could underneath pork chops, hamburger, and anything else he could find to hide the appendage.

He weakly supported himself with the handle on the ice box door until he got his act together. He knew he would have to relocate it soon. What if one of the girls came across it while searching for their next meal? That would certainly hang with someone until they died, right? "Hello – meet my girls, and yes they both have anorexia nervosa because when they were young, they almost cooked their dad's finger for lunch."

That was when he couldn't hold it in any longer and his breakfast came up like Yellowstone's Old Faithful, strong and proud.

He told himself to quickly relocate his finger as soon as he could deal with it.

Later that day, Rita approached Carl and wanted to talk. She wanted to share some information that Jackie had told her in confidence. Jackie didn't want her to tell anyone especially her dad since she knew how happy he was to be in their new home. Carl agreed he wouldn't say anything. After all, this was part of living in a family. Girls will be girls and boys will be boys. He knew when Stephanie and Jackie were born there would be many "girl" secrets he wouldn't be privy to. He accepted it, and privately hoped he and Rita would have boys in the future that would also give him the luxury of having someone to share private moments with.

It seemed that Jackie had been having bad dreams. Dreams that made her fear for her parents' lives. She had been waking up crying and most nights she had been fighting off demons. Demons that she knew would soon win and she had come to Rita begging that they move away. Far away, and quickly.

A couple hours before sunrise that same night, Stephanie awoke screaming and ran into her parents' bedroom. She said that they were all going to be murdered in their beds if they didn't leave. She had said that the old people in the basement didn't want them in the house and that they had to leave.

Rita and Carl thought the girls were just letting their dreams get the best of them, until a few nights later Rita awoke to banging sounds coming from the basement. Carl sprung out of bed and began to go downstairs when he realized that the carpet runner on the staircase was saturated with thick liquid, and he was unable to get a foothold without slipping. Holding onto the stair rails he yelled at Rita to turn on the hall lights. When she did it seemed as though the entire floor was soaked in blood. He had tried to gain a foothold, but it was no use. He came down the stairs like he was caught in a riptide. He hit the front door and as the hinges broke apart and the door swung outward, he was carried off into the front yard. He had been completely out of control.

His family escaped right behind him and as each of them found one another, they held on tight as they watched the house change. One minute it was an old wooden structure, the next it was a two-story hamlet. Minutes later it was an A-frame with a small winery surrounding it. In each setting was what looked like a family in the foreground. The family stared at them, glaring into their eyes as if daring them to fight back.

Rita and Carl Felton knew they were unwanted. They were being asked to leave as pleasantly as those old people knew how. It was clear they were used to winning and keeping their space.

The family never returned to their home in Prescott. That night they drove to a local hotel to try and get some sleep and figure out what their next move should be.

They weren't sure if they would ever overcome what had happened to them, but they could only pray that they could.

That night Carl's hand itched uncontrollably. Though it had plenty of time to heal, in recent days as the hauntings became more violent and consistent, it began bothering him again. It didn't make sense.

When his hand began to throb, his mind took him into strange thoughts. Thoughts that weren't his own. It was as though some sort of exterior entity kept pushing his awareness towards old memories that were new to him. He often thought of the old days. Days before time. Days before the house was even built. The ax. A history of horror that followed it was so intense that although he tried to turn away, his mind wouldn't stop seeing people, events, dark recollections of fear and neglect. Monsters.

As he laid in bed and scratched the finger that had somehow grown back, all he could do was smile as his eyes turned red and his pupils turned cat-like. He rolled over in bed, looking at Rita with an incredible desire to hurt, while an incredible feeling of relief overtook him.

He had been waiting much longer this time. Thankfully, he felt like he was finally becoming himself once again.

Carl was dead now, and things were turning out exactly how they should be, he thought as his new fangs penetrated his bleeding gums.

"Do not stand by my grave, and weep.
I am not there, I do not sleep —

I am a thousand winds that blow.
I am the diamond glints in snow;
I am the sunlight on ripened grain,
I am the gentle, autumn rain.

As you awake with morning's hush,
I am the swift, up-flinging rush
Of quiet birds in circling flight,
I am the day transcending night.

Do not stand by my grave, and cry —
I am not there, I did not die."

Clare Harner (1934) ~

THE FAMILY

CHAPTER ONE

There used to be a time when I loved to traipse about. I found myself drawn to back roads and pot-holed highways. Now I sit in my chair and wish I had more memories.

Youth was cut short for me, but not because of my exploration or my crazy ways. I just quit roaming. I'm not sure why actually. I've often asked myself why I stopped doing the things that made me so happy many times. I guess I just got tired. Of course, knowing that no matter where I wandered — no matter what time of year or how cold or hot the temperature, the woman with the scars on her face would always show up. She was often on a bus or a park bench. One time I even saw her exiting the men's room as I was walking in.

Her eyes were always dark and sullen, and although she would always look in my direction, it was as if she never seemed to really see me. It was as if she were looking right through me. She always appeared hopeless and lost, as if there was something she needed to say. Not necessarily to me, but to anyone. Then she would pass by, dropping her head, never turning around. She was young, I think, probably in her thirties, and at one time I believe she must have been beautiful in a plain sort of way.

I couldn't get her out of my head, in fact I never could. Even after years had come and gone, I felt haunted by her appearances. It was hard not to feel this way. Her clothes were always the same. They were of another era and looked very dirty. Her dress was torn and ragged. As I aged, I often wondered what ever happened to her, until I settled in Prescott.

CHAPTER TWO

Years later, and still many years ago, I was visiting a small western town on kind of a spur of the moment vacation and had to run some errands in town. I decided to walk rather than drive my old beat-up Chevy. I figured I had already put enough miles on the ol' gal and didn't want to add any more. It was a cool, breezy day and I knew I could use the exercise. The city was very small compared to most cities these days and the main hub was the Courthouse Square, in the center of the historic district. Hell, the whole town was in the historic district and that was exactly why I became so interested in it in the first place. Even though it's technically a "city," I refer to it as a town, as do all the residents. This is due to its small-town feeling, cozy atmosphere, and quixotic folklore. I'm referring to Prescott,

Arizona, by the way. Did I mention that before? Anyway, that was the day I walked past the only real estate office in town and saw some properties taped to the front window. It was then I decided to buy a chunk of ground. I was still a relatively young man, but it was time to stop wandering and find a place of my own; I could feel it. I was single at the time, hell, I've always been single. Now, here is where this story begins.

I fell in love with a five-acre spread, and immediately began searching for cabin kits to erect on the property. I knew I was capable of building the structure myself, and over time I could add the electric, plumbing, and whatever else was necessary. The septic system and the well came first, of course. After that it was up to me to get it all together and I loved every minute of the planning and construction phases.

I was never much of a guy that was good in coordinated efforts with others, but by myself I could always create whatever I needed and that was my good fortune. My preference was to try and live as close to the land as good ole' mother nature intended. In that way I fit right in with the majority of folks in Prescott. The town motto was that Prescott is "everyone's hometown" and it was, and still is, exactly that.

After a couple of years my hard work paid off, and now I have a sweet little cabin with all the amenities anyone would need. The only thing I didn't need were the twelve tombstones that stared down at me whenever I looked south up the knoll. I think they were one of the reasons I was able to purchase the land so cheap. I guess no one else wanted them either. Anyway, I never thought it was a big deal at all and I really liked the property. It was perfect for me, not to mention the tax break for having a cemetery. A penny saved is a penny earned if you ask me.

The cemetery is located high on the knoll as I mentioned, which overlooks most of Prescott proper and the surrounding mountains. I seriously wanted to build the cabin there but legally could not. Don't get me wrong, I still have a dynamite view, just not THAT view. I figure the dead earned their right to that hilltop and I'm okay with knowing that.

Some folks say the cemetery is haunted by the dead that lay in the ground up there; some say each person died at the hands of Indians while building their ranch. Farther down the west side of the hill there is an old burnt-out rock homestead covered by years of weather and wilderness. No doubt it was someone's home, and I've always guessed it was theirs.

I'm told the bodies up there are a family, and as far as anyone knows, they were settlers who tried to inhabit the area before Prescott was incorporated. Not much is known about them except that their deaths were tortuous and horrible. I've heard one story about how the Indians hung a little girl with her own long hair off a bough on the old tree that still stands nearby. They say if you look hard enough you can still find strands of her blonde hair stuck in the bark, although personally, I've never felt the desire to check. They also say that on full moons or after a strong monsoon in late summer you can still hear her gruesome and urgent cries for help if you listen close. Echoes never completely disappear, you know. Anyone who lives near the dead knows this is true.

The Wild Wild West lost lots of pioneers back in the day and this town wasn't any different. Everyone coming from back east knew the consequences and chances of foul play while crossing the wilderness were great. They either accepted them or stayed home. As it turned out, this brave family should have stayed home.

CHAPTER THREE

The first time I realized the folklore was true was on an unusually quiet night in July a great number of years back. I knew a monsoon was getting ready to blow, and if you've been in Arizona for any length of time you can always feel them coming. Between the heat lightning and the blasts of wind that seem to kick up in all directions, even a green-bellied easterner with hands as soft as a baby's bottom could figure out one's coming in no time at all.

I remember walking up the hill to retrieve my ax, which I left outside by the graves earlier that afternoon. Back then an ax was the closest thing to a weed whacker as they had. I always try and keep the cemetery tended to as best I can out of respect. Heck, I figure anyone would do the same. I didn't want my ax to get wet and run the risk of it weathering badly by the next time I needed it. I usually try not to destroy my tools until I've had them at least a year or two you see. Anyway, as I picked it up, and was taking a moment to appreciate the view, out of the corner of my eye I saw movement.

The sun had just gone under the horizon line. It wasn't full dark yet, but it was comin' and those dark storm clouds had moved in quick which helped speed up the arrival of the night.

I looked again where I thought I had seen something, maybe it was only a javalina or desert dog that had scurried by. I began to turn away but what I saw next stopped me cold. A woman and a child stood, also presumably admiring the view. The woman held herself in a tired and sorrowful posture. I couldn't see her face; looking back I was glad I couldn't. The child was carrying a bunch of dry and withered flowers in her hand. Instead of fear, I felt a stab of heartfelt sympathy as she turned towards me, and I saw deeply rutted gashes along her throat, her eyes sunken and glazed. I stepped back, my foot tangled in a mass of goat heads, and I fell; my eyes never leaving the two of them. The woman took the child's hand and together they walked away and disappeared.

My first thought was that the fading rays of sunlight had begun to play tricks on my eyes, but then I realized it had not. As the woman led the child away, with me still sitting on the ground, stunned, she quickly glanced back, and our eyes met. It was then that I knew I couldn't stand even if I had tried. I could only sit and stare at the place on the hill where they disappeared from my sight.

The woman's eyes were so sullen and full of sorrow. I had seen them before. But, where? It was that moment I remembered – how could I forget her? Those eyes. I had seen them so many times in my dreams. Could she have been with me all my life? Could she have been waiting for this moment to show herself to me again after so many years? My hands trembled as I brought them to my face. I was unable to make a sound.

I never again sensed being alone after that night and instead of wanting to pack up and head out of town in fear, I felt the need to stay. To my surprise I had the needful urgency to protect the property, especially the cemetery. It was as if I had the essential need to protect this unknown family.

Silly, but true. This family was dead and long forgotten. Even the weathered and faded engraving on their tombstones had forsaken them.

I began to routinely paint the fence surrounding their graves. I planted flowers and rose bushes, which in the harsh Arizona climate require constant watering and upkeep. I found myself wandering up the hill for no reason but to sit and spend time on the hand-crafted wooden bench I made myself to overlook the valley and have a smoke.

Sometimes in the evenings just after the sun would set, I could see others standing and looking out at the view. I saw an older couple and maybe a teenage boy from time to time. On those evenings, as one by one would drift out of my sight, I realized the last two figures to remain were always the woman and child. Every time I saw them, the child would turn to look down at the cabin and every time the mother would also turn and look in my direction as they disappeared. She never quite angled her head so I could see her face for any length of time. I never knew why. It was as if she would only glance back to see if I was still there.

I told myself the woman wanted to communicate but could not or should not.

CHAPTER FOUR

I wanted to connect with them badly. I wanted them to know me and I them. During the late afternoon of the last full moon in 1989, I took a large bouquet of roses and baby's breath up to the cemetery. I left them in a sturdy vase that I knew the wind wouldn't knock over with a short note that read "For you." There was no envelope, and I wrote in large handwriting so the woman should have little trouble reading it if she could.

The next morning the flowers were gone.

As the years went by, I left flowers more often and every time I saw the woman and child, the child would be carrying my flowers in her arms.

As they withered, I brought more.

I continued to paint the fence, trim the rose bushes that had grown large and dramatically beautiful over these many years, and of course I continue to go up on the knoll. Well, as often as I can. The arthritis has set into my knees and I'm sad to admit I don't get up there as often as I'd like to anymore, but I manage to take care of the things I started. It's my life, you see. It's what I've come to know. It's what I've come to love. I make it up that hill a lot slower than I used to, but I make it.

I'll be going on eighty-two in a few months. The town folk think I'm a recluse. I am I suppose. I enjoy it that way. From time to time, I'll get a visitor bringing an invitation to a new church or maybe a gift of lasagna in a pan. I think it's their way of checking on me. Everyone knows I'm alone. I can't say I blame them for worrying and I hate to admit that it feels good to know someone cares and tries to look out for me in such modern times as these when our government seems more concerned for illegal border-crossing aliens than they do for life-long tax paying Americans. It's sad times we live in.

I wrote a will the other day. I know my time is getting short. I have no one to bequeath anything to and certainly nothing much to leave behind and I'm fine with that. My life is simple. The only concern I have is regarding the cemetery and my wishes to keep it safe and well maintained. I'm sure it will be. Perhaps the next person that owns this land will do right by my request. I can only hope. My other request is that I want to be buried here. I've bought and paid for a casket and even marked out the area for my grave. In my almost eighty-two years I feel closer to that unknown family than anyone else. I know I can rest there and hope they will welcome me. I think they will.

It's February in Prescott and I think February anywhere is colder than a witch's tit, which is not appealing. I haven't been well, but since it's a full moon I will be making the long walk up the hill later today to deliver my flowers. I have hired a reliable boy who lives down the road to bring them to me as I no longer can drive. I've been saving money my whole life so on certain things I'm willing to spend the extra bucks for certain necessities to make my life easier.

CHAPTER FIVE

I threw on my boots and buttoned up as well as I could. I even brought out my parka and old ski gloves I bought over thirty years ago. I rarely have the need to use them these days, but I always like to tarry a while when I go up the hill and the winter temperatures drag a lot of life out of me as I go. I suspect I won't be going up there again 'til spring.

I put the flowers in the vase and walked over to my bench to watch the sun go down like I always do. I lit a smoke and got comfortable. Suddenly my arm began to tingle and went numb, but I was quickly distracted by the beautiful view. The best place on Earth I always say.

CHAPTER SIX

S hortly after the first day of spring, a family of four had finished unpacking their belongings and were beginning to settle into their quaint and wonderfully decorated cabin on the hillside overlooking Prescott, Arizona. It was simple but had everything they needed. It was perfect.

During the evening of their first full moon, they stood on the big hill watching the sun go down and admiring the view. As the children played along the path, the husband touched his wife's shoulder and pointed at the small graveyard. Maintaining the cemetery was in the purchase contract. It was written in as a contingency that the new buyer would have to honor. This duty would be carried over to the next owner as well. He held his finger over his lips so the children wouldn't be drawn to what they were witnessing.

First, they saw the child. A little girl in an old and worn pioneer dress carrying a beautiful bouquet of wildflowers and running to the edge of the hill. Following her was a woman, also in old clothing. She had long blonde hair that was thick and vibrant with shades of gold and white. Her smile was a happy one and her face was so beautiful, neither could have ever remembered seeing such a more stunning woman in their lives. Then a man walked from around the big oak tree and lovingly twirled the woman around and lifted her off her feet. As he slowly let her down into his arms they embraced. The child ran back to them, and the man picked her up and held her close. Together the three of them stood watching the sun disappear beneath the horizon.

Before they walked out of site, the man turned and looked at them. He smiled and tipped his hat.

"The night is darkening round me,
The wild winds coldly blow;

But a tyrant spell has bound me,
And I cannot, cannot go."

Emily Bronte (1818 – 1848) ~

THE HANGED MAN'S WIFE

CHAPTER ONE

I bought my first and only home about thirty-five years ago. I signed the papers in a room with two realtors, two lawyers, and two sellers. Feeling overwhelmed and lost under the bright and unforgiving conference room fluorescents, it didn't take long for me to interrupt the show as I attempted to excuse myself graciously. Unfortunately, rising out of my chair with my hand clamped over my mouth spoke for itself, and all I could think of was "please God, let me get out of this room before I ruin the carpet." The intimidation factor was horrific. When I returned, everyone knew I was humiliated, and I could see expressions of both compassion and humor. The realtors told me buyers often get sick and not to be embarrassed. Being who I am, I had to laugh out loud. Nausea had never occurred to me. Obviously, the stress of the past few days had taken its toll on me. The others chimed in, and humanity reigned.

I was relieved, however, when no one said a word about my wet hair. It had gotten wet when the water from the toilet bowl had splashed back at me from the force of the bile landing in the bowl. I had to rinse it out. Knowing it was impossible to hide, I sat with my hands shaking as proudly as

I could. I told myself "What the hell!" and the best part was that I meant it.

I had been working hard for many years towards the goal of purchasing my own home and I was thrilled to be able to finally cross it off my list. What's a little puke when at the end of the day you are the winner?

When the signing was finished, everyone shook hands and went their separate ways.

I danced out towards the parking lot, all thoughts of panic and doubt washing quickly away, and arrived to where my U-Haul rental truck sat with my old pick-up securely fastened and sitting atop a flat-bed trailer. The first challenge had been accomplished, which was getting the U-Haul all the way to Arizona. I figured it would take at least three days, and I was happy to say I was right about that. The bonus was that I made it the entire way without ever backing it up. That shit is a lot harder than it looks!

Prior to renting the trailer, I practiced backing up a friend's trailer and after an hour, realized it was impossible. I was given many precious traits from my parents, but unfortunately the "backing up a trailer" gene was not one of them.

Before I began the trip, I decided never to pull into a spot where I knew I couldn't pull forward to exit. It couldn't be that hard, right? Well, that was my plan. As it turned out, there were a few times this couldn't be managed, but when I got out of the truck and asked the nearest man to help, my request was met with a smile and a helpful response every time. I learned during those three days that chivalry wasn't dead and I exhaled deeply when I crossed the last state line into Arizona.

After driving the best I could and coming out in the end without an accident nor miles lost due to wrong turns or bad weather, I finally pulled into the gravel driveway and marveled at the home I could now legally call my own.

I first saw the property while on vacation visiting some old friends of my parents, who have since passed on, and before I caught my flight back to Maryland, I stopped in at a local real estate office. I was invited to sit down with an agent

THE HANGED MAN'S WIFE | 45

to discuss my interests in the home and my hopes of purchasing it. He was very understanding and helpful but told me it was not available. Over the years we kept in contact, and he often emailed me other listings, which I appreciated receiving, but none ever grabbed me like the original home I first saw.

I had been patient and knew the current owners were older and it was just a matter of time before the house would be listed. My goal was that one house, and I would wait for it. I don't know specifically what I loved about it the most, all I knew was that I needed to live there. It seemed to call to me and always stayed in my mind. The architecture, the intricate gingerbread along the porch's corners and along the gables. The white picket fence that gracefully accented its boundaries, the rounded living room, and bedrooms on the second floor all coming together in a powder blue with all the trim work in clean, bright white. It was stunning.

Arriving that first day was the best feeling I think I've ever experienced in my life. All that went through my mind was "Mission Accomplished!" They say that purchasing a home is the most expensive item most people will ever buy in their lives. I believe that is true. I would have sworn on a stack of Bibles it would be for me. I was so looking forward to planting gardens and watching trees grow tall and proud. I priced going rates to put in a pool and decks . . . The options were limitless! Homeownership was going to be wonderful!

The house is located in Prescott, Arizona's most exclusive neighborhood on Mount Vernon Street. The homes are all very old and most boast historical markers on their lavish gates. The town has an exciting and luring history and is well-loved among most all of the American historians. The town's motto is "Everyone's Hometown" and it surely is.

Chapter Two

After cutting off the engine and sitting, staring at the huge old place, my place, I could barely make my legs move to get out of the truck. I had only seen the house from the street; even during the escrow period I had never gone inside. This purchase was an odd one, as most home sales go, and my realtor almost insisted that I come out and look at it, but I didn't. For some reason I just couldn't. I had been so confident that this was "my house" that I suppose I wanted the entire experience to be a surprise. I wanted my opening the front door and walking over the threshold to be my special event. My dream event, and it was.

The realtor had sent me many videos of him walking through the home and asking for my opinions. I never even watched them. I only told him to make sure the house was structurally safe, all the inspections were good, all codes were met, and beyond that I would handle any minor issues. I was confident the many inspections I arranged would be accurately and professionally handled.

As I walked into the house for the first time, I stepped over the threshold and the instant I put my first box down, I heard a door slam shut. I jumped a little as it caught me off guard, then smiled. I assumed a window must have been left open or something else to create a pressure strong enough to slam the door closed and thought nothing else about it.

I found the house to be in fine shape. The prior owners took great care of the home, just as I knew they would have. The hardwood floors were stained and in perfect shape, the walls, the kitchen, everything was tip top.

I was amazed at how large each room was. The high ceilings and wide corridors were amazing. Every window was both tall and wide and the bathrooms were exceptionally spacious. Each contained an old water closet. I must admit they took some time getting used to, what with the water holding tank towering above the seat, I often worried about leaking, but I know it was just me being used to the modern versions of things. Soon it felt normal, and they fit the house perfectly. I just hoped to hell one wouldn't fall on my head.

The realtor must have hired a maid service to come and clean the home because there wasn't a speck of dirt anywhere. Even the baseboards were wiped clean. When I phoned him to thank him for taking the extra effort, he had no idea what I was talking about, but mentioned that the office manager must have arranged for cleaning. Again, I didn't think twice about it.

The first night I dreamed I heard someone singing. The songs were sad, and the voice distant as if it were coming from an entirely different age in time. The lyrics were melancholy and seemed to echo through the house. They captivated me in a way that made me feel incredibly sorry for the person that had been singing. I slept all through the long night and when I awoke, I still didn't feel rested.

When I went downstairs, I noticed a few of the items that I had brought from my home in Maryland had been reorganized. In fact, some of my belongings had been tossed into the basement. Looking back, I wonder why I accepted this without even a second thought. I must have been too overwhelmed with excitement and tired from the previous days of traveling to care.

I didn't have much furniture, but what I had didn't seem fitting anymore. So, I took most everything to a secondhand store and let it go. I kept my most precious keepsakes, those that reminded me of my life growing up and family; the ones that reminded me of old times I had shared with friends and loved ones. Something in my mind told me it was time to let the rest go. It was time for a complete change. I couldn't argue with the feeling. It was as if the house itself wanted me to start fresh. Looking back, I can't believe I was able to get rid of so many things in my life so easily.

I found myself needing antiques. I had never particularly been fond of them, and certainly never thought of purchasing any, but having them around me now seemed to suit. I needed something that would fit the atmosphere of the home. I found quite a lot of items in the local antique stores and more items from old estate sales. It didn't take long for me to fill the house with period furniture, and it soon came alive with all the old-world charm and character that I was sure it boasted years before. It felt wonderful to have been able to give the space life again. In fact, I may have given it more life that I ever thought possible.

The nightly singing continued, and not just in my dreams. I now began to hear faint footsteps in the hallways and on the stairs. Sometimes I heard crying. There was never anything frightening or harmful about it, so I didn't feel threatened. I found that if I left a fan on or soft music playing, even the television on, it covered up the sad voice. It never occurred to me to be scared.

By the fourth week I had almost finished decorating and completed most of the landscaping. My savings account had also dwindled by leaps and bounds during the process. I originally wanted time to get to know the town and get comfortable in the home, meet some new neighbors and friends before re-entering the job force. Now, however, I was okay with the decision to go back to work earlier than planned and looking forward to getting started on the all-American job hunt.

I ended up getting hired on with the Prescott Historical Society. My duties mostly included maintaining office appearances and answering telephone calls. I was a glorified receptionist at most. I also created files and organized pictures and events into the database of the Society's computer system. I liked the new responsibilities and enjoyed meeting and making friends with the people who came into the office. Everyone had so many questions I couldn't help with, but I learned a great deal about the town and it's past and it didn't take long for me to feel comfortable in my new surroundings.

One day as I was skimming through old articles, I ran across an old picture of my house. There was a man in the picture leaning against the iron gates of the front entry. He looked old and haggard. He was dressed in a top hat and black duster. His fingers looked long and thick and abused from a lifetime of hard work. His face was very hard and stern. Next to him was a thin woman whose eyes were dark and puffy. She looked very unhappy and if I could read her mind, I would assume she was scared to be standing so close to him. Her body language was intense and disturbing. Her hands were in fists at her sides as if ready to defend herself at any moment. Although the picture was only black and white you could see her face looked swollen. Needless to say, it bothered me, but somehow, I couldn't put the picture down. I kept staring at it and looking at the woman's face. I'm no empath, but the longer I looked at it, the more I became overwhelmed with emotion. It's hard for me to explain but I began to feel lost and greatly saddened.

Moments later, Kate, the woman who hired me, walked past, and noticed I was looking at the picture of the house.

"I was wondering when you were going to run across that. There are more in a box over there," she pointed to the back room. "The one you've got isn't nearly as bad as the ones in the box."

"It's so sad. Look at the woman's face," I said.

"I know. Those were the first owners of the house. The people you bought the place from were the second owners. They found a box in the basement and brought the pictures to us years ago. We kept them since they were so old but considering the history of the property, we haven't wanted to put them on display."

"History?"

"Well, yeah . . . Wait, you don't know? I mean, no one has told you?"

I could only stare at her. "Do I want to know?"

"I would. The man in the picture was one of the first men to be hanged in the town square. They found his wife in chains in the basement. She was barely alive. Poor dear. Word has it that he made her stay down there. All he let her do was clean the house and cook his dinner and then he'd chain her up again, like a dog."

"Are you serious?"

"Yep. He was a tyrant. There were stories about how he'd want to hurt anyone who looked at him twice. He was crazy. Crazy Joe, they called him. The town records indicate he killed two men in cold blood by shooting them both in the back over a minor lot line disagreement.

It was unbelievable that his wife lived as long as she did. What a survivor. The man had family money, so he wasn't seen in town much from what I understand. I guess the wife could never get away from him. Back then there were no immediate neighbors, so no one ever heard her scream. Heck, maybe she was afraid to scream."

"Maybe that explains it," I whispered.

"Explains what?"

"If I told you, you'd think I was nuts."

"Try me. I like nuts." She pulled up a chair, sat down, and stared at me with wide, concerned eyes.

"I hear crying at night. Footsteps in the hallways and on the stairs. If I leave things on the floor or laying around, when I wake up everything is in its place."

"You're kidding me, right? You're telling me the lady is still cleaning that house?"

We both laughed.

"Thanks. I needed that!" I told Kate. "You have no idea what's been going through my mind. I haven't felt any danger, but it's very unsettling. Now that I know what happened in the house it makes it all easier to deal with. At first, I thought I was homesick and imagining things. I had really begun to doubt myself."

"I heard that after her husband was hanged, she continued to live in the house. Gossip was that she even continued to stay in the basement. After some years they found her down there laying on a cot by a wall, dead," Kate said. "Evidently the mail was piling up on the front walk so a few men went over to check on her, that's how they found her. It must have been awful."

"The couple I bought the house from must have lived with the noises for years. They never left. I don't think I will either. I've loved that house from the first moment I saw it. I was drawn to it. The poor woman must have felt like she had nowhere else to go. It was her home, maybe the only home she ever knew. I guess a part of her will always be there."

Kate smiled. "Well, if you want to see those other pictures, feel free to get them out of the back room. You can even take them home with you for a while, but please bring them back since they are part of the Society . . . and honey, remember I told you that some are pretty disturbing."

"I remember, and thanks, Kate."

That night I sat on the front porch and looked at the old pictures. Kate was right. They were disturbing. At one point I could have sworn I felt pressure on my shoulder as if an invisible hand gently rested there.

One was a picture of the man standing by an overgrown bush next to the front corner of the house. He was holding a scythe with a long wooden handle. A dog was lying near him; its legs were bent in strange angles. It looked as though they had at one time been horribly broken. They were so twisted it would have been impossible for him to walk.

Another picture was of the wife. Her back was towards the camera, and she was washing windows. At first it wasn't bothersome, then on second glance I realized her dress was caught on one of the ladder's rungs and it showed the backs of her legs. Although the picture was black and white, you could see dark shapes across her calves and knees. Each was the entire width of her skin and looked as if they were marks from a whip or bruises of some other kind. The skin looked darkened around those places, and a few looked as if blood could have been trailing from the wounds.

I walked around that big old house and tried to imagine what life must have been like back then. In a strange way it brought me closer to the woman. I think the prior owners must have felt the same way.

Years of neglect and heartache . . . yet the woman chose to stay. Unimaginable.

The next day I took the morning off and went back to the antique stores. I bought a nice floor lamp, a small brass bed, along with an area rug and a few nick knacks to put on top of a beautiful white dresser I found for a great price. I also found a heavy iron picture frame painted white and put a picture of the woman inside it. I had found the photograph in the box from the Historical Society. The woman was young, and her smile was genuine. It felt to me it must have been taken during her happiest years so I kept it and hoped the Society wouldn't notice it missing. The kicker was also finding a small music box. It was brass, very lovely, and intricately designed. I put the music box, along with the photo, on a white nightstand that I positioned next to the bed.

I arranged all the items in the basement room where it was said she often slept and was found dead. In an antique store on the west side of town, I found a wonderful painting of a young woman standing on a hillside with the wind blowing her long blonde hair. You couldn't see her face, but she had an arm up to her head as if blocking the sunlight from her eyes. I hung it on the wall above the dresser. She was free.

If that woman was trapped in death and could not escape this existence, I hoped she found comfort in knowing she would always have a home as long as I'm alive.

It has been many years since I purchased the home in Prescott. Now I am old and as I tuck myself in bed at night, I oftentimes hear that music box turn on as I close my eyes.

I believe one day soon we will be friends.

"When I Saw you, I fell in love, and you smiled because you knew."
(Come ti vidi m'innamorai, e tu sorridi perche lo sai.)

Arrigo Boito (1802 – 1856)

MANDY

CHAPTER ONE

Jon P. Houghtin was a tough sixty-one-year-old guy. He was a smart guy. Everything he ever tried to accomplish in his life, he succeeded far beyond his expectations, yet he remained a humble man and that was what people liked about him most. He had many promotions during the tenure of his career, and when he retired his office walls boasted many awards and affirmations from co-workers and clients with nothing but kind sentiments and well wishes for a prosperous future.

In earlier years, Jon had always anticipated his retirement with great plans of traveling to exotic lands and beginning new hobbies; possibly even writing a book. However, as the years ebbed on, closer to this goal, his excitement began to dull. He began to worry about his age, his health, and he became fearful of possibly losing his mental capacity. He had begun to witness many of his friends and co-workers faltering in their later years. Jon saw them eventually needing the assistance of canes, having their driver licenses revoked, experiencing forgetfulness and, of course, dealing with the nightmare of being incontinent. Noticing his friend's eyes as their children would step in and insist they take part in making decisions for them was awful for Jon to witness. Seeing the humanity drain from their once strong and knowledgeable faces and watching them give up as they lost their freedom was the most heart wrenching thing of all for Jon to witness.

Jon had always been incredibly independent and losing his ability to make his own decisions or having someone try to take those rights away was what terrified him most in life. This was certainly never a concern or an issue he ever thought he would EVER have to deal with, and it scared him to death that it could be a possible reality now.

His portfolio was tip-top, and he had always managed his finances himself, never even considering the advice from professional brokers or others who came forward to assist in these sensitive matters. He was confident in the knowledge of his own empowerment and refused any outside support on any personal issues.

CHAPTER TWO

On a whim, Jon decided to buy a cabin in Walker, Arizona. He had never seen the property in person and the entire purchase was done via cell phone, videos and discussions online. He was okay with that after thoroughly checking out the broker's credentials, thus learning that the agent as well as the brokerage was in fact, very knowledgeable of the area with years of experience. His decision to sign off on the contract was an easy one, especially when the inspections came back positive.

Jon was very excited to visit the property and after his children's attempts at having him negate on the contract, thereby releasing him from all obligations to purchase, which is legal in Arizona within a specific time frame after signing, he promptly snuffed out their requests abruptly and harshly.

He loved his children and knew they loved him, but he adamantly refused to let them influence his desires about his long-awaited retirement. He had worked diligently for years. Putting in long, hard hours and devoted most of his life to his career. He was hell-bent on enjoying this time in his life on his own terms. He resented the fact that his children were so obviously trying to control him because they felt his decisions would inevitably take money out of their pockets and put it in someone else's. Jon knew that the decisions he made now, while nearing the end of his life, would greatly affect them, and so did they. His finances and his choices were still his own and he wanted to keep it that way. Besides, he had compensated his children in other ways so seeing their obvious greed upset him to no end.

Two weeks after the purchase contract was ratified, Jon rented a U-Haul trailer, loaded up his old 1980 Yamaha XS 1100 Midnight Special, a few yard tools, kitchen items, and other miscellaneous things that he had collected over the years and headed west.

His plan was to keep his current home, after all money wasn't an issue and he had many happy memories in that old house. His children had been born there, and his oldest son had even gotten married in the expansive backyard overlooking a seasonal creek where deer and other wildlife were often seen drinking the clean water and eating the wild blackberries that grew along the edge of the woods. He often would grab a book, a pillow, and throw a blanket down on the grass and lie, oftentimes with his old Canon A-1, waiting for something to stir. It never took long before he found himself catching some type of wildlife activity. He felt lucky to have those memories.

He had always wanted to explore the west and the wild frontier of Arizona seemed to be the best place to start. It had wonderful history and was smack in the middle of many popular destinations. Sedona, Flagstaff, The Grand Canyon, the Colorado River, Vegas, Mexico, Phoenix, and many more hotspots were all less than a day's drive. Jon was excited to explore these areas and knowing they would be in his new backyard was icing on the cake. He didn't plan on moving there permanently, at least not at that point in time, but he was thrilled that he had a place to call his own near such enticing attractions. He thought maybe he could bounce back and forth. After all, isn't that what a lot of retirees did these days? Summer here, winter there. Shit, maybe he'd buy a place in Mexico, too. That'd be puttin' on the dog, wouldn't it?

His GPS led the way and got him almost entirely there on the first try. Once he arrived in town, he realized his arm was sore from waving as everyone who passed him threw up a hello gesture. Yeah, he could get used to this, he thought. Hell, on the East Coast people only waved if they needed help or were giving you the finger.

He drove up the driveway and the house looked just like it had been advertised.

The asphalt ended about a mile from the cabin and turned into gravel. The road gently transitioned from pinion pines and high brush to large pine trees that scented the air with the wonderfully thick aroma of Christmas that up until now, he had only been lucky enough to experience once a year. He didn't have to see it to know he was home. He could feel it in his heart.

It was exactly as advertised.

The A-frame structure was full of windows, and the flower boxes that lined the deck were calling his name. A swing had been built which hung off the upper deck that overlooked the lush forest and wildflowers that grew randomly along the property line.

As he opened the front door, the entry dropped to a sunken living room. Along the diameter of the sunken area was a raised six-foot-wide path with rustic wooden railings separating the spaces. A spiral staircase led to the upper loft. The space was open, inviting, and couldn't have been more perfect. He sighed happily with relief and knew his decision to come was the right one.

The kitchen was off the living room and a large spit hung in the center with a huge exhaust tent just above. You could roast a pig in there if you wanted to from the size of it, he thought. The brickwork was astounding and the double ovens and counterspace were fit for a king. The place had everything. At that moment he was so thankful he didn't listen to what would have turned out to be bad advice from his family and friends. In fact, at that moment he thought even his children would have approved of the investment.

After a short power nap, he carted what he had brought from the U-Haul inside. Grabbing a Dos Equis out of the cooler, Jon carefully considered where he wanted things to go and began putting things in their appropriate place. There were a lot more items he needed, and he was prepared for that. A trip to Walmart was the first thing on his agenda.

It was at that moment he smiled and realized that he couldn't care less if he ever went back to Maryland. He was doubting his sanity forever having lived there in the first place. Nothing but Democrats and people working the system to get stuff for free. Yeah, he thought, maybe he would stay in Arizona for longer than he had originally planned.

CHAPTER THREE

Jon woke up the next morning to cool breezes and sunshine.

He walked out of his bedroom and onto the widow's walk that reached beyond the point of the home. It was an A-frame after all, and he couldn't begin to know the architectural standards that were involved in making a widow's walk work, but according to the building inspector he hired, it did, and he wasn't going to worry about it now. He just stood and breathed the Arizona pines into his lungs.

As he did, he suddenly felt a cold presence surround him. It was as though he was no longer alone, and he thought he smelled something. He couldn't quite place it, but it was like a flower or a perfume. He couldn't pinpoint the aroma, but it wasn't natural. There was no foliage or flora nearby that would give off such as pleasant fragrance. He wondered if honeysuckle was in bloom this time of year. He didn't know, but he liked it.

Jon's mind quickly drifted to his list of errands, and he began deciding which to do first. He started coffee and jumped into the shower.

When he went into the kitchen, he noticed his coffee was in a cup and absent-mindedly grabbed it and began drinking. It tasted wonderful and had the perfect amount of creamer and sugar. He sat it down on the counter and took a step back. He hadn't prepared it. He thought he had lost his mind for a minute and forgot, but no, he was sure he didn't.

Once again, he felt coldness overcome him and smelled the fragrance of honeysuckle. What the fuck was going on?

He wasn't going to let anything break his mood, though. He was happy and life was good.

The place was too perfect; it was exactly what he wanted and had been hoping to find for years. Nothing bad was happening. He was going to stay come hell or high water. Jon was a person who could handle things. He could deal and make most any unexpected event work towards his favor. Besides, it was only a fragrance and coffee. These were good things. They were welcoming things. The last thing he was going to do was get spooked and run out with his tail between his legs this late in the game.

Jon spent quite a while making his list for both the grocery store and Home Depot. Besides being incredibly organized he was a list maker and randomly forgetting something he needed while out and about was unheard of. Later, as he stood about three paces from committing himself to joining the checkout line at Home Depot, he had a hard, gut feeling that he was forgetting something. He wasn't sure what it was, but he knew that when he left the house, he had been anxious. Being anxious was a strange feeling for Jon and he wasn't quite sure how to handle it. Finally, he realized he needed some cleaning supplies and also wanted to look at the gas grills. How could he have almost forgotten that? A grill is right up there with oxygen. A man without cooked meat is a man without . . . pants. He grinned and started walking toward the barbeque section.

Even though it was nearing the end of summer he was happy to see the store still had quite a few grills on display. He picked out the one that looked like a big green egg as it was supposed to be the hot lick this year and all the consumer magazines were giving it a thumbs up. It looked ridiculous, but he knew he could always bring it back if it didn't hold up to the reviews. It wasn't very attractive, but it was only him he was cooking for, and he knew that probably wouldn't change any time soon.

When he got back to the house, he was greeted by music coming from the stereo. It was soft and weirdly romantic. He knew good and well he hadn't left it playing, and as soon as he brought in his bags, he turned it off.

He tried not to think about it. In fact, he refused to.

His phone alerted him to the time, as it always did in recent years. It had just turned five o'clock. That was when his workday ended, well that was when it was supposed to end. Once he retired, he just couldn't bring himself to cancel the alarm. No wonder his stomach felt empty, and his normally sunny personality was beginning to fade. As he walked back into the kitchen, he realized that the food he was planning for dinner, that he had placed inside the ice box, was back on the counter.

Maybe he was beginning to lose his shit after all. This was a thought he definitely wasn't going to dwell on. Forgetfulness was not a personality trait he'd ever had to worry about. Besides, it had been a busy couple of weeks, and between the drama of organizing his move across the country and setting up housekeeping, he knew he was more tired than he was willing to admit to. Jon made a mental note to take it easy for the next couple of days. He was always a go-getter and to be honest, relaxing just wasn't something he wanted to get used to doing. He'd make some adjustments in the future, after all he was no spring chicken anymore and it wasn't rocket science.

Jon marinated the meat while he set up the grill, then rinsed the veggies.

He'd had a full day and his body entertained thoughts of early slumber, which he didn't feel guilty about one bit.

Usually, he was a late night kinda guy, but not tonight. He fixed his dinner, ate it, and decided the dishes could wait until morning.

Although his body needed sleep badly, his mind was racing. It was also dreaming of weird things that were unsettling and when he awoke, he didn't feel well. He had pictures in his mind of a woman running through the rain. She was ill and there was no one to help her. When he looked out his French doors that morning, he remembered the scene from his dream. It was exactly the same view from his bedroom doors.

He wasn't sure if it was coincidence, or the fact that he still felt a little out of his element. After all he had only been there two days. The house was wonderful, but things were still strange to him, especially in the middle of the night. He resigned himself to knowing it would take a while for things to start feeling normal.

CHAPTER FOUR

Jon was feeling excited about a new day. After going on a short walk around his property and taking a quick shower in his first ever walk-in, he dried off, and dressed. As he opened the bathroom door to relieve the steam, he immediately smelled the pleasant aroma of bacon wafting up into the loft and into the bath.

"What the hell?" he thought to himself. It caught him off guard and he didn't know how to react. He walked as quietly and as slowly as he could down the stairs. He was hoping his daughter had flown to Arizona to surprise him and let herself in.

"Rachel is that you, darlin?" No response.

"If you're trying to surprise me, I sure wish you'd jump out and say hello."

Rachel was Jon's daughter who was in her late twenties, had recently graduated from the University of Maryland, and was part of the group who thought he was nuts to move all the way to Arizona on what they thought was a whim. She clearly didn't understand the urgency of "spreading your wings" at any age, because she had made it very clear she didn't want him to leave Maryland.

He tip-toed through the foyer. The living room was empty. No suitcases in the hallways. God how he hoped her black Lab, Charlie would come flying around the corner. "Come on Charlie," he thought.

He walked into the kitchen and saw a plate covered with paper towels and six pieces of bacon resting on top soaking up the grease. The table also had been set for him. Buttered toast and cheesy eggs sat on the counter in his mother's small warming tray. Jon had brought the tray to Arizona, not because he actually ever used it, but he couldn't bear to give it away since his mother had loved it so much. He was only attempting to clear the unnecessary clutter from his Maryland home.

Jon stared at the food that had been cooked for him. Just enough for one person.

He looked out the window hoping to see a familiar car. He opened the front door to see if anyone was in the driveway.

He was happy assuming Rachel had probably gone into town to grab a last-minute item; probably a curling iron or some other girly thing, thinking he was still sleeping yet still wanting to surprise him with breakfast. It all smelled fantastic and with little hesitation he sat down and began to eat.

Waiting for her return, which never happened, Jon decided to head into town for himself and give her a call on the way. If she was visiting, he wanted to make her stay comfortable and get some new bed sheets for her room and what not.

After contemplating his life while driving into town, he accepted the fact he was single, older, and in his heart, he wished he did have someone to share his life with on a regular basis although he never considered it a huge priority. He was used to being alone. He did have friends and unexpected adult sleepovers from time to time over the years, and totally accepted the cards that had been dealt for him. He was content and satisfied with being alone. He kept himself busy and he had his children to spoil. He was pleased and the new investment in Walker was a good adventure. For the first time in ages, he was looking forward to his new life.

Jon called Rachel and after the second time she finally picked up the phone.

"Where are ya, girl? Thanks for the breakfast. You in town?"

"Hi Dad, what? My cell isn't working right, I'm at the office and I can't hear you very well. I'm getting ready to go to into a staff meeting. Is everything okay? Are you settling in?"

Jon replied as calmly as he could muster, "Sure babe, I'm great. I just wanted to let you know the place is beautiful. You're gonna love it."

"I'm glad Daddy! But, hey I gotta run . . . I'll call ya later, okay?"

"Sure, hon, I just wanted to check in. We'll talk soon. Love you!"

"Love you, too, Daddy! Send me some pictures."

She hung up before he could respond.

At this point, Jon couldn't imagine who had made his breakfast. This was turning into a weird situation quickly. Normally, Jon would have been concerned, but nothing bad was happening. He hadn't been poisoned; no one had tried to burn his new house down or stab him in the shower. In fact, he was a little intrigued. He figured if he could see it, he could shoot it if he had to. Otherwise, until whatever it was began to show malicious tendencies, he would deal with it and consider it a learning experience in a spooky sort of way.

On the safe side, however, Jon did decide to have all the locks changed and add a home protection service immediately. He bought the "Ring" which was a home security system he could link to his cell phone. He could add as many cameras as he wanted to monitor any outside area or room within the cabin and be notified immediately upon any movement or activity.

This was both a challenge and an adventure for him.

Regarding the events he had seen thus far, Jon thought it must be a female. A nurturing type due to the nice fragrances, the cooking, and now otherwise kind interventions. He didn't feel threatened in any way, and somehow felt sympathetic towards whomever it was that was trying so desperately to invite and welcome him into his new space.

Jon wondered who she was. Who she had been. He wondered if this was a woman spirit, why was she still here, in this house? Was she as lonely in death as he might be in life? Was she searching for companionship and unable to fully cross over to the land of the dead? What could have happened to her to keep her here on this side with the living?

For a strange reason he couldn't explain, he felt more comfortable thinking of these occurrences as ghostly apparitions versus someone simply sneaking into his home all hours of the day . . . and night when he was vulnerable.

The following morning Jon visited the town office building where the land documents were kept and learned that his home had once belonged to a single woman. In fact, she was the first owner of the property back when the town was still young. After further research he learned that she had been a teacher and something of a renegade who had devoted her life to those who needed aid. She spread the news of peace and God until old age finally took her.

Although dead, she was still here in every way. He was sure of it.

As he read about her, he learned about her life, and his heart changed in many ways. She had accomplished so much towards helping others and teaching them to respect each other and love one another. Realizing she was still in the home made his heart warm. "My God. Could this really be happening?" he asked himself.

Jon had begun mentioning "her" to folks in town by making simple comments which included her in his daily activities. The people he spoke to soon began to have doubts to his lucidity, although they nodded reassuringly to him and smiled as they listened to his musings.

CHAPTER FIVE

Over the course of the next year Jon never saw the woman, although the house continued to welcome him with wonderful fragrances and kind gestures that varied from soft music greeting him in the evening hours to warm bubble baths prepared when he awoke in the mornings. He found himself bringing fresh cut flowers home for no reason and purposely removing his shoes before entering the house.

Although technically alone, Jon never felt lonely. In fact, he didn't even consider himself alone anymore. His days were full being thankful for "her" kind courtesies and his gestures such as bringing fresh flowers into the home and wiping his feet were his way to do thoughtful things in return.

One night Jon fell ill and could not care for himself. It had come upon him suddenly and his temperature at one point reached almost one hundred and four degrees. He knew he was hot. He had managed to make himself a little soup earlier in the day, but by this time it was after sunset, and he couldn't manage to even sit up.

His vision began playing tricks on him and as he lay, beads of perspiration dripping from his face, he wondered if he was dying. He thought without fear that maybe he was.

Moments later a woman in a pioneer dress with golden blonde hair which flowed over her shoulders, walked into his room, seemingly from nowhere. Her hair was swept gently back off her face and her smile was calming and lovely. He couldn't remember the last time he had seen such a beautiful woman. She was carrying a small bowl of water and a white hand towel. She sat on the edge of the bed next to him and wiped his face and neck, gently cooling him off and relieving the heat that saturated his bones.

As he stared at her, into those dark, ageless eyes, he tried to speak, but she only smiled and covered his lips with one of her fingers, graciously hushing him into silence.

He wasn't sure how long he had slept, but it felt like an eternity. It was early morning; his fever had broken, and he was no longer uncomfortable. In fact, he felt a little hungry and thought he would actually be able to hold a little food down.

Jon sat up on the side of the bed, noticing the bowl of water on the nightstand. The hand towel was still damp and neatly folded over the side of the bowl. He remembered her coming to him. Had he imagined it in his delirium? Probably, but it all seemed so real. He wanted to believe. Then he remembered her dark eyes, so caring and strong and he knew it was real. She had come to him. She saved his life and he now only wished he could have saved hers.

One part of him was thrilled to have finally seen her and felt blessed that she saved him. On the other hand, he wished he would have died so he could finally hold her in his arms. It was at that moment he realized he had fallen in love with her and for the first time he said her name out loud. Mandy JoHansen.

At that moment, downstairs soft music began to play, and Jon smiled.

CHAPTER SIX

Jon lived in Walker for the next ten years.

His family visited him often and continued to try and talk him into moving back to Maryland. To these sentiments Jon would smile and shake his head adamantly. Sometimes he would look up into the air as if he were making secret contact with an invisible entity. His family only looked at one another and they too, like some townsfolk, began to doubt Jon's mental clarity.

On their last visit to Walker, his oldest daughter, Evie, had commented that she and her husband had begun thinking about buying a second home in the area. It was after all a wonderfully quaint town with so much history. It had countless nearby attractions and was also a great place to raise a family. Jon thought this was a great idea, however it caught him completely off-guard.

Jon enjoyed the fact he was finally getting the validation that he deserved. "You just never know about family. Sometimes they come around, and sometimes they don't," he thought to himself and openly winked to "Mandy" who Jon knew was close by.

His family didn't mention to him that their reasons to move west weren't entirely true. They were beginning to worry about him being alone and so far away from town. They also had noticed during their recent visits Jon's gestures and expressions to a person no one was able to see except Jon himself. They didn't like that he was suddenly so mysteriously happy.

If he did have someone in his life, who, and where was she? They began to sadly believe his age was getting the best of him and his newfound companion didn't really exist. After all, he was now in his early seventies.

The next morning as he drove everyone to meet the Shuttle-U, which in turn drove them to Sky Harbor in Phoenix, the closest commercial airport, they took turns holding one another and saying their goodbyes. They were short and sweet as they all visited fairly frequently. Plus, between Skype and Facebook video chats it seemed no matter where you were in the world these days, you were never far away from the ones you loved.

Jon watched as the van pulled away and continued to wave as it drove out of sight.

CHAPTER SEVEN

After getting back to the house and doing a few chores he had decided to ride his vintage XS1100 down the mountain to Skull Valley and grab some lunch. It was a cool, clear day and he hadn't taken it out of the shed in a few weeks. It would do the bike good to charge its battery, and the switch backs along the mountain would do Jon good as well. Although he was seventy-one, he felt great. His health was good, he was in shape, and riding at his age was common for a lot of folks. "Today's seventy is like yesterday's sixty, and that's a fact, Jack," he mused to himself and Mandy, who he knew was nearby.

The bike started quick and reliable as always. Jon did a safety check, and as it warmed up a little, he put his wallet, keys, and other needed items in the magnet bag he had on the tank. As he rolled out of the driveway he turned back and winked. He always did that these days. The wink was for Mandy.

A few miles out of town as Jon headed south on I-89 he rounded a switchback and saw there was a doe with a fawn close behind her crossing the highway in front of him. Jon knew it had to be one or the other, but hoped there might be just enough space to get between the shoulder and the doe. There was absolutely no room available for him to stop and miss them both. Unfortunately, the doe heard his motor which created fear and she began to run in panic. She centerpunched Jon's bike and threw him sideways. The bike flew off the side of the highway but at that location there were neither guardrails nor much of a shoulder. Jon never stood a chance. He hit both front and rear brakes which made things worse. The front brakes locked up, the rear brakes slid the bike sideways and before he knew it, he was completely out of control.

He stood up on the pegs planning to jump off and clear himself from the bike so he wouldn't fly off the mountain with it, which was a good call, but unfortunately there were trees. As he jumped off the motorcycle the front end hit a little ditch which upended the bike and as it flew upward it pivoted forward into a juniper.

Helmet or no helmet, pads or no pads, a seventy-one-year-old body wasn't going to fare well during a motorcycle accident at any speed. Jon's once handsome and strong physique laid broken and bleeding on the ground among rocks and goat heads. He knew he was dying, and his last thoughts were about Mandy JoHansen.

CHAPTER EIGHT

Jon's mind cleared as he lay crumpled at the base of a tree. His first sensation was a warm hand gently caressing the side of his face. He smelled lavender and for the first time he experienced the most sensual kiss he ever had in his life as someone bent down over him.

As he opened his eyes, he found he was now alone and laying among daisies on a hillside, and the valley views were breathtaking. The beauty was astounding. "Was this heaven?"

The old hardwood trees along the side of the meadow were full and the leaves were green and large, and he felt good as a refreshing cool breeze blew over him. He closed his eyes again.

The next moment he heard the footfalls of a horse. They slowed and he found himself sitting up effortlessly. Jon was dumbfounded that he was no longer in pain and was free of shattered bones. The old age had also disappeared from his body, and he was in his youth. At that moment he opened his eyes to a new world.

Mandy was sitting bareback on a large white mare and gracefully held out her hand towards him. She was young, beautiful, and everything he had imagined in his dreams. At last, they were together. He stood, mounted her horse, and together they rode into the bright sunshine.

"Two lovely Sisters, still and sweet
As flowers, stand side by side;

Their soul-subduing looks might cheat
The Christian of his pride;

Such beauty hath the Eternal poured
Upon them not forlorn,

Though of a lineage once abhorred,
Nor yet redeemed from scorn."

William Wordsworth (1770 – 1850) ~

THE TWINS

CHAPTER ONE

This story began in 1975, when I was only ten years old. Although I was too young to remember the actual details, there have been many townsfolk for many years talking about the girls and their awful departure from this world. Some say they are still seen from time to time, but others say that part of the story is just crap. Personally, no one wants to believe in crap, but when it's thrown in your face, or you find yourself stepping in it, it's hard to not believe it.

The dead girls were twins, nine years of age at the time of their deaths. They weren't identical and one was very petite for her age. Their smiles were big and genuine. It was said they were so friendly even the unkind old lady at the end of Main Street enjoyed talking to them when they walked by. Each girl received good grades in school and had won the hearts of most anyone who had been lucky enough to meet them.

Their names were Tabby and Nelly Turner and they lived in the big white farmhouse next to the railroad tracks on the east side of town. The house still stands, although it's in bad need of painting and other cosmetic repairs, but they say the frame and foundation are still in great shape.

It's been many years, forty-seven to be exact, and the house has been up for sale numerous times. Many potential purchasers have walked through it, but no one ever ends up writing an offer. The location is perfect, except for the train tracks following alongside of the property, which some buyers love, and other buyers hate. I feel, however, and many agree, that the tracks add to the smalltown feeling, which is loved by so many. The house has that wonderful old-time character and quaint yet aristocratic curb appeal. The realtors all agree that when the house is shown people seem very interested until they go into the third bedroom at the top of the stairs. That was the bedroom that Nelly and Tabby shared.

They say the house is haunted, which is the "crap" part of the story I mentioned earlier. I'll get into all of that in a minute.

CHAPTER TWO

Our town is called Iamsville. The pronunciation is just as it looks, just lose the "A". It's located seven miles southeast of Frederick, Maryland. Iamsville is a wonderfully rural town that, back in the day, was best known for its Dairy Queen hot fudge sundaes and its only movie theatre which happened to be a drive-in. It only played G rated movies and was not to be confused with the XXX rated pictures they showed in Bowie, Maryland a couple hours away. The drive-in was a few acres of land that was wedged between Plunket's Dairy Farm and the Livestock Auction.

Nothing unusual or out of the ordinary ever seemed to happen in Iamsville. However, on Thanksgiving, at Christmas, the fourth of July, and Labor Day we did have the best parades in the state. Iamsville's GWG Majorettes and Drum Corp. (named after our town's founder) were the best along the East Coast and the whole town was damn proud of them.

One day in early April when the girls were coming home from school, they had decided to walk instead of ride the school bus, which was their normal routine. Their mother's birthday was three days away and Tabby suggested how nice it would be to walk through town on the way home and stop at the Five and Dime to see if they had any of those big boxes of assorted chocolates their mom enjoyed snacking on during the Lawrence Welk Show. Each girl had been saving their milk money for well over a month in hopes of getting their mom a great present that year. Nelly agreed, and that afternoon instead of hopping on the bus, they walked home.

Upon entering the Five and Dime, they both looked at each other, both feeling proud of their accomplishment. This was the first time either girl had been in town without having the watchful eyes of one of their parents on them every minute like a hawk. They were big girls now, little ladies, in fact, and it was about time they spread their wings a little and shopped like adults. After all, they were almost ten years old, they were almost two digits old.

Tabby and Nelly went immediately over to the candy selection. There were several choices of assorted chocolate boxes, and after they both agreed on the right size, they realized they still had money left over for something else. This excited them immensely!

On the way home, they visited numerous shops and decided to stop in an old antique store at the end of Main Street. While walking through the jewelry section which also boasted various kinds of fancy table lighters, gaudy broaches, and old liquor flasks, they both spotted a beautiful ring that they almost began fighting over immediately.

The ring was silver with silver leaves surrounding a large stone with an unusual shape that captivated them at first glance. It was very ornate, even larger than the average dinner ring. One could call it tasteless, but it was obvious it was very old, and the girls quickly discussed buying it and how they'd share it. The lady helping them said it was a blood stone and it was said to have many magical properties. The girls didn't care about that side of it at all, but only loved the glistening beauty that the stone provided while the lights were shining upon it.

After paying the saleswoman, they left for home with now empty pockets. It's been said that was when the horror in their lives began.

CHAPTER THREE

The next day at school during Tabby and Nelly's lunch break, Kirsten Nolan sat down beside them, as usual, and the girls began to eat their lunch.

"Oh my Gaawd! Let me see that ring!" Kirsten whispered, grabbing Nelly's hand to inspect the ring more closely. "Where'd you get it? I love it! It's gorgeous . . . with a hint of creepy. I can't explain it, but it's great." She held Nelly's hand right up to her face and gawked over it.

"We were at that antique store in town yesterday looking for a birthday present for our mom," Nelly said. "We're taking turns wearing it."

"Yeah, we're already fighting over it," Tabby added.

"Well, it's great. You wanna sell it? I swear I'd buy it."

"No way," both girls said at once. "Maybe you can have it when we're both dead and gone!" Tabby added, laughing.

That afternoon as the school bus arrived at their stop, the girls unloaded and began crossing the street as usual.

No sooner had Tabby breached the front of the bus, some redneck in a tricked out Chevelle SS blasted past the stop and almost hit her.

Tabby backed up as quickly as she could and knocked Nelly back as well. The bus driver honked, but it was after the fact and the driver of the car disappeared quickly. The automatic arm that swung out once the bus driver hit the yellow warning lights was torn off, and luckily, no one was hurt. It was alarming and the bus driver didn't even have time to catch the license plate of the car.

As the girls stood in the street, eyes wide, trying to figure out what just happened, they could only embrace one another, happy neither were harmed.

When they arrived home, they had a wonderful dinner, and their mother was so happy that the day ended well; she thanked God for his mercy and prayed for his continued love to look over them. Their dad, however commented that if God was really looking out for them, they wouldn't have had such a close call in the first place.

CHAPTER FOUR

The next day the twins were raking leaves on the side of the house. It was a sunny, crisp Saturday morning in October and the autumn colors that had been so predominately bright and eye-catching only a couple of weeks before had already begun to lose their brilliance and change into deeper and less stunning hues.

Much to Tabby's regret, it was Nelly's turn to wear the ring that day. But that was part of the deal. She wasn't particularly happy about it, but they lived in the country, and everyone knew that country people's word and a handshake meant everything - even with little girls.

Moments after they had finished raking all the dead leaves into one gigantic pile, the girls decided to destroy it by running into the center of the huge mound and having a leaf fight, covering each other in the dry fronds. They laughed and laughed until they finally grew tired and came to a rest laying buried and hidden from sight, each breathing hard and enjoying the heavy scent of the leaves surrounding them. What a wonderful smell.

Their mother was busy making lunch in the kitchen and poked her head between the curtains when she saw the girls through the window. She remembered when she was young, and she and her siblings had played in the piles of autumn leaves that her parents made them rake every year. Such good times, long before everyone owned leaf blowers and automatic lawn mowers that blew the leaves into a bag on their sides. Although her husband had brought one of the fancy blowers home a year before, she never used it. As far as she knew it was on the top shelf in the shed, still in its box. She wanted her children to grow up with the memories of leaves and playing.

"You girls be careful out there!" she hollered.

"We will Momma!" the girls hollered back, still playing.

As the sisters lay hidden, each girl heard a soft noise coming from the other side of the railroad tracks. They sat up and looked at each other, their minds forgetting about the leaves. The noise could have been a small animal, maybe even the fox kit they saw recently in the woods behind the house from their bedroom window. Maybe it had finally gathered its nerve and come for a visit. The girls looked at each other in sheer excitement and decided it was time for them to get up and investigate.

That was the last time anyone ever saw Tabby and Nelly Turner.

CHAPTER FIVE

As the following days turned into weeks, then months, the law enforcement detectives did their investigating. They asked their questions and put up their little flyers on the corners of all the intersections and in business establishments. Nearby towns got involved in the hunt for the Turner Twins. They were even on the nightly news. But no one ever heard a peep from the girls or whomever had abducted them. Back then, especially in small towns when people or things disappeared, they stayed gone.

After a couple of years, the Turners moved away from the beautiful neighborhood they thought they would live in forever. They had put the home they'd had hopes of entertaining their grandchildren in, the home that they would eventually leave for Tabby and Nelly on the market. No parent should outlive their children. It wasn't fair. They had no illusions that their daughters were still alive, and they simply could not bear to live there any longer. It had too many memories and although they did not want to forget them, they didn't feel it healthy to be reminded of them every day. Tabby and Nelly's father had been offered a "can't pass up" promotion with his company, which required them to relocate to Bend, Oregon. He accepted the position, and in June of 1977 they said good-bye to Iamsville, leaving the responsibilities of maintaining and selling the home to a local property management company. No one ever heard from them again.

The big house stood empty for almost another two years and in December of 1979 the house was rented by a man who had come into town hoping to refurbish an antique store that had been currently for sale. He was very knowledgeable in the business and had reviewed the past inventory of the store with great care. After the commercial real estate purchase had been completed the new owner decided to renovate the building to give it a more welcoming and up-to-date appearance. He planned to jump on that task as soon as he got settled into the house.

The man who moved into the old Turner house by the tracks was Harry Linley. Being a single guy, he didn't have a whole lot of furniture, just the necessities. He had been used to living in an efficiency that sat over his last store. Both his prior living accommodations and his store were very small, and he had been wanting to enlarge his business with a lot more square footage. He considered himself very lucky to have found the new property in Iamsville with such a perfect location to both shopping and other tourist attractions. He knew the home was over-kill for his needs, but there weren't any other housing options available so close to the store, and he didn't want to be more than just a couple miles away. He would make this set-up work and was very excited about his new home and beginning a new chapter in his life.

CHAPTER SIX

T he third night Harry was in the house he heard children's music coming from down the hall. When it started playing, he had been dozing in and out of sleep and thought he remembered leaving his cell phone downstairs. There was no way he was going down there to turn his phone off. It was late, he was now half asleep and since it didn't bother him, he ignored it. After only a few minutes it had conveniently lulled him into a deep and refreshing sleep.

The next morning upon awaking and climbing out of bed, he noticed his cell phone on his nightstand. Weird. He recalled hearing it during the night and thinking it was downstairs. He grabbed it to check the time. He also remembered that he had completely forgotten to set his alarm. Thank goodness Nina, his assistant, had the keys to the store and was able to open up for him. Also forgetting the music from the night before, he quickly showered, dressed, and ran out the door to begin his day.

Nina Cantrell had begun working at the shop about four years prior and was so glad Harry had kept her on. She knew every item in the store and could locate any piece at the drop of a hat. She enjoyed her job and wanted to keep it. At the time the deal was closing, the prior owner suggested to Harry that he would appreciate it if he would consider keeping Nina on the payroll. He had told her how valuable she had been to him and since she was so knowledgeable of the inventory, she would be a good asset. Harry agreed to keep her on without batting an eye and things had been working out very well indeed.

Later that night after he arrived home, he found two hair ribbons laying on the stair landing. The colors in the ribbons were faded and he noticed there were remains of old leaves clinging to the dirty and frayed edges. He often saw unusual items laying around in random locations. He was an antique dealer, after all, and clutter was his game. He didn't think twice about them as he picked them up and tossed them into the trash can in the upstairs bathroom before returning downstairs to make his dinner.

A few nights later as he was climbing into bed, he noticed a light reflected on the hallway floor coming from a room down the hall from his own.

After gently yanking the chain on the antique light which sat atop his bed side table, he threw his legs over the edge of the bed and slid on his bedroom slippers. Then he scuffled down the hallway. As he approached the door, he thought it strange that he would leave a light on in there. He never used that room, and he had no furniture or need to go inside. He opened the door and was immediately hit with cold air. It was freezing. He walked to the window to see if it had been left open and found it was closed and locked. He felt around the edges of the window and felt no breeze coming in from outside. Then he knelt to check the heat ducts around the floor, but they were warm. He shrugged it off that it was an old drafty house and made a mental note to get some of that clear plastic stuff that goes around windows. It was fall after all, and winter was just around the corner. He realized he should prepare now for the brunt of it.

As he left the room he looked down and saw another hair ribbon. This time when he picked it up, he was a little unnerved to see that one side of it was completely covered in something dark brown. Could that be dried blood?

He tried not to think about it as he put the ribbon on the basin in the bathroom. This discovery bothered him somewhat, but he would deal with it later. It was late, and tomorrow would be a busy day that was due to start early.

CHAPTER SEVEN

Harry had been in the house a couple months and although he didn't want to dwell on what was obviously turning into oftentimes unnerving events, he refused to buy into considering the house had a "spirit" in it. Absolutely no. If he started walking that plank, he would drive himself crazy, not to mention setting himself up for sleepless nights, and he refused to be uneasy in his own home. Nothing had ever jumped out at him or tried to hurt him. So far it was only finding weird things laying around and occasional music and lights being turned on. He was a big boy, and he could certainly deal with that.

The following Saturday morning he came downstairs in his flannel pajama bottoms, turned on some old Little Feat and began to make himself some pancakes and eggs. He reached for the big frying pan he kept in the cabinet over the refrigerator and put it on the stove. Then he began sorting through a wall cabinet for a good-sized bowl to mix the eggs in. As he grabbed one and turned toward the sink to rinse it out since he rarely used it, he thought he heard laughter. He found himself sliding the curtains open and looking outside.

What he saw shocked him and made his knees buckle. He had to grab onto the counter. Suddenly there were invisible hands on his shoulders, gripping him, holding him in front of the window. Harry couldn't turn around. He could barely breathe. He tried to fight the grip that was holding him but could not break free. Whatever was happening to him, whatever held him, wanted him to look out the window.

The day was glorious. Instead of seeing a barren, neglected yard he hadn't yet had time to work on, there were huge oak trees with colorful leaves everywhere. The lawn was a healthy green, thick, and lush. Bushes lined both sides of the driveway. The autumn flowers were in bloom and followed along the property line and at the base of every tree. Goldenrod, chrysanthemum in every color of the rainbow, aster in lavender and shades of pink, strawberry blonde marigolds, and the sweet alyssum, snow white in color hung out of the window boxes along every window!

Two little girls were raking the leaves into a big pile, and they were playing. The girls were smiling at one another and having a good time.

With no warning at all Harry yelled at the children, "You girls be careful out there!"

The girls waved at him, and he could have sworn they hollered back, "We will Momma!"

Without warning the curtains slammed shut and the hands that held him let go. Harry fell onto the floor. He lay there whimpering and in shock. His body was wet with perspiration and water was draining over the basin and onto the floor. How long had he been there? He didn't know.

He grabbed the counter and began to pull himself up, quickly taking the stopper out of the sink and turning the water off. As he did, he reached for the curtains and when he once again parted them and looked outside, he saw his truck in the driveway. The grass had gone, the trees were dead, the beautiful flowers and bushes were no longer there. The only thing outside was blowing dirt.

It took Harry a long time to get over that. He sunk back onto the kitchen floor and cried. What had happened here? Was he losing his mind? Someone had needed to show him something. Did someone want him to do something. If so, what?

He knew he wasn't alone any longer if, he ever was. He knew he wasn't in any harm, and he knew if someone meant to inflict evil on him, they surely would have. He was helpless, and completely defenseless against the hands that held him only minutes before. The hands that wanted him to see. What did it mean? All he could do was force himself to calm down and try to understand what was happening and what had already happened in this house. He needed to find out what evil took place here.

Chapter Eight

T he days following were met with dreadful expectations. Harry worked late hours and got to work very early in hopes of avoiding any more contact with those awful hands. He was afraid of another confrontation, but also knew there had to be another to learn more about what had happened. He wasn't sure if these occurrences would get worse and more intense.

When Harry saw the children playing in the yard, they were so happy. His heart went out to them. All he could do was wait and see what would happen next.

Two evenings later he had a dream.

As he laid in his bed, he felt the sense of being watched as he slept. Before he even opened his eyes, he knew they were there. He felt a pressure on his right arm. The pressure turned into a tugging feeling, and he knew he had to face what was touching him. He opened his eyes and recognized them as being the same girls, the twins from his daydream two days earlier.

The girls led him to that same bedroom down the hallway where he'd seen the light on weeks before. As the door opened and he was led inside, he realized he was being taken to the window. It was covered in condensation from the cold night air, but the words written on it were large and unmistakable.

"Find it."

Chapter Nine

W ithin a month or so after the shop had been redecorated and re-opened, a man in Lee denim jeans and a cashmere overcoat entered the store and walked up to the counter. He asked to speak to the owner and said he didn't mind waiting if he or she were currently busy.

"The guy was nice enough," Nina thought to herself as she walked towards the back room where Harry was sitting, eating his lunch, and going over invoices. It was close to the end of the month, and they had begun piling up.

"Nina, tell the guy I'll be out in about five minutes. I want to slam down the rest of this sandwich. Maybe we'll get lucky, and he'll buy something while he's waiting."

"Sure thing, Harry."

Nina walked back to the check-out counter and saw the man bent over the jewelry selection as if he was really interested in something.

"He'll be with you in about five minutes. He's just finishing something up and will be right out. Can I help you find anything in particular?" Nina asked.

"I don't know that you can. What I'm looking for was accidently sold at my grandparents' estate sale over five years ago. My brother and sisters and I stop at these kinds of shops whenever we can in hopes of finding it. It was my grandmother's family ring you see. It doesn't have much monetary value, but it's priceless to us," the man said.

"Hello. I'm Harry Linley, the owner," Harry said, not conscious of having interrupted their conversation.

"Hey, I hope I didn't catch you at a bad time," the man said as he looked up from the glass jewelry case. "I was just looking for a piece of jewelry you may have picked up. I don't know where you get your stuff, but this piece would have been from an estate sale quite a few years ago. I'm sure if you had it, it's probably gone by now, but I figured it was worth a shot to stop in."

Nina chimed in and said, "He's looking for a family ring that was accidently sold at his grandparents' estate sale."

"Oh wow, that's a bummer," Harry said. "What's it look like? We have a rather large selection of rings, plus some that we've recently purchased that we haven't put out on the shelves yet. Let's see if we've got it."

"Well, it was in a silver setting with leaves surrounding a large bloodstone." The guy smiled and added, "It's kinda' creepy, actually, but it had been in my grandmother's family, so you know how that goes. The stone is large and not completely smooth. It is almost eerily obscure and it's very old. I think once you've seen it, you're never going to forget it."

"Unless it's here right now, I won't be much help. I just recently bought the store and we've only been open a short time. I purchased a good part of the inventory from the prior owner," Harry said. "Nina, does that description ring a bell? Do you think you've ever seen a ring like that?"

Nina stood in disbelief with a half-smile on her face.

Tilting her head, she replied, "Oh my God, I think maybe I have."

The man looked at her dumbstruck. "Really?"

"Yes," Nina said. "I don't know quite how to say this. Some years ago, a couple of girls came in here looking around. They saw the ring and fell in love with it. They actually fought over it. They were sisters and bought it with plans to share it. It had to be the same ring. I mean you're right, once you've seen a ring like that you can't forget it. It was truly one of a kind and I've never seen anything else that comes close to resembling it. Anyway, they bought it and left the store."

"So, who were they, did you know them?" Harry asked.

"Sure. Everyone knows them. They were the Turner Twins," Nina said.

"Oh my God, this is awesome!" the man said. "Do you know where they live? I'll go there right now."

"A few days after they bought the ring, they disappeared," Nina said sadly. "The police never found them, and their family moved out of town. I heard the parents finally realized that their twins weren't coming back, and they couldn't bear to stay in the house any longer. It was awful. In fact, the story around town is that the house is haunted."

The man who said his name was Morgan, turned his back to them and grabbed his head. Nina looked at Harry, neither not knowing exactly what to say.

After a moment or two of awkward silence, Morgan said, "What I didn't tell you is that the ring needs to be found. You see, our family believes it's cursed. Nothing but tragedy and despair surrounds it. Nothing good has ever come from it. It's evil. I know it sounds crazy, but it's true. I would like to visit the home where the girls lived. Do you think that would be possible?"

"It's on the other side of town. You can't miss it. It's a big white three-story home that sits right next to the railroad tracks. People stay away from it for the most part. Since the twins disappeared, nothing grows in the yard, and for a long time people said they saw the faces of the girls in their bedroom window after midnight. Well, I guess people assume it was their bedroom window. I know I won't go there," Nina said.

Harry's face had gone ashen, and he didn't say a word.

Finally, he spoke, "If you plan on going over there, I'll lead the way."

"That would be great. So, you know the house then?"

"I sure do. I just moved into it," Harry replied.

CHAPTER TEN

Harry decided to close the store for the afternoon and the man followed him in his car to the house. Nina, who years ago said she would never go to the house, had decided she couldn't resist the adventure, so she followed the two of them in her little Dodge minivan.

As they followed one another to the house, Harry had taken the time to think a little bit. He didn't want to be a pushover to what might very well be a prank to make him look bad, but then again how could he explain the happenstances in that third-floor room, as well as the weird shit that happened on the stairs and in the kitchen recently? It was hard enough living alone in that house, the only house that was available when he needed it. Hell, he would have purchased an apartment in the heart of town if one had been available. He didn't need a house that size. Although, he must admit he did fall instantly drawn to it the first moment he saw it, all that extra room being perfect for extra inventory and what-not for the store. The house had called to him, and he thought it would be a challenge to fix it up and bring it back to life.

Yes, Harry would be happy in it. Now, looking back over the few weeks he'd been there he realized he may have been overlooking a lot of details. One, being that he was in denial of the fact he never truly felt alone. Something always seemed to be near him, and not in a very comforting manner. He had never felt in danger or frightened really, simply not alone.

Unfortunately, for Harry he had always been hardheaded in realizing his mistakes, or should I say admitting to his mistakes. But was this a mistake? Maybe it didn't have to be.

As he pulled into the drive, he realized it was true. The grass in the yard was replaced with nothing but dirt and weeds. The trees that once towered high had long since died. There were no longer any flower beds or bushes surrounding the house. Compared to the rest of the neighborhood, there was no reason why his property was so dried up and lifeless when the other neighboring properties were flourishing. Even the home itself had lost its character and beauty. What was happening here?

"I never saw it in its glory," Harry said. "I assumed since no one was here the owners just let the landscaping go. I dealt with a management company upon arriving in town and never met the owners before. I certainly never knew anything about their children."

Morgan asked Harry, "Have you noticed anything, well, "not right" about the house?"

"You mean have I seen any ghosts? No. Absolutely not. And to tell you the truth I'm not buying into all this shit. I have no idea who you are, and I have no doubt that you may be looking for a family heirloom, but don't try to poison me with all "this house is haunted" shit. You got me? For all I know I'm the new kid on the block and you might be the dealer down the street trying to turn me into a fuckin' joke. Well, I ain't having it."

Nina looked at Harry dumbstruck. She hadn't known him very long, true, but she had never seen him quite so edgy and certainly never as defensive as he was at that moment.

Morgan apologized, but the look on his face showed determination. It was evident that he wasn't going to give up.

Harry took a deep breath and stepped back.

"Go ahead, man. Look around. I'll play nice. Sorry I freaked out on you."

"No, I pushed you and I shouldn't have. I could have been a little softer in my approach. I guess my emotions got the best of me after Nina told me the story." Morgan took his right hand out of his pocket and offered it to Harry. "By the way, I'm Morgan Freeman. No relation," he said grinning.

Harry met his hand, and they shook. He was deliberately amused at Morgan's humor.

"I'm originally from Jonesport, Maine, but my family relocated to this area about twenty years ago."

Within a few minutes they were walking through the first floor living room and Morgan was trying to make Harry feel as comfortable as he could.

Nina walked a short distance behind them, remaining silent, eyes wide and waiting for something to grab her from behind or someone to scream.

After they had searched the home. Harry came clean and told him what had been happening since he had moved into the house.

Morgan listened intently. He was able to offer little help but let him know again that they needed to find that ring.

"The message written on the window . . . do you think finding the ring was what it meant?" Harry asked.

"You're damn right I do."

CHAPTER ELEVEN

That night Harry found himself pacing back and forth in the living room. His long strides and stocking feet gently distributing newly formed dust along the wooden planks. Mentally spent and not gaining any ground whatsoever in trying to figure out his dilemma, he finally left at about seven o'clock to pick up a pizza and a six-pack of Heineken and headed back to the house. Once he got home, he turned off the motor and sat in the driveway. Suddenly, his hunger left him, and his head began to fill up with thoughts of two little girls he wished he could have known.

The air inside his truck began to thicken, and Harry found himself straining to breathe. His chest was heavy. With an unsteady hand he reached for the window button. Nothing happened. Then he remembered the key was off and grinned at himself for being so easily shaken. Once lowered, the wind let in the cold November air. As it bit his face he breathed deeply and felt more comfortable.

Popping the top off a beer and taking a large pull, he once again leaned back and settled into the seat. As he looked out at the yard next to the driveway, he realized he was parked right next to the spot on the lawn where he'd seen the girls raking leaves.

What did Nina say about the last time the girls were seen? Were they raking leaves?

Later, as Harry sat down on the edge of the bed and tucked himself in for the night, he had two words on his mind.

"Find it."

CHAPTER TWELVE

Harry's eyes sprang open just after sunrise and he didn't even look at the clock. Within minutes he was dialing Morgan's cell phone number.

Morgan answered on the second ring.

"I think I know where it might be!" Harry said. "First, I need to go by the store and grab something. When can you get here?"

"I'll get dressed now and be there within a half hour."

"Perfect. See ya then." The line went dead.

When Harry got to the store, he was surprised to see that Nina had arrived early and had started pricing the new merchandise Harry had picked up at an auction just days before. With all the recent drama, the inventory had gone unattended to, and she was playing catch-up. The Christmas season was coming fast, and she wanted as much of the shelves stocked as soon as possible.

"What are you doing here so early? You are awesome, Nina. When was the last time I told you that?"

"You tell me every day, Harry."

"Damn, I'm good," he said. "Now, get your coat, throw the sign, and lock the door."

"Field trip?"

"Yep. My house."

"Harry, I keep telling you you're not my type," she said with her hands on her hips.

Harry laughed out loud as he ran to the rear of the store and grabbed a large box leaning against an old canopy bed frame and moved it aside to give them more room to exit through the back door.

They left the building together and she locked the door behind them.

Harry threw the box in the back of his truck, and Nina climbed in shotgun.

"So, what are we doing and why are you in such a rush?" she asked.

"You'll see."

CHAPTER THIRTEEN

The two of them pulled into the driveway right behind Morgan's Explorer. Morgan was sitting on the front porch swing drinking a large Starbuck's latte. There was a box balancing on the railing with two more drinks inside. As Nina and Harry walked up, he pointed and told them to help themselves. "I wasn't sure what you guys drank."

"Perfect, thanks, Morgan," Nina said happily as she handed one to Harry. "This is gonna hit the spot. Now, is someone going to tell me why we are here at the crack of dawn?"

"Yeah, I was wondering the same thing," Morgan said.

Harry cleared his throat and told them that he couldn't get out of his mind the fact that those hands forced him to look out the window where he saw the girls playing outside just before they disappeared. He started walking off the porch and motioned for them to follow.

As he walked around to the back of the truck, he dropped the tailgate and slid the box from the store onto it.

"Why didn't I think of that? Harry, you're a genius!" Nina said.

Morgan still didn't get it but waited until its contents would be unveiled.

Harry opened the box and pulled out a metal detector. "It's used, of course, but it's supposed to be a nice one. I Googled them before I bid on it. It's a mid-range detector that's good from about 8" to 16" deep. The cheap ones only go to about 5". I was going to sell it, but I think we need to break it in first. Shall we?"

"Let's do it! Great thinking. If that ring is out here, we should definitely find it with that thing," Morgan agreed.

Without notice, the kitchen windows blew outward, and glass rained down upon them as they each tried to dodge the shards as best they could. They looked at one another and wondered if something was trying to keep them from finding the ring.

They quickly turned on the metal detector. Each stood watching and listening for the alert sound which signaled the finding of something under the topsoil. Within the first half hour they had found a set of keys, a half-inch wrench, an old can, and fifty cents.

"We need to keep trying. I know it's out here. I feel it; can't you guys feel it?" Nina said.

"Yes. Let me take a shot at it Harry," Morgan suggested.

Harry handed the detector over to Morgan and joined Nina on the truck's tailgate.

Morgan was very thorough as he went over the entire yard area under, and around the kitchen windows, and along the driveway. Nothing.

"You know . . ." Morgan said, "no one has said this out loud, but I will. I think we are all thinking it. Even though the ring is lost, there is still weird shit going on around here and someday, someone will find it. It won't be us and we'll probably be dead and gone, but I betcha the curse will continue. This won't be over until it's found."

"Then let's find it," Harry added. "I think the twins' fate has been decided and we may never find them, but if we can find the ring, maybe we can keep this from happening again."

They decided that they should spread out a little closer towards the railroad tracks and see if they'd get lucky there.

Within fifteen minutes the alarm went off. Nina and Harry jumped off the tailgate and ran over to Morgan who had a broad smile on his face. "I gotta get one of these things," he said happily.

All three knelt and immediately started digging. About five inches down they found a ring. They hesitated as no one wanted to pick it up, but Morgan was the first to reach for it.

The silver had tarnished into a dull, blackish color, but it was clearly silver. Crust had hardened between the creepy leaves, and the blood stone was caked with dirt. Harry ran into the house with Nina and Morgan closely following and began to wash it in the kitchen sink. The stone was beautiful. It was a deep green with orange blazes running through it. They could see why the Turner Twins were so attracted to it. Though a little creepy, the ring was stunning in its own way.

"You should have seen their faces," Nina whispered.

"Whose faces?" Morgan asked.

"The girls. Nelly and Tabby. They asked if I would take it out of the display case. They were so excited." Her eyes began to tear up. "The ring was priced at fifty-five dollars and they only had four. I saw their eyes and I knew they both loved it. They were already talking about who would wear it first and how they'd share it."

Morgan and Harry looked at each other and remained silent as Nina stared down at the ring. Tears slid down her cheeks.

"It was pay-day. I was caught up on my bills and after seeing the look on their faces . . . well, I just wanted to be nice. I never told them. It was their first day ever in town without their parents and their first time feeling all grown up. I just couldn't say no. You should have seen how happy they were when I put it in the little box and handed it to them."

Nina looked up at Harry and he put his arms around her.

"I had no idea the ring would kill them. It's all my fault. How can I live knowing that?"

"It's not your fault," Morgan reassured her. "Please don't think it is." Morgan looked at Harry, and they both felt awful for her.

As they walked inside, Harry kept his arm around Nina's shoulders. They looked up towards the damaged window and abruptly stopped walking. They saw two beautiful young girls looking down at them from the third story bedroom window. They were smiling and waving at them.

Nina put a hand over her mouth and held her other hand out in a gesture of compassion and love. The girls smiled and reached out as well.

Nina was no longer afraid of the house. She had only love and sadness in her heart for those girls.

CHAPTER FOURTEEN

Harry made a call to Barnett Glass in town and scheduled them to come out and replace the kitchen windows as soon as possible. Morgan, Nina, and Harry had lunch that afternoon at the diner in town. For a long time, no one spoke. Nina broke the silence and said she was so happy that everything turned out so well and told Morgan he must be relieved to have found his grandmother's ring.

"What are you going to do with it?" Harry asked.

"I'm not sure yet. I guess my family will take a vote and I'll find out then," he replied.

"I don't mean to be forward," Nina said. "But I'm rather surprised that you are the only one who showed up for this big adventure. I mean once you realized the ring was here – why didn't anyone else show up for the hunt?"

"Okay, you got me," Morgan said bluntly. "There is no family. We've been searching many years for it. I've lost my entire family during the pursuit. That ring has brought many deaths. I'm the last," he admitted before he bowed his head with obvious sadness for the great loss of his family. "It's very powerful and I'm not sure how to put an end to this."

They looked at one another. Nina was the first to make a suggestion.

"Why don't you just melt it? Melt it down and bury it. That's what I'd do."

"That's a good idea. Maybe I will."

That night the three of them had a nice dinner together. They each felt good about getting to know one another on a more personal level and they had quite a few laughs.

Morgan seemed to become another person and said he was excited to be finally able to put all of this behind him and start a new life for himself.

That night as they said their good-byes and swore they would meet again, Nina gave Morgan a friendly peck on the cheek and asked him where he planned to go.

"To be honest, I haven't really given it much thought. Maybe I'll just let the wind blow me somewhere. I've been drifting most of my adult life," he answered.

Harry and Nina looked at each other, then at Morgan.

"Why don't you stay here?" Harry suggested. "You said you liked the town, and though it's small, there are opportunities. Why don't you take a few weeks off from drifting and stay? You can stay at the house, that is if you don't mind the fact that it's haunted! It's huge and it's only me, so you'll have plenty of room and privacy while you sort it all out. Plus, it will certainly save you a ton of cash instead of giving it to that damn hotel you're in."

Nina jumped up and down and clapped her hands as if Morgan already said he would.

Morgan looked at his feet and then up at them as he was obviously thinking what to say or do next. "You know, I really do like this town," he laughed. "I've been flying by the seat of my pants for so long, maybe it's time for me to try and grow some roots."

"Yeah, give your pants a rest, Morgan," Nina said smiling.

Harry held out his hand and Morgan shook it.

CHAPTER FIFTEEN

A year later Morgan closed on his own house just on the other side of the railroad tracks and less than a mile from Harry's home. As it turned out, he had a great knack for real estate investments and had earned his real estate license only weeks after moving in with Harry. More recently having earned his Broker License, Morgan decided to open his own business in the heart of town.

Harry and Nina had become quite the talk of the town in recent months when it became evident that their working relationship had blossomed into a full-blown love affair. People enjoyed watching them walking hand in hand along the streets and listening to them giggle during their meals at the local luncheonette on Clover Street. When they announced the birth of their first child and after the first sonogram, they were delighted to discover twins would be on the menu!

Life quickly returned to the old Turner home. The grass grew once again, thick, and lush. The flowers returned and even the trees had new growth.

Things sure were blossoming for everyone.

The only area in the yard that didn't recover was right next to the tracks where they dug up that awful ring.

The dead area in the grass used to be only as round as the hole that was dug to find the ring. Now, it had elongated into the size of a patio lounge chair. In fact, no one had even noticed that one side of the expanding dead spot had spread outward. With each passing day it was beginning to look like a path instead of a dead patch of grass, and the path was heading directly toward the house.

Unless one viewed it regularly, it's strange development was barely noticeable. If it wasn't for the hair ribbons tangled in the surrounding grass, one would never catch on to what was happening at all. At the rate of its progress, it would reach the house by the time the babies would be born.

"When I am dead my dearest,
Sing no sad songs for me;
Plant thou no roses at my head,
nor shady cypress tree.

Be the green grass above me with
Showers and dewdrops wet;
And if thou wilt remember,
And if thou wilt forget.

I shall not see the shadows,
I shall not feel the rain;
I shall not hear the nightingales sing on
as if in pain.
And dreaming throughout the twilight that doth not
rise nor set;
Haply, I may remember and haply may forget."

Barnabas Collins (1770 - . . .)

THE OLD MINER'S CEMETERY

CHAPTER ONE

J erome, Arizona was founded in the late eighteen hundreds, 1890 to be exact, and settlers were first lured to the area due to its rich abundance of copper. The old mining town is located on Cleopatra Hill between Prescott and Flagstaff and is historically known as "the wickedest town in the west" due to its many brothels, saloons, and opium dens.

During its heyday in 1930 there were as many as 4,932 residents but as the copper dwindled, most folks left except for about fifty individuals who chose to stay behind. During the census in 2010 Jerome had four-hundred and forty-four residents.

For years, homes and other buildings sat abandoned, and many were lost due to lack of maintenance. The surviving buildings are old and mostly structurally compromised due to the lack of proper architectural skills of the builders and drastic mountain slopes. In fact, many have collapsed due to neglect and have been lost altogether down the intense mountain grades. The buildings still thriving have been the lucky ones and have had modern structural overhauls completed to reinforce their decaying foundations. This is a sad fact, but also why the town continues to flourish. Although the residents are low in number, its wineries and tourism are what keep the town alive today. It is quaint, cool, and "real". Evidently, drinking is one past time that is still appreciated and encouraged by those who frequent Jerome.

The place has always been considered haunted by anyone who has visited, and at night it is a common happening to see people walking the streets in early nineteenth century attire. Halloween is especially fun because you never know who will join your group without an invitation.

A lot of the old brothels are now a combination of saloons and restaurant establishments. Typically, the rooms for rent are above the ground level, where the bar and bands are located. They are rented cheap due to the scant furnishings and lack of toilet facilities. It is not uncommon to rent a room and find the furnishings to be only a mattress on cinderblocks and a lamp on a box. Of course, the bathroom is always down the hallway, shared, and nowhere near the standards we see in hotels these days. In other words, they advertise "authentic" and that's exactly what you're going to get.

The good thing about Jerome is that this is exactly why so many are drawn to it. Unpretentious, honest, and truly a step back in time where anyone can be anything they want to be. The locals will defend its honorable reputation with their last breath. People say "Don't mess with Texas" . . . well, don't even THINK about messing with Jerome. Amen brother.

CHAPTER TWO

The Old Miner's Cemetery has headstones dating from 1897 to 1942 mostly. A few are as recent as two years ago. No one knows for sure when the cemetery was first established. It is said that many gruesome deaths have taken place there. Also, English, Spanish, and Italian inscriptions are on the headstones, and it is a known fact that many Chinese were enslaved and brought to Jerome to work hard labor during its heyday. The cruelty legends have been proven true and there was a lot of torment and tragedy in Jerome's past records.

All this being said, Jerome is not a town you want to verbally bash out loud. At least not while you're within its boundaries, and especially not when you're within the cemetery gates. This is a first-hand piece of advice from me. I'm not a local and my name doesn't matter, but I live in the next town over at the base of the mountain, and I've seen vengeance firsthand, and it isn't pretty.

CHAPTER THREE

Years ago, I used to be a realtor. I sold a house to a couple who was really excited about Humboldt, Arizona and wanted to start fresh and create a new beginning in their lives. They were relocating from the East Coast and fell in love with the romantic history of the west. I showed them a cute little home in my neighborhood, and they loved it. We quickly became friends and I thought we'd be friends forever. We used to visit with one another every weekend and have cook outs and honest, heart to heart conversations that only best friends would share.

As Kevin, Fatty (real name was Fatima; always a little nuts, and we called her "Fatty" for short), and I sat on my deck one Friday night in front of a raging fire we had been telling each other foolish stories of our youth and decided it was a good time to create a new story. Preferably one that would be better than the old ones. This is only a subject that pre-middle aged folks can relate to.

We decided to drive up to the Old Miner's Cemetery and explore headstones and see if all the folklore was really true about the walking dead or if all the town gossip was just bologna. Kevin in his blue jean shorts, Harley T-shirt, and Converse tennis shoes; Fatty, in her usual baggy, outdated slacks and Walmart flip flops; and me in my favorite pair of worn-out jeans and strappy sandals, headed out, completely unprepared for the night's adventure. We were all in our forties at the time and as we pulled into the old weed and cacti ridden parking lot; we took our time and enjoyed the thrill of the experience. We knew at that late hour the cemetery would be closed and figured if a cop found us while doing his nightly rounds, or whatever else cops would be doing in the middle of the night at a cemetery, we could talk our way out of most anything. Happy thought, right? Looking back, I don't see how even the cleverest of folks could talk their way out of getting caught in a graveyard after midnight, but it sure sounded good at the time.

As I said, it was late at night. By the time we arrived, it was probably a little after two o'clock in the morning. We pulled up to the old, rusted black iron gates in my worn-out Aerostar van. Its doors jammed often and a lot of times they wouldn't close all the way, or they wouldn't open at all. It was hit or miss in that van and extremely frustrating. I was poor at the time; too poor to fix them, and it was around 2008 when the recession was at its peak. Real estate was not the best field to be in, and I suffered a great deal, along with my children.

I'm not sure what round of drinks my friends were on by this time, I'm embarrassed to admit, but I must say their indulgence made the night a lot more fun. I was the designated driver, which meant I was the most qualified of the three to drive, plus it was my van. I had stopped drinking once the subject of going to Jerome was suggested and the night was still relatively young. I openly admit that it was still irresponsible of me to drive up the mountain in my slightly-less-inebriated-state-of-mind-than-my-friends that night. That being noted, I'll proceed with the story.

Even though I locked the doors, I left the back windows open. I am a city girl and being in a dark and lonely graveyard on a mountaintop in the middle of the night, I wasn't going to take any chances on losing the only key, so I stashed it on top of the driver's front tire. I kept thinking we needed a way inside if we unexpectedly had to flee for our lives and the key did disappear, so locked doors and open windows were my way of saving the day. Thinking back, perhaps I was a tad more inebriated than I thought.

The gate was locked as we half-way expected, and since we were still young enough at heart, we thought we could climb the iron fence. It was Fatty's idea and a good one at the time. Not stopping to think that three drunks, forty plus years old, had no business climbing a fence didn't occur to us. The spikes at the top were a challenge, but we all made it over unscathed. The only hiccup was the sole of my shoe giving way to one of the spikes at the top of the fence; I should never have tried to stand on it. There was a tree limb directly overhead and that was why I tried to stand. The rusty spike impaled the bottom of my sandal and luckily for me, it went right between two toes, never leaving a scratch. The spike continued right up and through one of the top straps as well. At the time it was easier to just slide my foot out rather than yank it off the point. For all I know that damn sandal could still be speared to that fence today.

Once on the other side and finding ourselves still alive, we had a huge laugh and proceeded to look around.

It was eerily quiet out there without the sounds of the town humming, and except for the occasional dog barking or owl hooting, the sounds of the night creatures were wonderfully spooky. We all felt so alive and excited. Growing

older doesn't have to be a slow-down if you have the right
people to spend your time with.

Chapter Four

A s we began walking through the graveyard and reading
the inscriptions on the tombstones, it didn't take long
for us to somewhat drift apart from one another. We
each had our own flashlights, although we tried to keep them
pointed downward as to not attract any unwanted attention
from nearby residents.

I had to watch every step as my left sandal was safely on
my foot, while the other was still stuck to the fence. Stepping
on a cactus, goat head, or other pointy weed was definitely not
in my plans for the evening, and I knew it would spoil all the
fun.

I bent down on one knee to get a better look at a date on
a tombstone when I thought I saw something out of the
corner of my eye. I stood up immediately and took a step
back. I saw a face peering at me from behind a marker. It was
the face of a child. It disappeared almost as soon as I saw it.
The eyes were large and black. I walked around a bit to see if
I could get another glimpse, but whoever the child was, had
quickly disappeared. I felt a chill run up my back as I realized
the grave I had been kneeling on was the grave of a little girl.
She had died when she was ten years old.

Without warning Kevin hollered, obviously in distress,
and I saw Fatty's flashlight quickly bob up and down as she
began to run in the direction of Kevin's voice.

As I turned and started walking toward Kevin, I heard a
noise behind me. Then I felt a cold chill. It was as if someone
ran their hand across the back of my neck. I almost called out,
but found I was too afraid to do even that. My eyes were wide
with fright as I saw the little girl was now standing right in
front of me.

I couldn't move. Without warning my flashlight began to dim and I felt my heart beat faster as I knew the light was close to going out.

The clouds had shifted in the sky and covered the moon. The air seemed thick, and I struggled to breath. I frantically looked around for my friends, but it was just so dark I couldn't see. It seemed their flashlights had also dulled and were close to winking out at any second. Before we arrived, we had stopped at a truck stop and purchased new batteries. There was no way the batteries could be dying so soon! I've heard when ghosts or unexplained paranormal phenomena takes place, the energy in batteries and other devices quickly drains. Could this be what was happening?

Fatty began to scream.

As I looked back to the child, I found that it wasn't only she who stood in front of me, but now there were at least six more children. Miserable, lost eyes looked at me. Each stood in their Sunday best outfits. A couple were fresh and looked new while others were dulled in color and the styles were old and not from even recent decades past.

Their skin was drawn and pale and I knew if the moon had been shining bright, I could have seen right through them.

They did not walk closer to me, nor did they reach out to me. They only stood, staring as if waiting for me to guide them somewhere safe. Instead of being frightened, I felt so sad and helpless. They wanted, needed, something from me, and I was unable to provide it.

I heard Fatty scream again.

CHAPTER FIVE

I caught up to her as quickly as I could. When I found her, she was at Kevin's side. He was lying at the base of a tombstone. He said he tripped over a rock, but after both Fatty and I looked around, we saw that there were no rocks to speak of really. There was grass and decorative landscaping, but nothing that would cause him to fall. We assumed it was only the drink talking. Until we noticed the four long gashes. Kevin's ankle was quickly swelling, and he was unable to even stand up on his own. His eyes were wide and wild, and I got the impression that he was hiding something from us. Looking back, I thought he must have seen something, maybe a child, or worse. He appeared almost at the panic level, yet it was obvious he was trying to keep his shit together. Perhaps to keep us from panicking, or perhaps it was what he knew he had to do to keep his sanity.

I didn't want to create a panic but told them that we needed to leave right away. I didn't feel as though the children meant us any danger but didn't want to hang around and find out.

At that moment Fatty pointed out a figure behind a tombstone to our right. It was in human form, or so I thought, and it was ghastly. It looked like a dead woman in an old and worn pioneer dress walking past us. She took no notice of us and continued walking. I'll never forget seeing her. She looked as if she was burned to some degree and her hair was unkept and wild. She walked slowly as if she was confused and was looking for someone. This reminded me of the children.

Knowing the history of Jerome and knowing the stories of hauntings and tales of neglect, slavery, and tragedy that occurred in those early days, I couldn't help but be pulled towards what I saw, wanting yet unable to help, and still completely terrified.

Fatty and I helped Kevin to his feet and as we turned toward the fence to make our escape, we saw the children. The six had more than doubled. Now there were a lot of Asian children among them with the same expressions of hopelessness on their faces. Misery in their eyes. Skin burned and a couple were missing limbs. They must have been the children of slaves.

As the three of us walked to the fence, we had to pass among them. The children parted and let us through. There was no attempt on their part to harm us or keep us within their gates.

We climbed over the iron barrier which separated our lives from their dead ones. Once we were on the other side, we each looked back, and sadly they were gone.

No words were conveyed. No signs of empathy or consideration were expressed. If I had another chance to go back and try to make things better for them, could I have? If those children could break out of their world for that short amount of time, what else could they be capable of? Were they limited to the confines of the cemetery grounds?

Kevin refused to speak of what happened that night. I want to know about those marks on his ankle, and why he was harmed while Fatty and I were not. I guess we'll never know.

Looking back, it would have been so easy for me to have run away, and in a way, I feel like I did. I wonder if someone ran away from them when they were alive, when they could have been helped. Remembering the lost look in their faces, the faces of children confused and desperately trying to understand what had happened to them. It seems that so many people run away from their responsibilities.

In those days, the owners of the mines imported people, slaves, to work or serve as cooks, or to fill whatever duties were needed. There were no laws to help them, and no minority's voice could change how life went for them. No one's could. We will never know if help or understanding would benefit the children now unless someone goes back and attempts to communicate with them again. I'm too afraid.

I hope it is never too late to change someone's existence for the better, even after death. I can only hope that at least it might be possible.

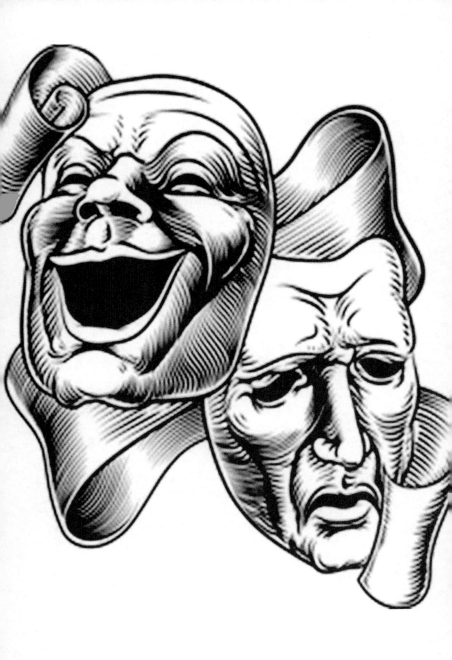

*"All the world's a stage,
And all the men and women merely players;*

*They have their exits and their entrances,
And one man in his time plays many parts,
His acts being seven ages . . ."*

William Shakespeare (1564 – 1616) ~

COLD HANDS

CHAPTER ONE

The first time the lights went out caught everyone off guard.

The band had been playing and were on their third set. "Not Dead Yet" was a metal band and a damn good one. They wrote mostly all their own tunes but would also play a few shout-outs before last call or when the crowd kept asking for them. They always maxed out the occupant limit wherever they played, and management never let them leave without booking the next gig. Life was good and they were making easy money.

They were an honest bunch of guys that originally only wanted fame and fortune, yet somewhere along the line found themselves all grown up, slightly greying, and accumulating responsibilities. Now having families that loved and depended on them they discovered that the love they had for their women and children outweighed the need for stardom. Being rich and famous with houseboats, Lear jets, and wads of cash didn't mean shit compared to the love they had for their people. The days of waking up smelling the breath of some nameless bitch that had been puking all night off the side of a grungy hotel bed was happily forgotten.

In recent years each band member acquired good jobs, were respected in their communities, and were appreciated for the way they kept their yards tidy and maintained. In fact, most of the neighbors who lived near them had no idea those guys played music at night. Their nine-to-five existences were all the neighbors saw. When you got right down to it, the band had the best of both worlds and who could argue with that?

As they began the second tune the lights went out, so did the music. It was a Friday night, and the house was packed. After a few minutes, the screaming began, and then the forceful shoving. Soon after, the rich, metallic, smell of blood filled the air and was accompanied by earsplitting blasts of sound, louder than any amplifier that ever enveloped the bar. Within minutes the huge glass wall panels exploded from the inside out and fragments rained down onto the crowd. Many never stood a chance due to being knocked unconscious from the heavy blocks and the deep wounds to their heads and facial areas from the smaller shards. People began slipping in the blood and spilled drinks on the floor. Attempting to quickly maneuver to the exit doors was useless. The cries of voices in the darkness were both terrifying and compelling.

Razzel, the front man of the band and lead guitarist was pushed into the drums by what felt like a Freightliner. His cherished Gibson, the favorite of the lot, was all but snapped in half as whatever collided into him sent it flying across the room into a table of girls, decapitating two of them in seconds. Cords of tendons swayed loosely down the sides of their necks, blood draining onto their now crimson-colored shirts. Razzel, feeling stunned and breathless felt cold hard hands pulling on his neck. Unable to free himself, he prayed this wasn't his final gig.

When the fire broke out it spread quickly and harshly. Most died in the flames, while others suffocated in the smoke. Only few managed to survive.

At the end of the evening, Razzel's band along with most of the crowd were dead. It all happened so fast. There was no warning, and no one was even sure of what started it. The lights had gone out and the darkness overtook everyone, except for the flames.

The building had burned almost to its stone foundation and became another town memory. Unfortunately, the owners had no choice but to sell the property.

Quite a number of years later the real estate was purchased by a middle-aged couple from New York City, evidently with a lot of money to back their big mouths. Faye and Harmon Kostalas rebuilt the property from the ground up and added about ten thousand square feet. The place was beautiful, and they had decided to turn it into a dinner theatre. They even added a second floor with balconies surrounding the stage and chandeliers that lowered and rose by the flip of a switch.

The drama students from the surrounding high schools flocked into the Human Resources department like moths to a flame. The positive feedback from the community was amazing and by the looks of the advertising, they spared no expense. Most everyone in town was looking forward to the addition of the dinner theatre and couldn't wait for it to open.

CHAPTER TWO

The night before the playhouse opened, one of the stagehands was adjusting the lighting bar on top of the center catwalk. Suddenly the rails beneath his feet shifted, and the man fell uncontrollably off the side of the pathway. When he landed, he was taken to the hospital and X-rays showed he had broken a hip and had fractured his right leg in two places. Later, after his surgeries, the stagehand disclosed to another one of the theatre's employees telling him he had been pushed. He didn't know by whom, but he knew he had been pushed. All he could say about the assailant was that their hands were very cold and very strong.

The dinner theatre opened on time, without a hiccup. The lines out front trailed down the street, and the employees were just as excited as the customers. The staff was trained well, and the owners couldn't have been prouder at the way the night played out.

The only minor issue was that shortly before the intermission the lights cut out for a brief span of time, but the new emergency generators kicked in quickly which saved the scene, and the pace of the show returned. The mood of the audience hadn't broken and with the casts' keen wits and professionalism; they were able to complete the first half of the show with a standing ovation offered from the audience.

The owners had spoken with the cast and praised the evening's performance.

"Always expect the unexpected and never lose your head. You all did a fine job, and we couldn't be prouder. See you all tomorrow night! Go home and have a night-cap; you all deserve one!"

The crew and actors applauded one another and left the building.

Faye and Harmon finished the office paperwork and closed for the night.

As Faye climbed into their SUV, she immediately began rooting through her suitcase of a handbag for her cell phone, realizing she had left it on the desk in the back office. Harmon had just come around to the driver's door and was about to get inside.

"Honey, I'm sorry, but I think I left my cell in the office. Do you mind checking for me?"

"Damn it, Faye, I'm gonna buy you a leash for that freakin' thing. If I wasn't so happy with the way things went tonight, I'd make you get it yourself." He leaned through the window and winked at her. "I'll be right back, darlin. Lock the doors."

He was always so good to her. They had been married for thirty-six years and each year that passed had been better than the year before. She considered herself very lucky. Not bad for a poor Jewish girl with an extremely limited education. She had to fight for every opportunity thrown her way, and thanks to Harmon's strength and support, together they did very well for themselves. She often said that without common sense all the education in the world couldn't turn a socially retarded person into a queen.

Prior to purchasing the property, they had a small restaurant in New York that offered stand-up comedy performances on Saturday nights. Harmon wanted to expand, but the place was just too darn small. Plus, he had gotten fed up with the landlord constantly trying to up the rent. They both knew it was time to go and when their lease agreement term ended, they couldn't run away fast enough.

As soon as the realtor told them about this place, they scheduled a showing. It was extremely rough after the fire and there wasn't much salvageable, so they did a complete rebuild. Only paying for the property, which had septic, city water, and electricity to the lot line, it left them with plenty of money to build. Plus, it would be all theirs! They were both happy to be out of the big city and Laytonsville, Maryland suited their needs. It was out of the hustle and bustle of the city yet was an easy commute for those that didn't mind the drive. It also boasted enough town residents to make a nice customer base. Their dreams of having their own place were finally coming true and they marveled in the thought of it.

CHAPTER THREE

As Harmon opened the rear entrance door to the theatre, he noticed all the lights were on. "What the hell?" He walked into the kitchen and found the door to the walk-in freezer wide open. He clearly remembered both he and Faye walking the place making sure things were put away properly and locked up for the evening. Shaking his head, he entered the office and gathered up Faye's cell phone and, again, turned the lights off as he headed back to the SUV.

"Man, you were gone a long time. Did you find my phone?"

"Yep. I also found all the lights were on, and the freezer was open."

"No way! We shut everything down and . . ."

"I know. It was probably the Phantom of the Opera."

She leaned over and gave him a kiss as she grabbed her phone and began checking messages.

The next afternoon, Angelo, the chef, arrived early to begin preparing the specialty foods that took a little more time. He didn't like feeling rushed during "combat" and enjoyed preparing a lot of the accoutrements himself. His assistants were very knowledgeable in the art of food preparation, but he liked things done his way and until they knew what he wanted he wouldn't trust a soul but himself to get it right. After all it was only day two. He was paid to make things perfect and that was exactly what he planned to do.

He grabbed the bulky handle of the freezer door and went inside to retrieve salmon and cod portions. As soon as both feet crossed the threshold, the door slammed shut behind him. He knew the handle satisfied a mandatory safety requirement with the Health Department, and didn't worry when he heard the latch officially click home, but as he tried to push it back open it wouldn't give an inch. It was as if someone stood on the other side of the door purposely holding the handle down.

He struggled to free the catch, but nothing worked. He yanked and tugged and began to feel the cold temperatures of the freezer affecting his body. He was rapidly getting cold, and he knew no one would be arriving for at least another hour.

Angry, there was nothing he could do but wait it out.

About forty-five minutes later he heard footsteps and knew someone had finally arrived for work, most likely one of his assistants. He immediately banged on the door and within seconds it abruptly swung open.

Angelo jumped out of the freezing temperature with wide eyes. "Oh, thank God you're here! It's cold as shit in there! The fucking door shut behind me and I couldn't get out!

I thought I was gonna die!" In seconds he went from English to Sicilian, which is where he'd spent most of his life. There was no doubt his words were the rarest and most genuine graphic profanity in existence, spoken in the most intense manner imaginable.

Harmon entered the kitchen as this was occurring and tried his best to find out what was happening. He walked into the freezer, and they examined the latch mechanism. There was nothing wrong with it. Harmon closed the door and it opened effortlessly and smoothly. Neither of them could understand what happened.

"Do you think you may have simply panicked?"

"No way. I didn't even worry because I knew the door was up to code and safe. But I swear it wouldn't work!"

One of Angelo's assistants came over with a throw blanket he had found in the office and threw it over his shoulders. He pulled it around his neck tightly.

Harmon offered his chef the night off with pay, but Angelo refused. "I'm fine. I'll be fine. I just need to warm up a bit. Thank you, sir. I'll stay. It's too late to call Alessandro anyway. I think he went over to visit his family tonight."

"Okay. But if you need to take a break or need anything, please let me know. I'll put on an apron myself if I need to." Harmon patted Angelo on the back, poured him a cup of coffee, and left the kitchen.

CHAPTER FOUR

At the end of the first act the lights went out again. This time the generators didn't kick on as quickly as the night before, and it happened during the dance routine when the actors were in the audience between the tables. One of the dancers ran full speed into a table with two little children and sent Shirley Temples careening onto new outfits and into first courses. No one became noticeably upset, accidents happen after all, and luckily the parents were very understanding.

Just as the lights went out, Linda Callahan, the coat check gal, was standing in the cloak room organizing and making sure each owner's name tag was clearly visible on their garments for a quick retrieval at the end of the evening. Without seeing anyone approach her, and not having any warning, she felt cold hands encircle her throat and push her down on to the floor. She tried to scream as loudly as she could but was unable to make any sounds that were audible.

At the table closest to the coat check room sat two women, Maggie Fagan and Ann Herold, who were patiently waiting on drinks when they heard a commotion behind them. It sounded too strange to ignore and as the lights came back on, they both got up to see what was going on. They saw Linda on the floor struggling and they quickly entered the coat check area to try and help. Although Linda was obviously fighting off an attacker, neither woman saw anyone other than Linda on the floor. The struggle abruptly ended, and Linda sat up out of breath and scared to death. She kept grabbing at her neck and commented on how cold "they were." Maggie and Ann looked at her neck and saw an imprint of what could have been fingers on her skin. The flesh looked very red and was very cold to the touch. It was as if frostbite had begun to set in. The women looked at one another and tried their best to comfort Linda.

All three women were questioned by the owners and the police. A report had been filed, but nothing amounted to much. Linda never returned to work again. In fact, she refused to even go inside to pick-up her paycheck and insisted they mail it to her.

Strange happenings seemed to have become a common occurrence at the dinner theatre since it opened. Some of the employees abruptly quit fearing the rumors that spread throughout the community. On the other hand, some people were intrigued, and business continued to grow.

Each night's performance was amazing, and the customers were drawn to the theatre like moths to a flame.

Harmon hired extra security to be on hand but made sure they were dressed casually, and he implemented a "no uniform" rule as to not worry the paying customers.

The final straw, which shook up everyone who was unlucky enough to witness it, was when a black van pulled up in front of the theatre. The driver got out and opened the side doors. He leaned inward and pushed a button from inside the van and the lift gate came from underneath the passenger side and rose to meet the van's floor. The driver entered and pushed the wheelchaired occupant onto the lift, then locked the safety harness onto the chair's wheels. Once secure, the lift lowered and met the curb at the entrance to the theatre.

The chair was a sip-and-puff system that the user was able to control via a tube that was mounted on the wheelchair. The user either sipped or puffed air to dictate what they wanted the chair to do. The man in the chair was a quadriplegic. He was in his early thirties and through the immense scars embedded on his ruined face, one could only imagine the one-time handsome, ruggedly strong face that was once underneath. It was obvious, he was miserably sad and beaten. It seemed with each facial movement he was lost and on the verge of giving up.

As he entered the theatre, he spoke with the ticket clerk and softly asked to speak with the new owners. He could barely be understood over the crowd that surrounded him. Within a few minutes Harmon and Fay greeted him in the lobby.

"Hello sir, thank you for coming out this evening. My name is Harmon, and this is my lovely wife, Faye. We are the new proprietors of this establishment. How can we be of service to you tonight?"

The man whispered to them in a voice that Faye and Harmon knew was as loud as the man could manage. "Thank you for being so kind. If possible, I would like to take a few minutes of your time and speak with you. Perhaps you have a quieter location. This will only take a few minutes."

Harmon looked at Faye. She nodded happily. "Please, follow us into our office. There are no steps, so I'm sure the chair will make it safely. Can I offer you anything from the bar?"

"No, thank you, Harmon, and thank you for taking the time to see me. I know you are busy."

Harmon smiled. "Well, we're busy, but that's why we have employees to take care of things." He chuckled. "The older I get, the easier I try to make things for myself. My goal is to just walk around and have everybody doing everything I should be doing. Does that make sense?" He laughed again. Harman's manner was always friendly and easygoing, that's why so many people enjoyed his company and visited his and Faye's establishment.

"It does, and I'm envious," the man said in a soft non-energetic voice.

Harmon entered the office and Faye held the door open so the chair could make it through the entryway without banging into anything.

They sat down and waited for the man to speak.

"My name is Razzel. I was the lead singer of *Not Dead Yet*, although it's been quite a few years since anyone has called me that. It was a stage name, and unfortunately my days of performing are over as you can clearly see. We were the last band to perform here prior to your purchasing this property. Has anyone told you what happened the night the building burned down? I can't imagine you being unaware, but I thought that would be a good place to start."

Harmon and Faye looked at each other and couldn't help but slide closer to him in their seats.

"We have only general details. We haven't spoken with anyone who was here during the fire. From our knowledge, the fire wasn't due to any breach of any fire codes, although the building was a total loss," Harmon said.

Faye watched as Harmon spoke, then turned her attention back to Razzel.

"No, I agree there were no code violations," Razzel said. "Would you like me to tell you exactly what happened that night?"

It was obvious that even though Harmon and Faye were experienced in the art of performing, they weren't sure if they could manage the art of hiding sudden natural instincts off stage. Both were somewhat afraid to hear what Razzel was about to tell them, and prayed they could handle it.

Razzel had approached them in an honest human way of wanting only to warn and protect them, not at all to intimidate or make them feel uneasy or on guard. He knew his appearance alone would be alarming, but still felt the necessity to approach them. Razzle knew it was the right thing to do. Truth be told, he couldn't rest until he did.

Razzel told Harmon and Faye everything that happened that awful night. He told them how the doors had slammed shut so no one could escape; how unseen hands, very cold hands, held people down and mutilated them. He told them that each person who perished died in agony and the duration of each attack was lengthy. He told them of the maniacal laughter he had heard after the electronic acoustics had been shut off. He told them that even though everyone he saw suffering was begging for compassion, the cold hands kept on squeezing, and the laughter only became more intense.

He had passed out after his initial strangling. It was just before the fire broke out that he had come to. Then once his faculties returned, he could only roll off the stage and hide among the dead. He had slowly slid his body into the kitchen under the sink where water had been dripping continuously. Although his body had been badly burned, being able to get to the sink was what had ultimately saved his life. The nerve damage was due to the other patrons who stomped on his neck and back as they tried desperately to escape. Looking back, it was unbelievable he was able to drag himself at all.

Harmon and Faye were speechless. They were both appalled at the stories Razzel told them and realized they had been right in worrying how to respond appropriately. They believed every word Razzel said was true and astonished that he made it out of the nightmare alive. They were even more amazed at how he had the nerve to return to the property and tell his story – to warn them. How does one respond to such disturbing information? If you were a God-fearing soul, how was one to believe such travesty?

As Razzel was helped back into his van, Harmon and Faye both grasped his hands and thanked him for coming to the theatre and telling them what he had experienced. They let him know how important his involvement meant to them and that they would keep him aware of any future drama.

As the van doors closed, the last thing Razzel said was, "The hands were just so damn cold."

Harmon and Faye didn't say a word.

Later that night as they laid in their bed, each thought silently to themselves that as Razzel's van drove away they could have sworn they heard a faint, but evil laugh coming from inside the theatre.

CHAPTER FIVE

Harmon and Faye decided to research the history of the property and the bar that had burned down prior to their purchase of the lot in hopes of finding something, anything, that may explain what was happening. Neither was particularly superstitious or believed in ghosts, but there was clearly something going on and they were determined to find out exactly what it was before it ruined them. As it was, there were many on the staff that didn't want to go into certain areas of the building alone. They knew they had a big problem, and they were determined to fix it. All they needed was for someone to get hurt, or heaven forbid, killed on the property. A lawsuit would destroy both their reputations as well as their life savings.

Faye went to the courthouse and asked anyone who would listen to help her find out the history of their property. She was advised to go to the newspaper and search back issues as well as the County Recorder's office and was advised that the Police Department may also be helpful. It was a good first day and she now had a direction of where to proceed.

She met Harmon for lunch, and they discussed closing the theatre until they could get more information. Faye was concerned about potential harm coming to the customers as well as possible lawsuits. Harmon was totally against closing, even temporarily. Every scheduled show was sold out and since they hired the rent-a-cops, he was confident everyone would remain safe. They would ride it out and learn what they could and then discuss closing again when they had more information. She agreed and proceeded with trying to obtain as much history of the property as she could.

She found out that the bar had burned down years prior to their purchase of the property and had only been operational for about three years. The previous owners purchased the property for a price that had been well-below market value. She learned the prior owners also had problems with late night disturbances and strange occurrences in which law enforcement had to be involved on a regular basis. This made Faye a little queasy and she realized she was glad to be sitting down.

The following day Faye decided to check past newspaper articles and learned that long ago after the town had been established, settlers used that property as a waystation for the mentally ill and for those who were unable to care for themselves due to various mental and physical disabilities. There were quite a lot of articles that had been found in the bowels of the newspaper's basement. These articles were so old no one ever felt the need to historically label them and transfer them into the newer file system. Therefore, they had remained in the old filing cabinets but were still available for those that wanted to explore older issues.

It seemed the property was witness to many horrors that were unexplained as well as uninvestigated in a proper way. Criminology was in the process of taking off, so to speak, and in that stage of the town's development, no one had pursued exploring old cases. Therefore, files and old records had gone untouched.

In a dust covered box with no lid, Faye discovered articles regarding an extremely deranged individual who had been battered and abused since birth. He had been admitted to the hospital and somehow continued to commit horrendous crimes against fellow patients. It was a man who had suffered horribly as a child and throughout his teenage years from abuse by his parents, who often kept him in cold water as punishment for countless minor offenses that they would not tolerate. These offenses were as menial as not brushing his teeth properly or choosing the wrong attire for school. On his twenty-first birthday, he had slain his parents and his younger brother by drowning them in a nearby pond. It was said that when they found him, he had been sitting outdoors in a large tub filled with very cold water and was nearly dead himself. If the rescuers hadn't discovered him, he would have probably frozen to death within hours. His body had reached the state of hyperthermia and he was non-reactive at the time of his discovery. The health officials took him to the hospital and there he stayed until the time of his death in 1926.

Shortly after, the hospital was relocated and the ground, which had many graves on the site, remained as the only memorial of the hospital. As the town grew, the graves were maintained by a local church, and it wasn't until the 1980s that the ground became too valuable to remain a cemetery and the graves were relocated to another part of the town. Back then, the records of each burial were sketchy at best, and it was uncertain that all the graves had been, in fact, moved.

CHAPTER SIX

This knowledge was a rude awakening to both Harmon and Faye. They knew it was up to them to make things right. They knew it was up to them to try to appease the poor soul who had died so unceremoniously, but how would they do this? And how many bodies were still under the building? If any graves remained buried on the property, they were completely inaccessible, and under tons of cement and building materials. There was no way possible to dig them out for proper burial. Faye and Harmon would have to think of something.

Within a week they arrived at a decision they were both very happy with. They were running a dinner theatre, after all. With "theatre" being the key word, they decided to advertise *The Phantom of the Opera*.

At the beginning of the first night's performance, Harmon walked on stage and a hush fell over the audience. He was beginning an unplanned announcement and it caught both the ticketholders, as well as the actors, with a sudden jolt of curiosity. As he began to speak, he told both employees and patrons alike, that he and Faye, (pointing to her as she stood from her balcony and waved at the audience, blowing a kiss to her husband, then gracefully sitting down), that together they had decided to dedicate the theatre to the souls that had fallen long ago while trying hard to survive under harsh conditions while the town was in its beginning phases of construction. He talked briefly as to the property and its history and added that in honor of those who had suffered and sacrificed their lives, that the theatre would be a haven for their lost spirits. He closed with a dedicational prayer.

The audience stood and clapped in thoughtful praise. A gentleman appeared from behind the curtain and joined Harmon on stage. He handed him a memorial plaque engraved with a touching sentiment. It was hung in the front lobby surrounded by ornamental flowers and blessings from that day forward. The plaque read: "This theatre has honor and compassion for those misunderstood souls whose lives were taken from them on this property many years ago with callous disregard for the love and good tidings they could have offered in life. You are welcome here and we hope we can give you peace."

Patrons stood in applause. The house shuddered with stomping feet and wails of "Amen" and praise. The lights went up and there were heartfelt emotions as many women cried and the men could only lower their eyes with respect for those poor souls.

After that night the theatre was never again troubled by threatening, unseen intruders. Although oftentimes patrons say that ghostlike figures routinely stand in the balconies and along the aisles. They say if you walk by them, you will feel a chill in the air, but they always smile and let you pass.

Employees who are at the theatre late at night often feel cold spots or feel that they are not alone. Most of them will talk out loud. Often about their day, or sometimes about their personal lives as if they are simply venting out loud or maybe even searching for an answer . . . an answer from the dark. Generally, the theatre now brings peace to all of those that need and want it. Most are grateful and feel the merging of souls, and it is a good feeling.

It seems that cold hands can be warmed with affection and honest hearts. Even dead ones.

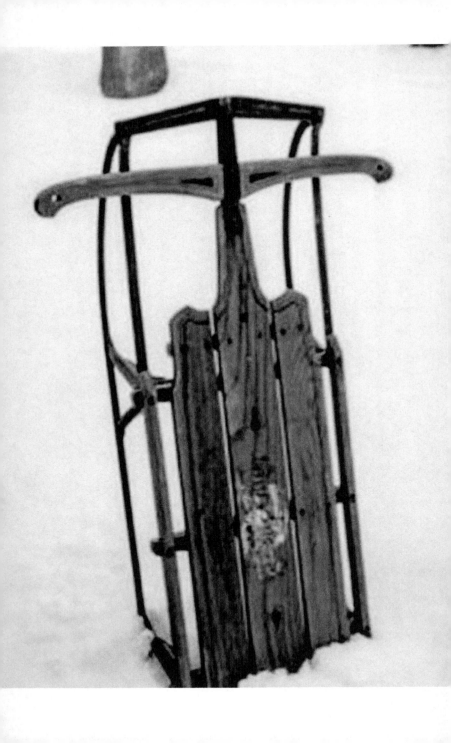

"Where holy ground begins,
Unhallowed ends,
Is marked by no distinguishable line;

The turf unites, the pathways intertwine;

And, wheresoe'er the stealing footstep tends,
Garden, and that domain where kindred, friends,
And neighbours rest together, here confound.

Their several features, mingled like the sound of
Many waters, or as evening blends . . ."

William Wordsworth (1770 – 1850) ~

THE SECOND PATH

CHAPTER ONE

When I was a kid, I used to hang around with a girl named Terri. She was in my grade and our moms were best friends. We used to spend most weekends together, as it was common for children that age to often sleep over at each other's houses. We were good kids and never got into much trouble. Terri was a lot smarter than I was and she got much better grades than I did, but we still got along. In grade school it didn't matter who was smarter or who was prettier, it was all about fun. Fun was everything. If you enjoyed the same stuff, everything just fell together.

I'm Madison O'Shay and my folks moved here before I was born. This story takes place where I grew up and lived until just after college.

Our neighborhood was, well still is, called Mill Creek Town. It used to be quiet and surrounded by fields on every side. We were actually a suburb of Washington D.C., but back in those days it was still country for the most part. Every night at three a.m. the freight train goin' through would blow their horn. I hated it then, but funny how I miss it now. I haven't been there in years, and I have no doubt that I'd be lost if I had to find my way around that town now, and after the memories from that winter long ago, I wouldn't want to.

I've since moved to the other side of the country and although I have wonderful memories of growing up, and I know the bonds I shared with many schoolmates made me the person I am today. Unfortunately, I still get a feeling of dread when I think about that area. I remain grateful for my time spent there and the memories made, but also know that sometimes, you just can't go back. Sometimes you find that all those old memories often turn into new nightmares. Bad dreams you can't forget no matter how hard you try. It's just not healthy. Moving on a little further down the line is the escape some people need. It's the escape that cures that aching heart and clears the mind and soul. That's how it was for me.

CHAPTER TWO

I'm sixty-two now and I'll never forget that one Friday in February; looking back it's still the worst day of my life. The powers that be closed the schools due to a heavy snow fall that had swept in without warning and caught our little town with its pants down, to say the least.

Terri showed up at my house with her Flexible Flyer and asked if I wanted to come along to find a good hill to sled on. My mom was fine with me going out but told me not to venture off too far. I agreed and we left the safety of the neighborhood for one of the pastures on the west side of town. We were excited because we knew we'd probably have the whole place to ourselves since most people used to sled on the big hill at the elementary school. There were always so

THE SECOND PATH | 129

many people on that hill there were oftentimes pile ups of sleds and bodies at the bottom. It seemed that every year someone wound up going to the emergency room with a broken arm or needing stitches or something, which was another reason to try the pasture. Its solitude wasn't an issue at the time.

By the time we got out there about eight inches of snow had already fallen, and the skies were still heavy with more snow that was predicted to come.

The snow wasn't packed down yet, and it was so deep and fluffy that trying to go sledding became more work than fun. After a few rounds of walking back up the hill, having to drag the sleds which were getting heavier by the second, we realized sledding was pointless and decided to check out the pond to see if it was frozen.

The pond was located not too far away from where we were, and it was popular with everyone in town for playing hockey and ice skating during freezing temperatures. If I could go there today, I'd probably call it a puddle. But as memory serves, it felt huge.

The pond was home to many neighborhood cookouts where each family would bring something to throw on the grills. No one would lug their big grills all the way out there, but there used to be many of those little Hibachis lined up along the edge of the water. You know the kind I mean, the ones that only had enough grill space for about four burgers at a time?

I remember my dad teaching me how to ice skate on that pond. I remember his old faded black skates were creased and worn from years of winter fun. They were scuffed and torn in spots from old, failed attempts at fancy turns or clumsy crashes. I remember him skating backwards and crossing his legs as he made each turn. I remember his patience as he taught me how to balance properly and carry myself through each glide. It was one of the sweetest memories of my whole life. If I could go back to any time in my life, I swear I'd go back to that time. Just to see him again in those old black skates and his old dark grey hat with ear flaps blowing up and down in the wind. We used to tease him about being from "Mother Russia" because that hat was stuffed with so much white fur. Yep. If I closed my eyes right now, I still see him like it was yesterday. So many recollections. So much love.

There were two paths that went to the pond. The first path took a little longer, but no one ever seemed to care. It was nice and wide and easy to walk on.

The second path to the pond saved a good deal of time but went through a swampy area that was very dangerous. Not only because of the dark water that was said to be bottomless, but because the ground you had to walk on wasn't very stable. There were lots of rocks and the terrain was very rutty and not friendly.

The worst part about that path were all the stories surrounding it. People had died down there. It'd been said that those people who took the second path simply lost their way, or the swamp would take them. The older kids talked about seeing demons and apparitions walking the swamp's shores hoping to find little kids to grab and drag under the water. They said ghosts would hide behind big rocks and bushes waiting to spring on their innocent victims. Parents told their children never to take that path and no one ever did. No one wanted to. Back then kids listened to their parents for the most part and respected the rules.

When people passed the entry to the second path, their conversations always seemed to faulter, and their eyes would become fixated on what may be down there. They would stare, desperately hoping they wouldn't see anything, but also secretly wishing they would. Even if it were high summer, you'd get a cold chill up your spine just thinking about taking that second path.

CHAPTER THREE

On the day of the heavy snowfall, Terri and I were on the opposite side of the surrounding swamp where the good path was located. We tried to get our bearings and needed to decide exactly how we could reach the pond without wandering near the swamp.

We thought we had it all figured out and happily began our journey. It was exciting because it was like a new frontier we had never explored. Nothing was familiar. On one hand it was crazy fun, on the other it was also scary. In a weird way it felt like some kind of rite of passage that every kid needed to accomplish.

As we walked and walked, our sleds became too heavy to keep carrying so we decided to leave them standing on end at the base of a tree. On the way home we'd just head back the same way and get them. We knew if we propped them up the snow wouldn't cover them, and we'd be able to find them easily. Well, that sounded like a good plan at the time.

We kept hiking and after a short time we noticed the sun wasn't high in the sky anymore. The heavy storm had blocked most of the sun's rays and it began to feel as though it was late afternoon. Being winter we knew it got dark about six o'clock. What time was it anyway? Terry arrived at my house around 1:30 and by the time we left it was about 2:00. Had it really gotten dark so soon?

The cold had started to get to us, and the weather hadn't let up one bit since we had been out there. Everything was covered in deep snow, and it was coming down so thick that we couldn't see very far. It was hard to tell exactly where we were walking.

We began to realize we had been stupid to be out there, especially at that late hour. If only we had known what we were getting ourselves in to.

It was then we realized we really were lost. The only thing we had going for us was that we were dressed warmly, and our feet weren't cold. Not yet anyway.

Terri had begun to cry. It was then we decided to turn back the way we came and go home. If we walked fast, we would be out of there in no time.

As we turned around and began walking, we soon noticed that we could barely see our footprints any longer. They were rapidly filling in with snow and we knew that shortly we would lose sight of them altogether.

We kept walking.

Tears were freezing on Terri's face and there were bright red streaks lining her cheeks.

I began looking for the sleds. I knew we couldn't have passed them, yet we had been walking a long time. Neither of us could remember exactly where we were when we left them. With the snow getting so high, everything looked different. The trees, the bushes, and weeds were covered up. Nothing looked familiar. We weren't even sure if we had walked in that exact direction before.

"I think we're going to die out here!" Terri cried. "I'm getting so cold!"

"No! Just keep walking, Terri. Come on!"

I grabbed her arm and held onto it hoping it would make her feel better. We were exhausted and needed to sit down, but we dared not. I had watched enough television to know that sitting down would be like giving up hope and that's when people died. I was damn certain I wasn't going to die, and I wasn't about to give up or be stuck out there all night. I knew we were both worried about the swamp but neither of us mentioned it. We said nothing about it, as if by not mentioning it, the thoughts would go away.

"Where are the sleds? Did you even see them?"

I had been hoping she wouldn't bring up the sleds. I didn't want to say anything because I knew it would upset her. "No. We haven't passed them yet. Come on. I'm sure they're still up ahead."

"They can't be! We've gone way too far. Oh my God, we really are lost, aren't we?"

I felt my own tears starting to come. I tried my best to hide them from Terri because I knew one of us had to be strong.

It was quickly getting dark. Neither of us could see the sun. The clouds were too dark in the sky, and we couldn't tell if it was above or below the horizon.

We had to stay focused.

Each step we took we held our breath not knowing if the snow would give way to drop us in freezing water. The swamp had to be close, we knew that.

As it turned out, that was exactly what happened.

CHAPTER FOUR

After another few minutes we began to breathe a little easier as we recognized a large oak tree in the distance. It stood fairly close to the pond and people would frequently hang scarves and sweaters on its lower limbs when they accidently got wet, or their bodies would get too hot from expending so much energy skating. We both sighed in relief, although we also immediately knew where we were, and we weren't happy about it.

Without warning, Terri sank waist deep in snow. She immediately began to scream as her boots filled with water, and that made her begin to sink deeper and faster. She couldn't kick them off as they had Velcro tighteners around her calves, and they wouldn't go past her ankles. I remember yelling, "Get on your belly, don't try to stand!"

She found a root from a tree sticking out of the snow and she was able to grab it.

In her struggle she was loosening and breaking up the snow around her, which in turn, created weaknesses that caused her to sink even deeper. It looked hopeless.

Terri tried to reach for my hand. She grabbed it once but wound up pulling my glove off.

I tried to get closer to her but as I did, I, too, began to sink.

The more she panicked the quicker the swamp rose to meet her. Meet us both.

As Terri and I began to flounder and try to stay above the black water, a figure appeared just above the snow. It was a woman and I swear I could see right through her. She was offering her hand and telling us to come with her. She said that we needn't be afraid, and she was here to help us. Help us get out of the swamp.

She seemed to be our only escape, but she also seemed to be a bad choice. I can't explain it, but I can tell you that when I looked into Terri's eyes, she had the unmistakable look of doom. She looked at me and shook her head. As her eyes widened and her lips tightened in a look of grimace, I knew she'd rather die than accept help from that woman.

"I can't feel my legs anymore, Maddy," Terri whispered. "I think we are going to die here. I can't feel my hands now either. I can't move!"

For some reason, Terri had no more tears on her face.

"Don't let go, Terri! You can't let go!"

I could no longer see her legs at all, and she was up to her chest in snow. I knew she had to be soaking wet and the swamp had her legs. I kept trying to inch towards her to get close enough to grab her. Even when I could grab a sleeve or the collar of her coat . . . I continued to drastically sink farther down as well.

It was full dark now. There was barely a sunset, and the sky was still very heavy with snow clouds.

I looked up and again saw the woman. She was closer now and almost within reach of Terri.

"You just keep back! You stay away from my friend! You can't take her, you hear me!"

The woman looked at me and smiled in a very sinister way.

She stood on the snow fully within Terri's reach. But how could it hold her weight? I looked again and realized that she wasn't standing on the snow, she was hovering about an inch over it.

When I looked back at Terri, she was beyond help. She knew she was at her end. The woman once again held out her hand and this time Terri, out of shear desperation for rescue, managed to flutter her shoulders and move her right arm in the woman's direction. As her arm slowly dragged across the top of the snow the woman moved closer and clasped her hand over Terri's. Terri let go of the tree's root and sunk into the deep dark tunnel of snow that filled in with black water. As her head disappeared her eyes never left mine even after the water covered them.

The woman was gone. She had disappeared the instant Terri did.

I screamed from the very top of my lungs. I kept screaming until I found myself almost in the same dark hole that my friend had vanished in moments before. I found myself clutching at the same root, from the same tree, and felt my body being slowly pulled into that same awful water. I looked up in disbelief as I saw that same woman walking back. She was walking toward me now.

I kept screaming.

CHAPTER FIVE

Some of the kids we went to school with were riding their quads around the fields in the snow that day. Four-wheel drive quads and teenage boys go together like peanut butter and jelly. As it turned out, there's nothing sweeter than the smell of two-stroke engines in heavy falling snow on a winter's day.

They were older and being out after dark was evidently allowed in their family, thank God.

They stopped and turned off their quads when they heard me screaming. Minutes later I could hear them, and they were getting closer. I continued to scream and held on to that root with all my strength.

I saw their headlights and seconds later they were running towards me. How they were able to hear my screams was totally beyond me.

As I looked at the woman her face began to change. It had become black and sunken in. Blistered and diseased, crepey flesh hung off her muddy skeletal frame.

She looked at me with one cloudy eye, the other lost and forever gone. She took my friend away from me. Away from all of us, and now she wanted me.

Tears flooded my eyes, and suddenly I felt a strong hand yank me away from a horrible death beneath that black water.

CHAPTER SIX

The boys found our sleds leaning against the big tree. Thankfully, Terri had her name written on the top of hers in big black permanent laundry marker. They knew Terri from the bus stop and thought it strange to find her sled way out there in the middle of nowhere and so close to the swamp's edge. Mark Behanna, one of the neighborhood kids, thought it best to take the sleds to her house and make sure everything was okay. This alerted our families and neighbors that we had to be out there somewhere and no doubt in danger.

Since it was getting dark and the storm hadn't let up, a search party was quickly rounded up. Everyone with dirt bikes, quads, and the like stepped up and joined the pursuit. There were even a few people on horses looking for us.

Leaving those sleds behind and Terri having her name on hers is what saved my life. Without her name being visible to the boys, they never would have known to bring them to her home thereby alerting her parents.

Three years later, the pond and swamp were filled in and a mid-county highway project was underway and due to be completed a year later.

That was over forty years ago and since the highway had been opened, it is said that after the sun goes down drivers often see a woman and a young girl wandering along the highway walking hand in hand.

On one occasion, it was said that a couple pulled over and stopped to offer them help thinking their car must have broken down. It was a snowy winter's evening in February, and it had just turned dark. After they offered them a ride, the woman only replied that they were out looking for her daughter's Flexible Flyer that she had accidently left in the field by mistake earlier that day.

"Unmindful of the roses,
Unmindful of the thorns,
A reaper-tired reposes
Among his gathered corn;
So might I, till the morn!

Cold as the cold Decembers,
Past as the days that set,
While only one remembers
And all the rest forget,
- But one remembers, yet."

Christina Rosetti (1853, published in 1884) ~

THE ASBURY HOME

CHAPTER ONE

The waves breaking on the shore got louder and stronger as the storm came closer. Normally the waves were soothing and peaceful, but not that night.

The folks in Calvert Cliffs, Maryland had been preparing for the worst and the younger folks believed all the preparations were overthought and basically, bullshit. They didn't offer as much help as they should have, and as with a large percentage of the young people today, they were counting on. and depending on, the veterans of the town to orchestrate and deliver all the prep and hard work so they wouldn't have to. Young Democrats no doubt, and as the days that followed played out, it was evident most of them regretted their decision to kick back and watch the party as the storm unfolded.

Never before in the town's history had there been a storm like this one, and no one ever thought a storm of this magnitude would ever come around to show its ugly face in their world. Being a coastal town, it was amazing that this was the first seasonal storm that ever threatened the community in any real way.

The storm was stronger and more intense than the weather stations had predicted, and thirteen persons within the town's limits lost their lives that night when it was all said and done. Lucky thirteen. Mostly the sick and the very old or infirm who weren't strong enough to hold on went first. The high winds brought down some homes, and those unlucky enough to be inside, were trapped beneath the structures' weight and didn't survive. Then, of course, the low areas disappeared under the seawater where some drowned. But what took the heaviest hit were the cemeteries.

Many of those were on land very close to the water line and between years of natural erosion, along with the non-funding of needed programs to reconstruct and maintain the land's original integrity, the graveyards never stood a chance.

In all honesty, and with due respect to the Board of Supervisors, the cemeteries had been considered to be on high ground and the county advisors never felt the need for the cemeteries to have any type of flood emergency plan or insurance for that matter. Now, in hindsight, the planning and zoning committees agreed that they should have rethought the issue and were sorry they hadn't. Most anyone of any intelligence could have told you that this travesty should have been expected eventually, after all they were on the coast, but no sense kicking a dead horse now.

The Gate of Heaven Cemetery which was one of the most beautifully maintained cemeteries in the county was hit the hardest. The cemetery boasted ninety-two acres and was well over three hundred years old.

A wonderfully elaborate mansion had been situated next to the cemetery for years prior to its formation. It was called the Asbury Home. It was owned by the highly affluent Asbury family and part of the original tract of ground when it was a cotton farm up until the farm was purchased by the state of Maryland in the late 1800s. The name was kept, and the

Asbury Home became a retreat for veterans and individuals who had helped the war efforts from past invaders and conspirators. It was one of the country's first and most honored places for our military's brave and loyal soldiers to live out their lives in peace and comfort. In fact, over the years most of the soldiers who lived in the Asbury Home had been laid to rest in the cemetery.

The section where they were entombed took the brunt of the storm damage. Their graves, being the oldest with less family members still alive to demand proper reburials and the like, were unfortunately the ones that had gotten the least attention in the clean-up and refurbishment efforts. This seemed very unfair to the old-timers still around; but who would listen to them? Most were too old to complain and if they did, they were easy to brush aside and quieted. Almost.

CHAPTER TWO

Trenna Marlo, her husband, Scott, and their three dogs came to town about a year after the storm hit and began renting the parcel of land just on the northern side of the cemetery which overlooked the bay, and they loved every minute of it.

They came from Arizona and were used to dust storms and one hundred plus degrees by early May. Both had heard about how awful the humidity was in the coastal states and had been mentally preparing for it ever since she and Scott decided to pull up stakes and make the long haul to the eastern shore. Neither had ever been farther east than New Mexico so this move was an enormous adventure for them.

Scott and Trenna had both graduated from ASU the prior year. Scott with a degree in Business, and Trenna with a degree in Nursing. Being young and impulsive they decided to begin their married lives doing something new and completely off the wall; something they would remember for the rest of their lives. "No Fear" isn't that what the bumper stickers say? Knowing that bravery went hand in hand with young adulthood, they knew if they hated living in the East, they could always go back home to Arizona. They felt awful leaving their parents and going so many miles away but knew it would be exciting. Both were smart enough to know that once jobs were obtained and working relationships were established in Arizona, it would be hard to break ties and move forward into the unknown. They knew now was the best time for them to explore, and not having children or other ties that would bind them to anywhere in particular was icing on the cake. They were confident they were making the right decision and happy they had their families' approval to go for their dreams.

CHAPTER THREE

U pon arriving in Maryland and finding their rental house, Scott and Trenna were so tired they almost didn't make it up the entry stairs before collapsing onto the wonderfully huge Futon couch that faced the sunrise. They noticed it was completely under the deck roof so the hot sun and bad weather wouldn't stop them from enjoying the view. They loved it already.

After going inside and being pleasantly surprised to discover that their landlord had turned on the air conditioning, they dropped everything and looked at one another. Seconds later the dogs bounded past them, instinctively knowing this was home and logically seeking out every scent they could and of course, searching for their food and water dishes.

Trenna obliged by immediately filling up the necessary bowls to appease them and stared at Scott in happy amazement.

"I CAN'T BELIEVE THESE PEOPLE RENTED THIS PLACE TO US WITH THREE HUGE DOGS! Who does that?" Trenna asked bouncing up and down.

"Seriously! We are so fucking lucky! I just want to find out what's wrong with it. Plus, this place should be way out of our price range."

"Oh, Scott I am so happy right now. Why do you assume something's wrong with it? So far, it's beautiful."

"Will you marry me?" Scott asked holding out his arms and raising his eyebrows.

"I already did, but if you want me to do it again just set a date, but you get to buy the dress this time. I'm always up for a new dress."

"Screw that. Get me a beer, woman! But seriously, the landlords could have gotten triple the rent for this place. Why is it so cheap? I assumed it would be a lot more run down, but it's in great shape. There's gotta be something wrong with it."

"Well, if you look hard enough, you're bound to find something. Don't kill the moment. Besides, it could be fate. Did you ever think of that?"

Scott nodded. He loved that Trenna always saw the good in everything.

Trenna turned around and started making trips out to the car and Scott followed her.

That night they enjoyed margaritas on the deck which overlooked the bay, and the views were amazing. Trenna and Scott were night people, and a sunset over the water would have been perfect, but from their east facing deck the best view was the sunrise. It was all good because their lives were just beginning, and as far as Scott was concerned, a sunrise on the bay was a hell of a lot better than a sunset in the desert with no foliage. The beach was always better no matter how you sliced it.

They both had planned to walk the beach before bedtime, but it was already late, and they decided to crash instead. They were exhausted.

The dogs had a large fenced in area along the western edge of the property with a doggie door creatively inserted in the sliding glass doors off the deck, so having to let them in and out wasn't ever going to be an issue. Scott laughed to himself as he thought that alone, was worth relocating 2,400 miles.

In the middle of the night Scott awoke and looked over at Trenna. She breathed deeply. Scott didn't want to wake her, so he quietly put on his slippers and tip toed out of the bedroom.

He went outside to feel the night air and reflect. It was cool and fantastically comfortable. Being from Arizona he had always heard how most people freeze at the drop of a hat when outside of their normal Arizona temperature range, and he thought for sure he'd be one of them. He was happy to learn that he couldn't have been more comfortable if he had wished for it.

As he looked at the waves, he thought he saw a person standing on the shore. It was a man in a uniform, an old one. Military by the looks of it, but Scott couldn't be sure. He was walking as if he was looking for something along the beach. Scott watched the man and soon realized that he didn't seem solid, or for lack of a better word, he didn't seem real. It didn't alarm him and in fact, he thought it was very cool. It reminded him of old black and white movies with romantic themes.

Scott shook his head and smiled. Heck, he and Trenna had covered a lot of miles driving and it had been a long day. After a half-frozen beer, (thank God he had to get up to pee and remembered he threw a couple in the freezer, otherwise they would have exploded by morning), Scott decided it was time to go back to bed.

They awoke in each other's arms excited about their first day in their new home and laughed as they jumped out of bed and raced toward the shower.

CHAPTER FOUR

After breakfast Scott made a quick trip to the local hardware store to get a few things he needed to arrange the garage to his liking. Trenna tended to the dishes and began sorting out the kitchen. She was glad they labeled the boxes appropriately so organizing things took half the time it would have otherwise. When she finished, she decided to check out some new scenery, as well as take the dogs for a walk to stretch their legs along the beach. This was what she had been waiting for and she was eager to get her feet wet.

After walking about twenty minutes she came to the Asbury Home. She had seen it in the distance, and it looked like something out of a movie. As she approached the side that she felt was the front of the home, she could only stare at the size of the huge picture window. She imagined how people over the years would have gathered around that window looking outward at the magnificent views during fancy parties or holiday get-togethers. It was beautiful. She wasn't sure how long she had been standing there when Scott walked up behind her and gently moved her hair aside and kissed her neck.

"You scared me!" Trenna said smiling, still looking at the big house. "Look at it. Isn't that place gorgeous?"

"It is. I'd love to walk through it. I hear it holds a lot of history. Sorry, darlin if I scared ya." He paused and said, "The kitchen looks great, you've done a lot since I left."

"Thanks. Did you find what you needed at the hardware store?"

"I did. I also learned a few things that I wasn't particularly prepared for," Scott said.

"Like what?"

"Well, evidently the owners of our house have been trying to rent it out for months. Seems everyone leaves. They just walk out and break the lease."

"Huh? Why? The place is great. Do I want to hear this?"

"Probably not," he confessed.

"Then don't tell me, Scott. I don't want to know." Her eyes turned dark.

"Really?"

"Yep, don't tell me. I love this place. Please don't spoil it."

"You're right, it's probably just bullshit anyway. Let's go home, I'm starving. Let's cook some burgers; I stopped at the grocery store and bought all the stuff."

"That's perfect, I'm hungry, too. Did you get those BBQ beans I like?"

"Of course, I did. You would have sent me back if I didn't."

They jogged home along the beach. The dogs ran around them, splashing in the water.

CHAPTER FIVE

The following day they woke up early and continued organizing the house and emptying boxes with great care to put everything into just the right space. Most people hated to move and turned the event into a nightmare, but Trenna and Scott found it exciting, maybe because of their youth. They loved knowing they had finally entered their future, and this made the whole experience enchanting, like a love story unfolding before their eyes. They even had a feeling the dogs could feel the magic in the air. Of course, if you asked the dogs, the magic was probably the smell of groceries on the counter.

That afternoon during lunch, Bronson, their red Dobie, showed up with a huge bone in his mouth. "Hey babe, check this out! Come here will ya? I think Bronson found something that's pretty fucked up," Scott hollered, as non-emotionally as he could. "You're a nurse . . . what does this look like to you?"

Trenna walked onto the deck, handed Scott a glass of sun tea, and stared at Bronson's new find. She bent over and looked up at Scott. "Well, I think we need to make a phone call, darlin."

"Who are we callin?"

"I think we need to call the cops for starters. That looks like a human femur bone."

"Yeah, I pretty much figured you'd say something like that. It's a tad too big to be from a cat."

"I'm always up for a little drama, but I didn't figure on any drama happening so fast, did you?" Trenna asked.

"Nope. But let's make the call," Scott breathed. "And if you don't mind, I'd rather let you take the thing away from him. I'm pretty sure I can't handle it."

Trenna had placed the femur bone on a towel in the center of the kitchen table. Scott thought to himself that dinner would have a whole new meaning after that day as he couldn't help but sit there and stare at it.

A half hour later a squad car pulled into the driveway and two cops got out.

Trenna and Scott met them at the front steps and invited them inside.

They introduced themselves as Detective Jurgenson from the homicide division and Dr. Christine Butler from the Coroners Division of the Sherriff's Office. The cops informed them about the storm that had upended the town's cemeteries prior to their arriving.

They had heard all about it but hadn't stopped to think about the cemeteries being dislodged and their dead inhabitants laying all over the beaches, willy nilly.

"Unfortunately, you both may see something like this again in the future. We have no way of knowing how long it will take to find all the missing . . . well, you know," Detective Jurgenson offered. "Especially, since you live in such close proximity to the Gate of Heaven. As you may know, it is the largest cemetery in our county, and we believe this issue may be a long and drawn out one."

"We have no reason to believe that anything you may find is dangerous or could pose any health issues to you or your family, so that really shouldn't be a worry for you. But if you need to report any other findings, please contact me at this number and I'll come right out and gather it up, day or night." Dr. Butler handed Scott her business card, which had her phone number and cell number highlighted in neon yellow.

She slipped on a pair of sky blue, thin rubber gloves that reminded Trenna of her residency program at the hospital, grabbed the bone and put it in a large zip lock bag and quickly tagged it with a little white sticker. The bag was so long and oddly shaped that Trenna realized you would never find one like it in the grocery store trash bag aisle. Ever.

Later that night Scott found himself wondering how Dr. Butler had labeled the bag, and how in the world she would ever be able to find its correct owner. Maybe it didn't even matter. The owner was long dead and buried. Who would it matter to? It was then that Scott looked off the deck toward the beach. Like the night before, he saw a man in uniform. Except this night it wasn't just one man, it was two men and they both looked downward as they slowly walked, looking at the sand at their feet. Scott thought nothing of it as many people often walk beaches at night.

Trenna nudged up beside Scott as he stood at the railing. She was in a long white night-gown that seemed to glow in the moonlight. Scott could see her full breasts as the moon shown through the thin fabric. He thought she looked beautiful in every way possible. She handed him a White Claw and smiled.

"Big day, huh?" she asked.

"The biggest so far."

She laughed a little as she came back with "And we're only on day two." She looked up and their eyes met. They kissed, long and passionately. "What do you think tomorrow will bring?"

"Hopefully, not another huge-ass bone. The dogs are gonna get spoiled as hell."

CHAPTER SIX

The next morning was cool with blue skies and smooth seas. Scott had two interviews on his agenda, which he looked forward to. He and Trenna had originally planned on taking the first couple months off before trying to land jobs. This was the luck of the young with no credit card debt or major pending obligations other than their new home rental. The bills and rent payments had been planned for and were already sitting in the bank. Most of the funds were from wedding gifts and the like, but also from their own efforts as the move east had been in the works for almost two years. They both were able to tuck quite a lot of money away in preparation for this adventure, so the pressure hadn't hit full force yet. That being said, they were both already getting eager to begin job hunting.

Trenna stood at the stove checking on a sausage, biscuit, and gravy breakfast casserole she had found on YouTube the week before and couldn't wait to try it out. Another word for husband, was "victim" which poor Scott would learn soon enough.

Scott came downstairs in his underwear and flipflops and sat at the table. "Can I help ya with anything?"

"Nope. Not yet. Want some coffee?"

"Sure, hit me."

She poured him a strong cup in his favorite mug and handed it to him.

"This is great java."

"Honey, you're a bad liar. It's instant. I dropped the coffee maker in the street unloading stuff."

"I pick my battles, baby. What are you gonna do today?"

"I'm not sure yet. Besides unpacking, there's still lots to do to get the house the way I want it. But I want to learn about that Asbury Home. Maybe see if they could use a nurse. It sure would be great to be able to walk to work, especially along a beach. That'd be the bomb, right?"

"I knew you were going to say that eventually. Sounds good to me."

As she checked the casserole and pulled it out of the oven she asked, "Hey, last night I was out on the deck after you went to bed, and I saw a few guys walking around the beach. They weren't kids with surfboards either. They looked like military guys. Should we be worried?"

Scott looked up at her. "I saw a guy our first night here. He was also in a uniform, an old one. He looked young. I thought he was looking for something in the sand. I didn't think anything of it. I also saw a couple guys last night, too. I was going to mention it, but people always walk the beach. They're probably people out there all night long. I'm not worried about it. How many did you see?"

"I didn't really count, but a few. I'm just a little edgy after finding someone's leg, ya know?"

She placed a plate of biscuits and gravy in front of him and a couple pieces of toast. He began eating enthusiastically.

"This is really good. Another YouTube recipe?"

"Yep."

"Needs a little hot sauce, but I like it. I really like that funny black dude. His recipes are always great. You should make more of his stuff."

Trenna smiled. He wanted hot sauce in everything. "He's a bartender, all his videos are about drinks."

"I know, that's why I like him best. I'm gonna jump in the shower and head into town. My first interview is at 10:00. Do you want me to bring anything back?"

"Nope, I'm good, thanks. If I change my mind, I'll pick it up myself."

They kissed; she wished him luck, and they planned to meet that evening on the balcony. Trenna had planned to surprise Scott with another YouTube recipe. This time it would be a new cocktail recipe from the funny black guy. Scott was right, his drinks were always amazing.

Scott jumped in his old Dodge and when he got behind the wheel there was a piece of paper balanced on top of the steering wheel. It said "check the tests" in bad scribbling. He wasn't sure how to react to the note, but the thought weighed in his mind the entire day.

When he arrived home Trenna wasn't there.

About six o'clock that evening Trenna showed up with a stupefied grin on her face and a cardboard box with an extra-large pizza with sausage, mushrooms, and pepperoni in her arms. They looked at one another, each figuring neither would have arranged dinner. Scott had some Ragu warming on the stove with grated mozzarella in a bowl on the counter and some noodles ready to go in the pot of boiling water he had kept at bay, knowing she'd be home any minute. A loaf of garlic bread at the waiting was also on the counter.

"Shit," Trenna said almost laughing. "You went out on a limb and here I am! Well, what do you want to eat first?"

"Let's make it all, I'm hungry!"

"Sounds good. Hey, I've got news."

"Does it have anything to do with YouTube?" Scott asked.

"No, I got a job! Of course, I told them I needed to discuss it with you first before officially accepting their offer. I went into the Asbury Home and spoke with the Human Resources Department and didn't even ask about a job, but I did have questions about the history of the place and wound up being invited to lunch with the Administrator. I guess she liked me and long story short, they asked for my nursing credentials and BOOM, they offered me a job! How crazy is that?"

"I love it! And I love you! But, what about our plans to hang out and do stuff before we commit to jobs? I'm fine with it and happy for you, but it's your call."

"That's the best part . . . I told them all about our plans and they are fine with them. They want a date for me to start and they said there is no real rush, although they are hoping I can start in a couple weeks. I guess between my resume and our proximity to the hospital, it gave me brownie points. Can you believe it?"

"I think it's all terrific . . . and I don't want to be a downer, but I vaguely remember hearing you say, numerous times, that you wanted to get into emergency room stuff. This definitely won't be that. On a scale from one to ten I'd guess the excitement level would be about a one. Are you okay with that?"

"I know, I thought of that, too. I also knew you'd remind me." She smiled and walked over to the deck railing and looked out. "I know it's all happening fast, and I know some time in the future I might wish I would have thought a little harder about accepting the job so fast. But, for right now it feels right. Heck, I can always quit if I don't like it, and besides it will be good on paper, right?"

"I couldn't agree more! Congratulations, Nurse Ratchet. Now go get your purse!"

"Why? Where are we going?"

"I'm taking you out for an impromptu congratulatory meal."

"But we have pizza and spaghetti!"

"It'll keep. Let's go."

As they were pulling out of the driveway in Scott's Tahoe, they never saw the six uniformed soldiers lined up along the beach watching them as they drove off.

CHAPTER SEVEN

The next few days were uneventful, and Scott and Trenna enjoyed visiting the local Home Depot and Lowe's stores nearby. They purchased decorative lights for that all-important nighttime ambiance, as well as a new grill, a weedwhacker, and other items of comfort. Basically, spending a good amount of wedding money and feeling damn good about it. They were happy.

Scott got a call back from one of the interviews he'd had days before. He felt he had done well during the meeting and expected to hear back from them with good news, but as the days went by, he had begun to wonder if he misinterpreted his instincts. It turned out he was right after all and after talking with Trenna, he accepted the position. Their lives were really shaping up and things seemed to be moving fast. It was as if they were meant to live in Calvert Cliffs and they were both excited about calling their parents and letting them know the happy news.

They both started their new jobs on a Monday of the same week. No fear in jumping in with both feet they thought. Every pun intended.

Trenna seemed to get along fine at the Asbury Home with both the residents and the other nurses. There were a few snobs among the staff that Trenna thought needed to be firmly put in their places, with emphasis on their attitudes being a little less high and mighty. But she wasn't going to point any fingers to the supervisors. Trenna knew employees of mostly low character acted this way when they had something to fear, or often when a new threat to climbing the rungs of the ladder was introduced, especially in smaller, closer-knit businesses. But she was not going to let them get the best of her. They were much older, and she had her whole career ahead of her. That was HER attitude and Trenna would be sure and let them see it in her smile, too.

Trenna was on one of her many errands to the basement, this time to drop off a box of old medical records. It didn't take her long to discover that at the Asbury Home, nursing duties didn't only cover one-on-one patient related tasks, but also quite a few administrative duties as well. This didn't bother her since she was fresh out of school and considered all hospital responsibilities a part of the whole and a learning experience. She knew it would help her better understand the "big picture" and Trenna was in it for the long run. The little things were easy for her to overlook, at least for now. So, she smiled and gracefully did what was asked of her.

She found a section of older patient records neatly stacked in an isolated corner of what she thought looked like a dungeon. She supposed due to the horrific storm that had recently blew through town, the staff was pulling old records left and right. After all, if her dog could bring a femur bone home, no telling what the other neighborhood dogs were finding.

She quickly glanced through a few of the boxes and the contents of one were newspaper articles regarding the Asbury Home and some of its staff around the year 1920. It seemed there was concern centered around a doctor who had been accused of tampering with the dead in a not so socially acceptable way. A big coverup had ensued and in its wake, highly newsworthy gossip, evidently taken as fact, covered both the major and local news publications. She went on to read that the doctor, Dr. Morgan Malarkey, had left the Asbury Home shortly after the crimes surfaced and no one had heard from him since. Foul play was never confirmed, and he was never absolved of, nor tried for his potential crimes.

Later that night she relayed all her newfound knowledge to Scott over cocktails as they relaxed on the deck enjoying the fractions of light that the sunset threw among the clouds and the melancholy sound of the breakers.

"Scott, something bad happened at the Asbury Home. I know it. I think the storm churned up a lot of it that most people have been trying to forget. And the soldiers, what about them? We can't deny we've seen them on the beach. We've talked ourselves into believing that they're just a few guys out there walkin' around. But you know as well as I do, they aren't just a bunch of guys. They aren't real. Don't you feel it? I feel it, I know it."

"Trenna, how many drinks have you had?" Scott smiled a one-hundred percent fake smile and looked away.

She continued, "We said the other night that for some reason we knew we belonged here, we felt it. Well, maybe this has something to do with it. I need to know. I'm beginning to feel that this Dr. Malarky, did some bad and perverted stuff and got away with it. I'm also feeling that maybe we are here to help those boys who have been walking around out there (she pointed toward the beach) figure it all out. If that's true, we . . . I can't just walk away from this, can you?"

"I can't talk about this now. It's just too much. I'm not disregarding it, and I'm not ignoring it. I just need some time to think. Can you give me that?"

"Whatever you want. I said what I needed you to hear. But Scott, this isn't over, and I want to help. I want to set the record straight, for the boys."

"Geez. This is turning into a movie." He hesitated. "I know. It's the right thing to do."

Later that evening when they laid in bed, silently holding one another while both of their minds spun, the soldiers were no longer on the beach searching for their lost treasure. That night they were lined up on the deck just a few feet away on the other side of the French doors watching them. Neither Scott nor Trenna could see them in the darkness. The moon cast no shadows.

CHAPTER EIGHT

The following morning as Trenna was leaving for the Asbury Home, she happened to look down on the front stoop as she closed the door. There was a filthy, stained, vintage nurse cap lying on the cement step. It was faded and worn but undeniably authentic. "What the heck? What are you doing here?" she said to herself as she bent down to pick it up. "You are just a little too creepy to suddenly show up at my door." Trenna went back into the kitchen, put the cap in a zip lock bag, put it in her purse, and left for work.

She found she was actually looking forward to a reason to go into the dungeon that morning and when it came, she found herself walking a little too fast to get there. Within minutes she had her nose in several boxes and learned quite a few things about Dr. Malarkey. She wasn't surprised that the information began to frighten her.

Dr. Malarkey had quite a hankering for the younger nurses on his staff. In fact, over the years, four of them had disappeared without a trace. None had given notice of wanting to leave their jobs, none showed any desire to leave town, and each seemed happy in their professional roles at the Asbury Home. Each woman was single, with no family to speak of in or around the nearby vicinity. Their disappearances were, of course, duly investigated. Questions had been asked, background checks were examined, and the police assured the town that they had discovered no suspects or interested persons in any of the cases. The bottom line was that the detectives felt there had been no evil intentions acted upon and presumed the girls must have simply left town and moved on.

The only ruckus that anyone kicked up was for Thelma Burhmer. She had been twenty-three and was engaged to a then Private Jimmy Runion. They were due to be married after a one-year courtship, but she went missing a week prior to the wedding. The police and those who didn't know Thelma assumed she ran off with cold feet, but Jimmy knew better.

Friends of Thelma's told the police that she loved Jimmy very much and would never have left him at the altar like that. Thelma had often told people how lucky she was to be marrying into Jimmy's family. Those close to the couple knew evil had struck her down. The police only checked the boxes on their forms and closed the file on poor Thelma. Jimmy did everything in his power to keep the investigation open, but it was closed just the same. Friends said they never saw a man so devastated.

They held a prayer vigil along the coastline one evening to pay their respects to Thelma. Jimmy cried.

Jimmy stayed in the Army until his death some thirty years later from a sniper's bullet on an island during Vietnam. His body was flown back to Calvert Cliffs, and he was laid to rest at the Gate of Heaven next to the Asbury Home in 1961. Jimmy never married and beside his name and rank, his tombstone read, "Jim and Thelma at Last Together in Heaven."

A shock went through Trenna as she realized Jimmy must have known for years about the town gossip and newspaper articles regarding Dr. Malarkey and the suspicions of his depravity.

Instead of taking screen shots with her phone of her newfound information, she grabbed a manilla file folder from the supply room and just started taking things directly out of the files. She figured no one would care. Who would even notice? It wasn't as if the nurses' disappearances meant anything to anyone after all these years. It wasn't as if she was stealing valuable information. They weren't patient records; only moldy old newspaper articles and she knew she could easily explain them. Plus, after she discussed things with Scott, she could always put them back.

CHAPTER NINE

Trenna couldn't wait to get home to fill Scott in on what she learned.

Upon entering the house, she dropped her bags, kicked off her shoes, and went straight for the Jim Beam. She poured herself a shot and threw it back. The heat hit her throat and she had to take a deep breath. "This stuff's worth every penny," she mumbled to herself and poured another as she began making dinner.

When Trenna and Scott sat down to the table, she began to talk non-stop.

"Why don't you eat something for a minute. Your food's gonna get cold, honey. You did leave some room in there for a little food, didn't you? I can smell the booze on your breath a mile away."

"I can't eat. I haven't eaten anything all day. In defense, I've also drank a lot of coffee today, too! I spent my whole lunch hour in the dungeon digging stuff up. You're gonna die when I tell you."

She filled Scott in on what she had learned that day and showed him the papers she confiscated.

"Jimmy must have known everything for years, and no one would listen to him or help him reopen Thelma's case. Imagine knowing someone you love was murdered at the hands of a psycho and even the police department didn't care enough to help bring the killer to justice. It's enough to make you go crazy," Scott said.

"I was wondering if the cops were covering it all up."

"What do you mean?" Scott asked.

"Well, it all happened about a million years ago. The town was very small, most people were poor, and Malarkey was a very prestigious man. He had money, no doubt, and probably could talk his way out of everything. He might have had the politicians and the police department under his belt. Back in those days bad things happened to people who made too much noise, and a crazy doctor could make anything happen."

"Are any of the missing nurses in this?" Scott held up a picture. It was an old black and white of what looked like the Asbury Home's nursing staff.

"I didn't see that."

"It was stuck to the back of a couple newspaper articles," Scott offered and handed it to Trenna.

Emotion left Trenna's face as her eyes focused on the photograph.

She remembered.

"Look at this." She ran to her purse and pulled out the zip lock, handing it to Scott. "I found this in front of the door this morning when I was leaving for work. I forgot all about it until now."

There was no doubt about it. The nursing cap that Scott pulled out of the bag was identical to those in the picture.

That night just before sunset Trenna saw soldiers on the beach. The man on the far left was pointing at the sand. Trenna wasn't afraid. She grabbed Scott by the sleeve of his shirt as she walked out of the kitchen. He reluctantly followed.

The soldier pointed into the sand and got down on one knee. His posture signaled to Trenna and Scott that he wanted to help. It was obvious to them both that he wished he could.

Trenna dug up another bone. By the looks of it an upper arm.

As Scott looked at the young men in their old military uniforms they were no longer in a line, but now were various distances away from one another, each pointing at sections of beach. It was clear what the soldiers were asking them to do.

By the time the sun set behind them they had exhumed numerous bones. Some were still barely wrapped in the old cloth they had no doubt been buried in.

Trenna uncovered a skull. Her hands carefully held it up toward the soldier that was now kneeling in front of her. When she looked up at him, she noticed that he was not a young man as all the others were. His uniform was not one from the 1920s, but he was middle-aged, a man that had lost his youth many years ago. His uniform was new. It was almost exactly like the Army uniforms from today. She noticed his cheek glistened in the moonlight as if it had been touched by a drop of ocean water and then saw his ranking and name plate.

Trenna was looking at Lieutenant Colonel James Runion.

Scott walked up beside his wife and held her right elbow as if to support her weight.

The moment the last bone was unearthed a woman appeared next to Colonel Runion. His head slowly turned as he felt her presence. They turned to one another and immediately embraced. When their eyes met, Trenna and Scott could feel the love between them. The air seemed to lift and there were no words as the couple once again found each other after so many years.

"We will make this right. We will be able to prove some of the bones are women, and with the nurse's cap . . ."

"We will lay Thelma next to you," Scott added. "They will all be at rest. You will be at rest."

Lieutenant Colonel James Runion smiled and nodded. He and Thelma walked toward them knowing that there was no way to properly convey their indebtedness and contentment. They held eye contact, then slowly turned, and walked away.

The soldiers followed them and slowly vanished into the night.

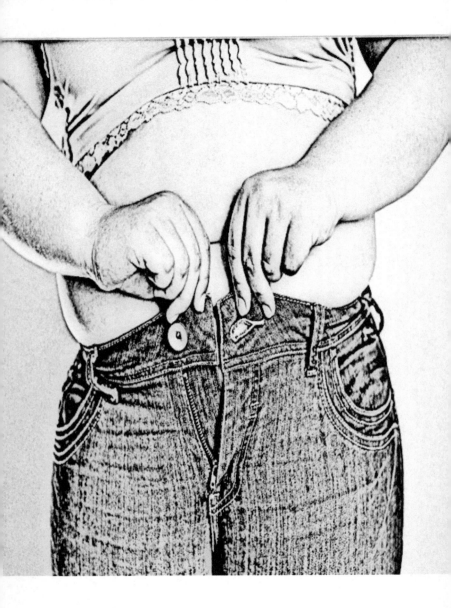

"They are not long, the weeping and the laughter,
  Love and desire and hate;
I think they have no portion in us after
  We pass the gate.

They are not long, the days of wine and roses:
  Out of a misty dream
Our path emerges for a while, then closes
  Within a dream."

Ernest Dowson (1890s) ~

DUDLEY'S REMORSE

CHAPTER ONE

Before the highway cut through the fields and the KOA Campground was established, the people who travelled through these parts were usually in some type of old beater or RV that was on its last legs and blowin' smoke like a chimney. If they didn't stop at Dudley's, they would be toast and they knew it. It got awfully hot in the late summer months and if you weren't prepared to be stranded, you could be in a whole lot of trouble real fast.

Dudley's Auto was located off the last exit before the Mohave Desert. The establishment made most of their money rescuing folks that didn't heed the advice of their motor's whining or wobbling front ends. Dudley made his fortune from those unfortunate individuals that were either too stupid to keep an eye on their dashboard gauges or just not man enough to admit their vehicle needed some work and kept putting off most general maintenance.

Dudley took pride in the fact that he was able to suck people dry at their weakest moments and he couldn't care less if they were inconvenienced by having to hole up at his other business, which happened to be a flea ridden motel, conveniently located about three-hundred feet from his service station. In fact, most of his customers found themselves in just that fix. Within an hour or so of stopping at his station they would find themselves walking down the dirt road, dragging their luggage (or worldly belongings) to Dudley's Rest for a nominal fee, of course.

He had it all goin' on and wasn't ashamed to admit that he had most of the town's revenue in the bag. He worked very hard at what he did and spent long hours throughout the day, and most nights as well keeping the money rolling in.

Dudley wasn't the cleanest guy in town either. In fact, most of the time the aroma he carried around both nauseated people and caused them to avoid him whenever possible. He had been told this fact on various occasions, but also didn't really care. Everything stank in the desert, especially in the hot months (which were basically year-round) and footin' the bill for air conditioning wasn't something he was going to do. Besides, it never seemed to affect his businesses and until it did, he wasn't going to worry about it.

One day an older woman pulled up to the pumps and Dudley noticed it took her most of about four minutes just to get out of her car. Her legs were so big he was amazed there was enough room in front of the steering wheel for her to get them both under it. As she managed to pull herself out of the car and stand up by gripping the driver's door, he noticed the car leveling itself as her tremendous weight was taken off the shocks. The woman's face was bright red, and her mouth was drawn up into a grimace of both pain and fear. Huge wet spots on her blouse underneath massive arms that were almost as large as her upper thighs glistened in the afternoon sun.

"I sure as hell wouldn't want to be in that car right now without a gas mask," Dudley mused to himself as he watched her struggling.

He had a quick moment's thought of wishing Karl, his night attendant and inspiring mechanic, was there to witness this event as he was always up for a good bet. Karl had a much more forgiving heart than Dudley did, and Dudley knew he'd bet that the lady would make it inside the office. Dudley, however, had his doubts but knew it would have been an interesting wager.

She lumbered into the station and complained of chest pains as she leaned onto the greasy counter. Dudley was waiting for the glass top to crack and was amazed that it didn't. That's all he needed was some chunky old lady goin' through his display. There would be no way in hell he could lift her out of it, and he sure as hell knew he couldn't sell her.

Dudley quickly phoned the emergency dispatcher in town.

The line was busy, and he became immediately angry. He was starting to fear the old birdie would drop dead in his shop. He hated to be inconvenienced when he had work to do.

Not sure of what to do next, he offered her a seat and went to fetch a glass of water, hoping she was only dehydrated from the desert temperatures, which he knew often caught people off guard. It was surprising how quickly the dry heat could suck the life out of you if you've never been in this type of climate before.

The woman tried to drink but only wound-up drooling most of it down the front of her outdated tunic top. It was then Dudley realized just how bad off she really was. He made no attempt to try to hold her up as he was probably a fraction of her weight, and he was probably older than she was. He knew he hadn't the strength to support her in any real way that would benefit her, so he tried to ease her to the littered floor of the office.

He tried to settle her down as best he could, but his harsh manner only intimidated her and upset her further. It was quite obvious that she disgusted him, and it only made things worse for her condition.

He knew she was failing. He was beginning to feel badly at how he had treated her. He knew his actions weren't subtle and knew she had to be aware of how he felt. He tried to push this uneasy feeling aside.

The second call to 911 went through and the operator answered on the first ring. Dudley made the call from his back office which was probably twenty feet from the cash register and was a relatively close distance from the counter at which the woman currently lay directly on the floor in front of.

"What's your emergency?" the operator said in a monotone voice.

"This is Dudley at Dudley's Auto. Is this DeeDee?"

"Hey Dud, what's goin' on? If you're calling to ask me out again you can't do it on this phone line. This is for emergencies only. I can't believe you don't get that!"

"No. DeeDee and I do get that. I have a woman here with chest pains and she's fucking huge. I need an ambulance right away."

"Okay, Dud, I'm sending an ambulance now. It should arrive within ten minutes. Is she alert?"

"Yeah, she's breathing like she's just been in a bull fight and her fat ass is on the floor of my shop."

"Okay. Are you looking at her now?" DeeDee asked.

"Yeah."

"Okay I'd like you to ask her for her name?"

DeeDee could hear him in the background as he asked her what her name was, and Dudley quickly returned to the phone. "Hey, she's breathing but her eyes are closed and she ain't answerin."

"Dud, I need you to try and wake her up."

"Shit, DeeDee, these people who eat and eat . . . don't they know it's a death sentence? For Christ's sake, okay, just a sec."

Dudley shook her and again, there was no response.

"DeeDee, I don't know if she's even breathing anymore. This is so fucked up."

"Okay. It's gonna be okay. I need you to listen to me darlin. Now put something under the back of her neck like a towel or something that lifts her neck a little so she can breathe easier. It will open her airway. Then I need you to put one palm of your hand over your other hand and press on her chest between her boobs. Can you do that for me Dud? Press hard."

"Fuck."

"Now press hard and release. Do it thirty times then stop. Then I want you to pinch her nose closed and breathe into her mouth three times and then press on her chest another thirty times. Keep doing this. Do you understand me?"

"Yeah, I understand. Fuck."

"Great babe, you got this. I'm going to stay on the phone with you, put me on speaker if you want, but I'm here. The ambulance will arrive soon and I'm going to stay with you." DeeDee was speaking in her professional voice now and she was good at it. Her voice was soothing, caring and exactly the type of voice that was so suited for emergency dispatch. She had been trained not to break when dealing with frightened people under stress and she enjoyed it.

She had known Dudley since high school, and he had been constantly trying to get in her pants over the years. He was very annoying and rude at times, but she had a way of dealing with him that both put him in his place but didn't offend his manly honor.

"Alright. If this fat bitch dies, I'm not liable, right?"

"Dud, just do what I say and tend to her until the ambulance shows up."

DeeDee was amazed at how callous and uncaring Dudley was regarding this poor woman who never harmed anyone and was only unfortunate enough to land in their town and get sick. She never thought much of Dudley and whenever he would call or when she would run into him on the street or at the local bar, she felt a faint stab of nausea as she knew he was all about the dollar and could care less about anyone but himself. She knew a man like that was only interested in a piece of ass, and she had no desire to communicate with him in any way beyond the scope of normal day-to-day chitchat. Not to mention his personal hygiene was non-existent and it took all her willpower to even stand within three feet of him, and that was on a good day. They lived in an incredibly small town and burning bridges was not a good idea. Not a good idea at all.

Especially since he was practically the only auto repair place in town.

CHAPTER TWO

The ambulance arrived and carted off the woman, whose name was Gloria Cashell, a hardworking gal, back in her day. Her obesity became too much for her and at the tender age of thirty-eight she became unable to work any longer although she remained very active in her social circles. It's easy to stay abreast of things when you have a computer.

When the ambulance pulled into Dudley's Auto, Gloria's vitals were very low. Although Dudley did his best to keep her alive, even though he was thoroughly repulsed at having to enact mouth-to-mouth resuscitation, he could honestly say he did what he had to do.

Unfortunately, she died before being transported to the hospital. Her last words in the ambulance were, "That man didn't even know me." She said this as a final tear of humiliation streaked down her face.

Dudley watched as the ambulance quickly pulled out of the lot and entered the main drag towards town. He stood there, his hands in his pockets, and realized that no sooner than the ambulance had gone about a hundred feet, its speed decreased, and the driver turned off the lights and siren. Dudley knew the woman must have died. Being the selfish bastard that he was, the first thing that came to his mind was what a pain in the ass it was going to be to get rid of her car which was taking up valuable space in his parking lot.

CHAPTER THREE

D udley wasn't sure quite how to react. He thought about closing the station for the day, but he had too much going on. Besides, he never knew that fat hag. He felt bad for her, sure, but she chose every day to eat and eat. It was her own fault for letting her weight get out of hand like that. He grabbed a voltage meter and a crescent wrench and wandered back into the bay and continued working.

Later that evening as he was closing the shop, he just couldn't shake the feeling that something wasn't right. Maybe the morning's drama got to him after all. Maybe he just needed to go home and have a few beers and try to put the day behind him. That sounded like a good plan and that was exactly what he did.

The next few days were uneventful, and his life continued to revolve around his shop and the motel. Business was good and he hadn't thought of the fat lady at all. In fact, he almost had forgotten about her altogether.

Before he left the shop for the night he walked into the men's room and as he looked in the mirror, he saw words written on the glass in thick black bearing grease. They read: "You didn't even know me."

Assuming a customer had written it he shook his head and said under his breath, "Yeah, and I don't want to know you if you're going to pull shit like this." He yanked a handful of paper towels from the dispenser on the wall and some WD-40 and began to wipe the mirror clean.

At the end of the day as he walked out to get in his pickup truck, again he saw the words "You didn't even know me," written on his windshield.

"What the . . ." Now he was feeling inconvenienced, and it was starting to piss him off. He cleaned the writing off the windshield and decided to stop by Lou & Joe's, which was a bar that a lot of the home boys in the neighborhood often stopped at for a few drinks before heading home after work.

He thought about reaching for a clean shirt, but decided it was too much trouble, so he grabbed his keys and locked up.

When he arrived at the bar he parked, got out of his truck, and saw a woman leaning on the light post just outside the entrance. He thought his eyes were playing tricks on him as he realized she looked like the same fat chick who died at the shop. If it wasn't her, she definitely had a twin. "Poor her," he laughed to himself as he hit the door lock button on the fob and began to walk inside. He glanced up again and saw that the woman had gone. Where did she go? She didn't have time to go anywhere. Weird. Dudley saw a few friends sitting at the bar, so he walked up and dragged a stool over and joined them. He ordered a Corona from the bartender and told him to hold the lime.

At the corner of the bar by the wall he saw the same woman sitting alone and staring at him. The sides of her thighs drifted off the edges of the chair. The light was very dim, but he knew it was her. She was wearing the same clothing she had been in when he last saw her. Maybe she hadn't died after all. He slid back his stool and began to walk over to her. He told his buddies he'd be right back and looked at her. Again, she had vanished. This time it caught him off guard because there was no way she could have gotten past him without running right into him. He returned to his seat and ordered another Corona. The bartender handed it to him, and he reached for a cocktail napkin and laid it on the bar. Just before he placed the beer on it, he noticed the words, "You didn't even know me" written in a shaky hand, glaring at him. He quickly stood and pointed at the napkin. His friends looked over at it and Dudley saw that the words had disappeared. What was happening? They looked at him inquisitively and Dudley blew it off and took a long pull from the Corona. It tasted funny but he drank it anyway.

On the way to his truck, he thought about the woman, and found himself looking around as he walked. He looked in the trees and behind each vehicle he passed. It was as if he was waiting for her to jump out and grab him or something. He didn't like what was happening or how he was suddenly feeling.

When he arrived home, he was glad to be there and was looking forward to checking his emails and getting a good night's sleep. He thought about taking a quick shower to wash the sweat and grime off his body, but decided he was too tired. He had a hard day and the beers made him unusually worn out. Going to sleep was exactly what the doctor ordered. Tomorrow was going to be an early day for him, and he knew he'd be getting dirty again anyway so what the hell. Bed was all he wanted. He began to quickly scan his emails before hitting the sack.

He bumped into the door frame as he entered his office and dropped his keys on the floor. "Fuck," he mumbled to himself and bent over to pick them up. He turned on the computer and sat down with a thud on his squeaky chair. He had been meaning to oil the wheels but had been putting it off. He'd get around to doing it sooner or later.

As he opened Yahoo Mail, he saw that he had over fifty new messages. He was surprised and figured they were probably all spam because he never got that many messages in one day. Then he noticed they were all from the same person. Gloria Cashell. "Who's that?" he wondered as he opened the first message.

His breath caught in his throat as he read, "You didn't even know me."

All the messages were the same, over and over. He began deleting them with fury settling into his bones. Now he needed to know who this Gloria Cashell was, but in his mind, he thought he already knew.

The following morning, he visited the hospital to follow up on ol' Gloria. Sure, enough she was the woman who was at his shop and died on the way to the hospital. Now he wasn't so mad as he was unnerved. If she died, who does he keep seeing? Her ghost? Maybe if he left out a shitload of cheeseburgers or maybe a pan of lasagna she would come back, and he could tell her to get lost or get a grave. He sighed. Then his demeanor changed as he wondered why she would come back. Was she haunting him? Maybe she was pissed because of his attitude that day. He had disrespected her and although sick she had to have known it. Now the game had changed, and he didn't like it. Now he thought he may have something to worry about.

He wasn't particularly in any rush to get to work that day as Karl had recently requested some extra hours at the station, so Dudley had changed the schedule and put him on two mornings a week to help him out. He was pleased and it was nice to be able to sleep in a little later on those days.

Dudley got to work at about ten o'clock and his day proceeded routinely with no surprises. He hadn't mentioned the weird happenings to anyone as he was worried people might think he was finally falling off his rocker. He had decided to keep all the "I think I'm being haunted" shit private for now and deal with it himself.

The next morning Dudley got up and took a much-needed shower, got dressed and went into the kitchen to grab something quick before heading to work. As he reached for the ice box, the door handle was so cold it burnt his fingers and pain caused him to flinch and step back. On the face of the freezer door "YOU DIDN'T EVEN KNOW ME!", was written in capital letters his time. He heard a woman's laughter. It was so loud it caused certain items on the sink to jiggle. Dudley ran out of the house praying his keys were in his pocket. They were.

As he drove to the shop, he stopped at the old Benjamin Franklin's to grab some food. It used to be the only store in town, but that was a million years ago. It was basically an old Five & Dime, with a counter along one wall with the best food, the only food, in town. Now it had a new owner. Although the food counter remained unchanged., the new owner changed its name to The Last Call. Despite the fact that most of the residents called it the Shit and Git, it was still popular among the locals. They still had the best milkshakes and malts in the state. They didn't get much business these days and Dudley, and the rest of the town for that matter, were amazed they were able to keep their doors open since it was located on a now very desolate road that highway travelers never knew about. Dudley ordered a large coffee and two BLTs on white toast with Miracle Whip. He had every intention of eating them in his truck on the way to the shop, that is, until he was waved down by a guy pushing a dirt bike along the dirt road that followed I-10 parallel. It was a short cut and Dudley often took it to avoid the highway traffic.

The guy was probably in his late teens or early twenties and Dudley knew it would be easy money, so he stopped to help him out.

The guy seemed nice enough and honest enough and Dudley couldn't help but like him right off the bat.

At first glance he realized that the cylinders of the bike weren't getting a spark, so Dudley asked him if he'd fetch his black tool bag off the back seat of his truck. The kid shuffled over to the pickup and seeing the keys still in the ignition, he opened the driver's door and jumped in. He started the engine and threw it in drive. Dudley looked up, caught completely off guard, and watched the kid smile, and gas it while keeping his foot on the brake and began power braking the shit out of it till a mixture of blue smoke, dust and gravel flumed up behind his truck. The kid only whooped and hollered.

Now, having an immediate attitude, Dudley got up off the ground and began walking over to the truck and the kid. His plan was to drag him out by his collar and beat the shit out of him. Unfortunately, just as he got a few feet from the front of the truck, the kid let off the brake and came at him with lightning speed.

The passenger headlight hit Dudley's hip and threw him about fifteen feet off the highway and down an embankment. When his body stopped rolling, he also noticed that besides his hip, he had evidently broken his collar bone and maybe an arm. He basically couldn't move at all. Dudley realized he was completely hidden, and out of view from anyone who may happen by. This section of road wasn't very well traveled, and Dudley immediately got worried that he was in a hell of a mess.

As his truck went by him the kid stopped, threw it in reverse and backed up. As he got on the shoulder closest to where Dudley lay grabbing his side, the kid laughed and said, "In case you get hungry you filthy, stinking bastard!" and threw the bag with the BLTs as hard as he could at Dudley. It flew past him and would have gotten him square in the face if Dudley hadn't spun a little sideways to avoid it. The bag hit a rock and rolled another couple of feet away.

All Dudley could do was scream at the kid as he watched in disbelief as he drove away and left him in the desert alone and bleeding.

CHAPTER FOUR

Dudley had laid flat on his back for what he had guessed to be at least five hours or so. Although he was never a Boy Scout, Dudley knew that at noon the sun was straight up no matter what time of year it was. Now it was way off to the west, and he figured it would be below the horizon fairly soon. This thought made him nervous. The last thing he wanted was to be laying out in the desert, helpless after dark. The kicker was that he was so close to town. Hell, he was right on the edge of it. Someone had to jog by soon. Someone fucking better.

He knew he slept a little because he remembered waking up but was unaware of how long he was out. All he knew was that he couldn't move at all. His hips were singing, and he thought that besides his collar bone and arm being broken, he must have also messed up his pelvis. "Damn, why did I trust that little fucker," he said to himself as he tried to keep his thoughts together. He didn't want to panic. Panic never helped anything or anybody. He knew he had to keep his head straight for as long as he could. He had to ride this out. He could do this!

It became obvious that no one knew he was out there, and he was very thirsty. Not only thirsty, but hungry. He knew he had to try to make it over to his sandwich before the Miracle Whip went bad. He knew he'd probably eat it anyway, but why put himself through that.

He wasn't about to die less than three miles from his house for Christ's sake. But it wouldn't come to that. Would it?

He managed to drag himself over to his sandwich bag, thanking God that the kid thew it out for him. The crawl to the bag hurt like hell having to maneuver through all the goat heads, hog weeds and other weird desert shit that stuck to him. Plant life in the west was incredibly unforgiving.

As the daylight began to wane with no sight of any passing cars, pedestrians, or evidence of any human life, whatsoever, Dudley began to get scared. His legs weren't responding, and he knew he couldn't move now if he had to. He was a sitting duck for snakes, coyote, or any other predator that happened along.

He had one bite left of his sandwich and he was so thirsty he already thought he was going to die. He had been in the Mohave Desert all day. It wasn't high summer, but it didn't have to be. The temps were always hot there and he was truly scared now. That first night as he tried to sleep, he remembered Gloria. Sometimes he thought he could see her nestled in between two bushes barely out of sight and sitting there, staring at him. Grinning at him. If she had been there, he was thankful that she kept quiet.

Now it had been two days. He slept as best as he could, but the morning didn't bring any hope. He still had no water and couldn't move. His tongue began to feel like a log. It was hard to keep from choking on it. He couldn't speak any longer and trying to holler for help was impossible.

He had tried to drag himself up the embankment numerous times with his arms, but the pain was too intense, and he didn't have any strength left. He knew he was dying.

What did the kid tell him when he drove away? He tried to remember but could not. He called him something . . .oh yes, he called him "a filthy, stinking bastard." If he ever got out of this mess, the first thing he was going to do was find that kid. He was gonna find him and nail his ass to a wall. Oh yeah, you better believe it. There would be no mercy for that kid. And to think he'd actually liked him; he even trusted him. What a chump he was, so gullible.

Day three. Dudley was done for, and he knew it.

Now Gloria was close to him. He could feel her. She'd probably planned this whole fucking thing just to get even with him for being so mean to her. She was enjoying his misery; she had to be. She was relishing watching him, laughing at him. Knowing that he was getting exactly what he deserved. How could she be so cruel? How could she be so hard on him, knowing he was laying stranded in the wilderness? Dudley felt helpless.

As he slipped out of consciousness the last words Dudley spoke in a whispered and breathless voice were "You didn't even know me . . ."

"How doth the little crocodile
  improve his shining tail,
And pour the waters of the Nile
  On every golden scale!

How cheerfully he seems to grin,
  How neatly spreads his claws,
And welcomes little fishes in
  With gently smiling claws".

Lewis Carroll (1832 – 1898)

WHAT A BARGAIN

CHAPTER ONE

Martha Murdaca woke up extra early this particular Saturday morning, jumped in the shower, and began to list in her head the items she would be looking for. She was to meet up with her two girlfriends, Katie and Mariah, for a trip to a local swap meet in town by eight o'clock.

The swap meet began in April and ran through Labor Day. It was opening day, the beginning of the season, and she refused to be late. The competition would be fierce, as always and she wasn't about to let anyone beat her out of a good deal.

Besides her regular job at a local café during the week, which she hated because the manager kept cutting back her hours and scheduling her to work odd shifts, Martha sold her swap meet finds on eBay as well as Amazon and she also had her own website. She considered herself to be well versed in purchasing and selling used treasures. If she wasn't, she sure did a good job of faking it. She sold toys, clothes, tools, old motorcycle parts – you name it. If it wasn't too beat up, scratched, or worn out she would drag it home and try to re-sell it, especially if it was a challenge. Martha believed that there was someone for everything and if she could clean up whatever it was, she could peddle it. She was actually very good at it, too, and since she began doing this, she had been able to make double payments on both her credit card and her car. This was no small task, and she was damn proud to be able to do it, so far anyway.

Fifteen minutes after she finished dressing, Katie and Mariah showed up at the house, each with pick-up trucks. Martha greeted them at the door with three travel mugs, that Martha had purchased from previous yard sales, filled to their lids with hot black coffee.

"I just need to grab my keys and I'm ready! Come on in. Does anybody need the bathroom or anything?"

"Not me. Thanks, this is gonna hit the spot," Mariah said as she grabbed for the coffee.

"Nope. I just wanna get there before the good parking spaces are taken. I love doing this but lugging all the stuff out to the truck sucks. Java Java Java! Thanks girl," Katie said.

"I hear that," Martha grabbed her keys, kissed Cooper, and locked the door.

Martha used to take Cooper, her twelve-year-old Schnoodle, which was a charming mix between a Schnauzer and a Poodle, with her to all the swap meets, yard sales, and estate sales she went to. In recent months however, Cooper's hips had begun to bother him, so knowing he was more comfortable at home, she would leave the doggie door open so he could come and go as he pleased until she would arrive back home. Most times he would be wagging his tail from his gigantic dog bed instead of greeting her at the front door as he always had before.

Martha used to kid around saying that damn dog bed was more comfortable than her own, although she secretly meant it with all honesty. For the last couple of years, she had been falling asleep on a used pillow top she abducted from a neighbor's garage sale. Pillow top wasn't the correct phrase anymore, now it was more like lumps that had gotten rock hard by the feeling of it. She needed to add a new bed to her list of "to-dos" but for now she was making it work.

It made her feel sad not being able to take Cooper with her anymore, but she knew it was the best thing for him. Leaving the television on took away a lot of the guilt. He was spoiled rotten. Exactly how it should be.

As Mariah and Katie looked at each other through dirty windshields and waited for Martha to climb into her old step van that she purchased used from a UPS auction three years ago (she never seemed to purchase anything brand new), each held their breath as the old battery cranked and finally kicked the motor into life. Relieved, they left Martha's pot-holed driveway and caravanned the eight miles or so to the swap meet. The van starting was always hit or miss as she didn't drive it often, only for her swap meets and estate sale adventures.

They pulled into the lot, lucky to find three spaces next to one another, and exited their vehicles. With shining faces, good attitudes, and dreams of finding good cheap shit, they walked with quickened paces into the already growing crowd of enthusiastic junk gatherers.

CHAPTER TWO

As expected, they found tons of cool stuff and Martha felt that by the end of the day all three of them would find lots of items that would make money upon resale.

Katie and Mariah had known Martha since high school. They weren't into the whole making money *thing* like Martha was since both were married and their husbands brought in most of the dough, but they enjoyed the hell out of the shopping end of it and felt good that they were able to contribute to the family pot even if the money was very little.

They had a good eye for knowing what would sell, and what would not, and Martha would give each of them a hundred dollars and trust them on the decisions they made toward purchases. Then at the end of the day, Martha would take them out to dinner, and they'd head back to Martha's house to unload their treasures and party on cheap beer and pizza delivery until everybody was fat and happy. The opening day of the swap meet was always on their calendars and the three of them had begun to call it tradition.

The following Monday morning Martha got up at her usual time to get Lydia, her daughter, ready for school. She had just entered the fifth grade and didn't miss a chance to let everyone know how proud she was to finally be one of the oldest in the school. Martha kissed her on the cheek and wished her a happy day.

Once she returned home, she stared at the huge pile of items she had purchased the previous day with her friends. She first organized the items into separated piles, with one special pile for cleaning and doing the obvious prep work needed to make each item look appealing to future buyers and made a comprehensive list of each. Once the lists were completed, she began to clean each item and get it as sparkling and pretty as she could. This often took time, sometimes as much as a few days. Then she took pictures and added descriptions for each and listed them on her website where she would advertise them. After that she basically sat back and waited for the bids to come in. Easy money.

She was very happy with the purchases they found and was confident it would be a good year. She considered herself lucky to have two great friends that enjoyed spending her money for her own personal gain. She also wondered why neither Katie nor Mariah wanted to join the fun, and try to sell things themselves, but was very happy they did not. Competition wasn't something Martha enjoyed, and she certainly didn't want to compete with her friends. Yes. She was lucky to have them.

CHAPTER THREE

During the cleaning process, Martha had been working on a vintage doll that she clearly remembered having as a kid herself. It was a vintage 1969 Krissy doll. Long red hair, lacey mini dress in bright orange, and still in the box although it was very dirty and vaguely smelled of a campfire. It looked as if it had been covered with soot, and smears of it remained on the outside of the box. It was amazing. Katie had found the doll, bought it, and Martha was so happy she did. In fact, it hit home with her so much, Martha wanted to keep it for herself and after a minute of contemplation, she decided to do just that. After the thrill wore off, she would in all probability add Krissy to her website, but for now she would enjoy playing with her. Girls never outgrow their favorite dolls.

When she was a kid, she loved her Krissy doll. You could press a button in her back and if you pulled the ponytail her hair would pull out long and shiny, all the way down her back to almost her feet. What great memories she had playing with that doll.

Yes. There was no way she could part with it. Martha decided to keep it and was very happy about her decision. She brought it inside her home and put it on her bedside table. She looked at it as she fell asleep that night and was so happy to be able to relive the memories that it had brought back to her.

That night she didn't sleep well. She kept hearing noises in the house that alarmed her. Cooper had been acting strange and didn't want to leave his bed. Normally he would follow her around the house, but not that night.

As she roamed around, she didn't find anything out of place and decided the noises were simply the house settling. It was an older home and it often creaked and groaned especially in stormy weather and when the humidity was high.

When Martha walked around her bed, she gently caressed the lace on Krissy's dress and smiled. She didn't notice that her white socks were dusty as if she had been dragged across the floor.

Cooper whined as Martha began to close her eyes and she realized he wanted to be on the bed with her, so she picked him up gently and cuddled up next to him. She fell asleep almost as soon as she closed her eyes. Although Cooper remained still, he didn't sleep. He kept staring at the Krissy doll, lips pulled back, teeth barred.

The next morning before sunrise, she sat up and began looking for her slippers. She looked everywhere and couldn't find them. She religiously put them on the floor next to her bed. In fact, she was pretty anal about it. Finally, she found one on top of the bookshelf in her room and the other in the clothes hamper in the bathroom. She thought Lydia must have been trying to wear them and although annoyed a little, she had to smile. She slowly put them on and stood up.

She noticed Krissy wasn't on the table where she had left her. Frowning, she walked around the room and out into the hallway. She noticed the doll on the floor in front of her daughter's room. That was strange. Perhaps her daughter, Lydia, had come into her room, saw Krissy, and began to carry her back to her room. After all, a great doll is hard to ignore for a kid. Odd that she would have left her on the floor though. She must have been half asleep. Lydia had never been big on dolls. In fact, she had always been the rough and tumble type that enjoyed toy cars and superheroes over girlie toys. She affectionately thought how much her daughter took after herself.

Martha walked down the hall to pick her up and carry her back to her room. As she reached for Krissy's shoulders it suddenly felt like a pin had gone right into the palm of her hand. She drew back in pain and immediately thought there must have been a pin or something in her dress that pricked her. "Shit," she whispered to herself as she stood up and went for the light switch in the bathroom to get a better look. A few drops of blood had moistened the toilet paper she used to dab the wound. Without even thinking about it she once again went back into the hallway and reached down, picked up

Krissy carefully and walked her back to her spot beside the bed to place her back on the nightstand table. Blowing off the whole ordeal she began her usual routine of going downstairs to make breakfast for Lydia before sending her off to school. Martha was in a carpool with a neighbor mom who also had a child at the elementary school. They took turns being the kid's chauffeur on school days.

"Time to get up! Breakfast is almost ready," Martha hollered upstairs. The usual complaints filtered down the stairs as Lydia began to come alive.

"What the heck, Mom?"

"What do you mean, what the heck Mom?"

"The toilet started clogging up last night and when I tried to come in your room you wouldn't let me in. What was that about?"

"I have no idea what you're talking about, darlin. Say again?" Martha said as she lifted the pancakes out of the frying pan.

"Your door was locked, and you wouldn't let me in when I banged on it. You never lock your door. I would have called the police, but your light went on, so I knew you weren't dead or anything. Why didn't you let me in?" Lydia asked.

"I have no idea what you're talking about; I must have been dead asleep. When I got up my door was open and yours was closed."

"Mom, can I have some butter?"

"Oh yeah, here ya go." Martha slid her the butter from across the table and didn't even stop to think about mentioning Krissy laying outside her door.

Another day had begun.

Chapter Four

After Martha got Lydia off to school and finished up the breakfast dishes, her cell phone alerted her to an incoming call. It was Mariah who had already begun speaking before she could even say hello.

"Hey, what are you doing?"

"Just the dishes right now, why what's happening? You sound freaked out. You never call this early, what's going on?"

"I'm standing in the street."

"You're what? Are you suicidal or just having a senior moment?"

"Some chick just ran into the back of my car. I can't believe it," Mariah said.

"Oh man, you just got that car! Are you okay?"

"Yeah, I'm fine, just pissed."

"Was she texting?" Martha asked.

"I don't know what the fuck she was doing, but she wasn't paying attention, that's for sure. Would you come and get me? They're gonna tow my car to Winger's garage. I want him to fix it. Tommy does good work, at least he always has in the past when I needed him for stuff. Anyway, the tow truck is filthy inside and I'm wearing white today like a freakin jerk."

Martha couldn't help but laugh. "Sure, I'll be right there, just tell me where."

"Thanks Mart. I'm at the corner of Miller Fall Road and Wheat Fall Drive."

"Okay I'm on the way. Do me a favor will ya?"

"What?" Mariah asked.

"Get the fuck out of the street."

They both laughed.

Martha grabbed her purse and went for her keys which she always hung on the hook by the door. Not finding them there really set her off and she began to worry about keeping Mariah waiting. Martha was a woman of habit. She did things routinely and rarely, if ever, misplaced things. A few minutes later she found them on a table in the living room. Relieved, she hurried out of the house and hopped in her car. Unlike the van, it started right up with no hesitation.

CHAPTER FIVE

When she arrived back home and began going up the stairs, she realized Cooper hadn't greeted her. Knowing in her heart that something was terribly wrong, she ran back downstairs and began looking for him. He wasn't in his bed or in any of his favorite spots, so she went out the back door and began searching the yard.

Martha was always afraid of snakes and prayed he hadn't gotten bit by one. When she was a kid her best friend's dog had gotten bit by a rattler, and it wasn't pretty. The poor thing died a slow and horrible death. To this day, she had always had a strong fear of those little bastards. Even having the doggie door made her a little nervous, but in her mind, it was so incredibly unfair to keep a dog in the house all day while you worked a job. I mean when you think about it, how would you like it if somebody told you to "hold it" all day?

Cooper wasn't outside. In fact, Martha couldn't find him anywhere. Now she had begun to worry a lot more than she already had been. Realizing she hadn't checked the upstairs, she ran back inside, through the kitchen, and across the living room to the stairs. She braced herself and began searching the second floor. Nothing. The last place to look was her own bedroom.

As she opened the door, and walked around her bed, there he was. Blood was puddled on the floor around him, and his eyes were wide with fear and surprise. His mouth hung open and his tongue lolled outward and rested on the carpet. He had gashes across the sides of his body and across the top of his head. Blood was drying in his already cloudy eyes. It was obvious that he had been defending himself, but against what?

Martha screamed and fell backwards against the dresser as her legs gave out underneath her. "Oh my God, Coop!" She immediately felt the remaining warmth in Cooper's body and began to cry.

Without hesitating, she looked up and tried to pull herself together, realizing that whatever had killed Cooper may still be in the house. She reached for the phone and called the police.

When the police arrived, it was decided that nothing had been taken from the home. The home hadn't been broken into, and outside of the obvious death of the animal, there seemed to be nothing unusual except for what they had found in a spare bedroom. Again, no sign of theft but things were on the floor and items had been rearranged on top of the furniture and in the closet. She knew she hadn't left it that way. In fact, Martha told the cops she rarely entered the room at all. Not being able to honestly tell the police officers that her daughter didn't reposition any of the objects, they didn't consider it was anything to worry about. But Martha knew it was strange and Lydia wouldn't have done it.

The police couldn't offer much help regarding Cooper's death, although evidence of a battle had taken place, and there were no clues as to who the offender had been. The police suggested that maybe a racoon came inside the doggie door and killed him when Cooper turned to defend his territory as they assumed he would have.

When Lydia came home after school the police were still at the house. The anguish of losing Cooper was heartfelt by the police officers and Martha did her best to comfort Lydia.

"Mommy, how could this have happened? Was he trying to protect us? What did this to him?"

"I don't know, sweetie, we're going to find out. The police will help us. It was probably some kind of wild animal that came in through the doggie door, but I don't know. I'm so sorry you had to see all of this. I wish I could have been able to help Coop. Right now, let's try and be strong and concentrate on trying to find out what happened."

"Ohhhh Mommy!"

That afternoon Martha and Lydia took Cooper to the vet to be cremated.

Mariah and Katie showed up unexpectedly to visit that evening. They brought KFC and beer in hopes of trying to take Martha and Lydia's minds off the awful experience they'd had that day with Cooper. Poor Cooper.

Martha and Lydia both were very happy to see them and appreciated the food and friendship. After everyone had eaten and Martha had a few beers in her, Katie had gone upstairs, changed the bedsheets, and did a quick cleaning of the master bedroom for Martha. She knew it would be very hard on Martha to face it and wanted to make things easier for her.

That night after Martha tucked Lydia into bed, the women stayed up and went over all the drama that had taken place that day. None of them were happy and couldn't believe so much horror could have transpired in one day.

After the girls left, Martha picked up the glasses and plates left behind from their feast, threw them in the dishwasher, and began getting ready for bed. Her usual routine was to shower at night as she had always fought with insomnia, and a hot shower just before bed always seemed to help her relax and make it easier to drift off. Tonight, however, she knew sleep would be hard to find no matter what she did.

After the day's events Martha only had thoughts of Coop and already missed him. She wanted to know how he died. What was he fighting off? She was angry that the police couldn't offer any definitive answers, but she was also aware that she needed someone to blame. It was all just so sudden and awful.

As she lay in bed and got comfortable in her blankets, feeling the warmth they provided and holding onto the soft pillows that surrounded her, she looked out her bedroom windows and marveled in the views which overlooked the moon swept mountains, and peacefully sighed.

Martha smiled as her gaze fell on her bedside table and saw Krissy. She slowly reached for her. She needed the comfort of all the fond memories of her past and drew her closer. All Martha wanted to do was hold her close and fall asleep.

As she drew Krissy close, she saw that Krissy's fingers were mis-shapened. It looked as if they were chewed and horribly destroyed. She also noticed that Krissy's dress was torn and that there were drops of what looked like dried blood all over her fingernails. As she examined the doll, she also realized there were bunches of red nylon hair laying on her dress. Further evaluation found red hair on the floor of the room. This would have been normal, Martha thought, if Krissy would have been found on the floor somewhere. But she wasn't. Krissy was sitting upright on the nightstand, exactly where Martha had put her the night before. Martha knew she hadn't picked her up that afternoon and she also knew the cops didn't either. If they had and would have noticed the blood on the doll's nails, they would have told her. Then she remembered Katie had cleaned up for her after . . . well, after. She obviously didn't look too closely at Krissy, or she would have noticed the torn dress and blood. Martha would wash her clothes and wipe her off in the morning.

The afternoon she had found Coop was a blur. There was so much emotion running through her mind. She tried to think and recall exactly what happened that day. She needed to know the precise chain of events that led to her finding Coop, dead on the floor. "Think. Just think," she said to herself as she laid in bed.

CHAPTER SIX

Awaking early, Mariah had planned to hit a local estate sale and had high hopes of getting lucky. Martha had told her the night before that she wasn't ready to get back in the groove of it all yet and wanted to sleep in. She knew it'd be a good day to mourn.

The weather channel had been calling for thunderstorms later in the afternoon and Martha told her where the key was hidden to the back shed so she could get whatever tarps she might need in case of rain. She even offered to give her a better cut of the profits, although she knew Mariah didn't really care about the money; it was the hunt she loved.

Mariah arrived at the house while Martha was dropping Lydia off at school. The low hanging clouds looked heavy with rain, which sucked, and even though she had no idea what good things she might find at the sale, she knew it was always best to be prepared.

As Mariah was searching the garage for the tarps, she thought she heard a strange noise towards the rear of the building. Curiosity overtook her and she followed the noise. Nothing. "Probably just a mouse," Mariah thought to herself and grabbed the tarps and left.

CHAPTER SEVEN

Martha made a mental note to phone Mariah later that night to see how she made out at the estate sale. The advertisement in the paper indicated that they had a great variety of things available, and she knew how excited Mariah was to attend. Still, advertisements always suggested great finds, but Martha on the other hand, knew better. She, herself, wasn't excited at all. She was still in shock about Coop and didn't feel, in any way, ready to jump back into her life quite yet. After all, what was the rush?

Martha was determined to hunker down in her room for an undetermined amount of time this weekend as Lydia was staying at her father's house for the next couple days. He and Martha had been divorced for two years and he lived across town. Which wasn't far enough away, as far as Martha was concerned, but they agreed it would be best for Lydia if they remained close to one another for their daughter's sake.

Although Martha loved her daughter to the moon and back and always enjoyed their time together, she also enjoyed taking every advantage of her alone time when she could.

Martha had kept a stash of a pills from over three years ago when she had needed to have a dilation and curettage ("D&C") procedure done. Being the now responsible mother that she was, yet remembering herself as an old hippie, she couldn't bring herself to throw away the unused meds. The fact they were seconals made the decision to keep them a no brainer. Not particularly caring how politically inappropriate it was to save them, she figured what the heck and sealed them up, good and tight in a zip lock and happily threw them in her freezer. One just never knows how things are gonna go, and in this particular circumstance surrounding Coop, she was damn glad she'd held onto them. A good couple of downers was exactly what she wanted.

As the day dragged on and as the two hits Martha ate were kicking in quite beautifully, she peacefully napped and happily let the entire world drift away. Her dreams of Cooper as a puppy and happy days enveloped her mind as she lay on her bed and looked at old pictures, sometimes having to close one eye at a time to get the best visual. She never even took notice of the fact that Krissy wasn't in her spot by the bed. But none the less, she felt as content in that very moment as she knew she could be. In fact, when Mariah knocked on her front door, she didn't even notice.

CHAPTER EIGHT

Mariah fumbled at the front door, rooting through her purse for the keys to Martha's house and not finding them quickly enough, she decided to just go around back to the shed to deposit her finds from the estate sale. It turned out Martha was right; the sale wasn't quite as wonderful as she originally though it would be, but she did manage to pick up a few items.

Mariah knew Coop's death affected her in the worst way and she knew she was probably laying up in bed in front of a depressing old black and white movie crying her eyes out, or just drunk and reminiscing. She would leave her alone. With Lydia visiting her dad, Mariah wanted Martha to enjoy her solitude while she could and no amount of small talk she could offer would help her feel any better. Yeah. She'd give her a buzz later, maybe the next day, to tell her about what she purchased and see how she was doing.

She unlocked the door to the shed and slid it open. It was really an old garage that was barely safe. It had a lot of years on the old wooden floor, and it was obvious that the weight of a vehicle would most likely cave it in. That's why these days Martha always used the driveway for parking the vehicles and stored only yard sale and estate sale items for the business inside.

As she was entering the back of the garage, arms weighed down with boxes of old toys and for the most part, other worthless crap, she heard a noise to her right. As she turned to see what it was her ankle got caught on a loose board. She fell over dropping everything and landing hard on the floor now covered in dust and cobwebs, which blew up in her face. When she sat up and brushed herself off, she heard a sinister laugh and attempted to spin around to see where it was coming from. As she did, all she could see was orange lace coming at her. The small and once cute little face with pink cheeks and a soft innocent smile had changed into a hideous visage, and now showed nothing but hatred and malice. The ashen and grisly painted face with pallid lips peeling around sharply carved teeth came at her with an unsightly grin that only could be described as pure evil. Short arms bore down upon her and grabbed her head with small strong hands, and Mariah felt them begin to twist her neck upward until she was face-to-face with the Krissy doll. She tried to defend herself and cried out as Krissy pulled her face towards her massive teeth and began to bite into her soft cheeks. Then Krissy began twisting her neck and she had no time to gather her wits nor enough strength to ward her off. Within seconds she heard the sound of her own neck snapping and felt the sensation of her body giving way to paralysis. The last movement Mariah's body ever made was the dropping of her eyelids around wide, now vacant eyes.

CHAPTER NINE

The next morning Martha woke up to a glorious sunrise and felt infused by the good fortune of another new day.

She wondered why Mariah never stopped by after the sale to show her what she had purchased, but also knew that she may have, and decided she didn't want to bother her if she hadn't answered the door promptly. Mariah was such a good friend and knew that she wanted time to adjust and be alone for a while after Cooper's death.

Around 11:30 Katie called and wanted to know if lunch could be on their agenda that day because she needed to know how to list the new items Mariah found on the website. She also wanted to know if Martha had heard from Mariah because she hadn't been answering her phone all morning and it was weird.

Martha hung up the phone and tried to get her act together. The previous night was a blur due to the effects of the seconasl, and she couldn't help but feel in her heart that something was wrong, although she had no idea what it could be.

She felt both hungover and sick at the thought that something wasn't right. She was a mom after all and this whole feeling was completely out of character for her. She dressed and got ready for the day and decided to venture outside into the garage to see what new additions lay waiting for her from Mariah's shopping spree.

There were some new things. One being the fresh corpse just beginning to rot in the warm spring sunshine which spilled in through the garage windows.

In total shock and almost pure panic she had phoned the police minutes later after stumbling backwards and falling on her knees in horror at the site of her friend. Shock filled her body as she knew that she could not hold Mariah and grab her as she had wanted to. It only seemed right to hold her; she was a friend, a best friend, she couldn't leave her there on the dirty floor. That wouldn't be moral. The police arrived at Martha's house within fifteen minutes and the time of Mariah's death was undisclosed until further investigation.

Katie was a mess and had completely fallen apart when Martha broke the news to her. They both sat on the back porch, speechless, only gazing at the sky and the crime tape, which now surrounded the old garage.

"You know," Katie slowly said as she reached for a tear that had begun to roll down her cheek. "Nothing like this has ever happened before. We've never had any bad luck, and now it seems every freaking day something is going wrong. What's happening?"

"I don't know. I'm just glad Lydia isn't here. Oh God, how am I going to explain all of this to her?"

"Fuuuuck."

"I know this is gonna sound paranoid, but it seems like things have been going badly ever since we got back from opening day at the swap meet," Martha said.

"What do you mean?"

"Well, besides Coop's and Mariah's deaths, which were both horrible, a few things I haven't mentioned have happened. I haven't really thought about it or saw the pattern until right now."

"Okay, now you're starting to freak me out. What are you talking about, Martha?"

She told Katie about finding Krissy in the hallway that first night, and about finding things out of place around the house recently. She also told her about finding the doll right after Cooper's death with blood on its chewed fingers and torn dress, but assumed it was from whatever killed Coop. She told her how Lydia had confronted her, telling her about hearing noises and telling her she wanted to sleep with her door closed from now on. In fact, when her dad had invited her over that weekend, Lydia was more excited to get away from the house than she was about spending actual time with him.

Katie sat, not saying a word until she had finished. "There is something I never told you either."

Why is my heart pounding? Martha thought to herself.

"What is it?"

"When I first saw Krissy at the swap meet that day, she was in a row with other dolls behind a section of carnival glass near the cash register. I saw her but didn't really take full notice of her because I had just gotten there, and she was at the first booth I had come to. I wanted to walk around first to see what all was available. That's how I normally shop, before I start grabbing things, I like to see what else is for sale first. It's a good way of saving money. Anyway, then I saw her again near some old snow skis a few aisles over. I thought it was strange that they'd have two Krissy dolls and not have them side by side, but I didn't think twice about it. Then I saw her again in a completely different booth at least ten exhibits away by some ice chests and yard decorations. That was when I really took notice of her. I picked her up and began seriously thinking about buying her."

"What are you saying, Katie?"

"I have no idea what I'm saying, except . . . well except maybe there really weren't two Krissy dolls. Maybe . . ."

"What? Maybe there was only the one and she was following you around the swap meet in a box? Oh my God, that is so lame!"

"I know how it sounds but look what's happening to us!" Katie said.

"Let's get in the car tomorrow morning, early. It's Sunday and the swap meet will be open. We can go talk to the person running the booths and find out if there is another doll, and if not . . . well, we can find out if they know where they got her."

"That's a great idea, Martha. We keep records and accounting on all our inventory. I bet all those venders keep track of where they get their stuff, too. It's their bread and butter for Christ's sake."

As Martha fell asleep that night, or tried to, she began to reach for Krissy, then thought twice about it. Instead, only looked at her. Krissy's eyes were soft and gentle.

Days earlier she had washed and mended her orange lace dress and carefully had taken a fingernail file to Krissy's fingers, sanding down the gnarled and chewed fingers to try and restore them to their original shape as best she could. Then she took some sandpaper, 2000 grit, which was the softest sandpaper mostly used for polishing rather than sanding to further perfect the hands. When she was finished working on her, Krissy was almost as good as new.

There was no doubt in her mind now. She definitely planned to resell her, as quickly as possible in fact. She would put her on the website as soon as she and Katie returned home from the swap meet.

As Martha turned off the bedside light and rolled over, she never noticed Krissy's eyes change from soft and gentle to hard and brutal.

CHAPTER TEN

The women arrived at the swap meet bright and early and were the first to enter through the gates upon its opening. They immediately went to the first booth and questioned the exhibitor. The woman was genuinely happy to speak with them, but as Katie began questioning her about the Krissy doll, her attitude turned grim and short.

"Look. That doll was sold weeks ago, and I can't be expected to remember everything about every item that comes through here."

"We know that, but in all honesty, we purchased it and now we've been having some strange things happening. Do you remember where you found her?"

"Or at the very least, anything about her history or anything that may stick out in your mind about her?" Katie interjected forcefully.

The woman had started to nervously re-fold some children's clothing on the counter next to her, then put them down. Taking a very deep breath she looked at them with reproachful eyes.

"Okay. I feel for you, believe me. I can imagine what you may be going through. Follow me." She called over to another gal who was working the space with her to cover for her for a few minutes. The gal walked over smiling and told her to take off and she'd be fine alone for a bit. The three of them walked out into the sunlight and sat down on a bench by the entrance. Katie and Martha waited for her to begin speaking.

"I got that doll as part of an inventory from a friend of mine. She usually had the space over there," she pointed across the dirt area toward another row of exhibits. "We were very close."

Martha and Katie looked at each other and remained silent.

"My friend, Kiera, found her from an estate sale. There weren't many things recoverable, but the Krissy doll was found among only a few items that weren't burnt. You see, there had been a fire. All I know was that the doll belonged to an elderly woman who was unfortunately killed in the blaze. The woman almost made it out alive, but the smoke inhalation was what ended her life. She was found clutching the doll in her arms. Kiera told me the elderly woman had dementia and was terminal. She had been living in a privately maintained home for the insane. The firefighters had found her. They said her arms were so tightly wound around the doll that it was hard for them to pry the box out of her grip. Evidently, she had been very violent, and the woman would go nowhere without that doll."

When the three stood up and said their good-byes, Martha and Katie watched as the woman began walking toward her exhibit. Just as she reached the entrance, she turned around and looked at them. "Kiera was murdered in her sleep. Before she died, she told me stories that seemed to surround that doll. If I were you, I'd destroy it before it can hurt you or anyone else." Then she was gone.

"So, the doll is possessed with the spirit of a demented old woman? Are we supposed to believe that shit now? I don't think so. I don't believe in ghosts, Martha."

"Me neither. But you said yourself it was weird how you found her and how do you explain what happened to Mariah and everything else? Ghosts have been known to take the form of things, right?"

"Ummm, you mean like possession? Is that what we're talking about now? Oh, this keeps getting better and better!" She wanted to laugh but did not.

When Martha got home later that day, the phone was ringing. It was Katie. "I'm sorry I acted that way. I guess I needed time to sort through everything."

"It's okay. No worries."

"After thinking about all of this I agree, it's all just too fucked up to believe that a senile dead woman can be inside of a doll like something in a late-night horror movie, ya know?"

"Yep."

"So, what are we going to do now?" Katie asked.

Martha heard a noise coming from upstairs. At first it scared the shit out of her, then she looked at her cell phone to get the time. Whew, 6:30 already!

"Hold on Katie, I'll be right back." She put the phone on the kitchen counter and hollered upstairs.

"Lydia is that you?"

"Yeah Mom, I just got home a few minutes ago. I was just going to jump in the shower."

Martha met her at the top of the stairs.

"Where ya been?"

"I was with Katie. Why don't you come down as soon as you get showered and dressed? I need to talk with you, okay?"

"Sure. I wanna talk to you, too. We had a great time this weekend and I want to tell you about it."

"Awesome, honey, I want to hear all about it." Martha stood on the stair riser and heard the water in the shower turn on. She quickly walked back downstairs and returned to the phone.

"I'm sorry, I'm back. Lydia's home. I dread telling her about Mariah. Her hearts going to break."

The phone was silent for a long moment. "I bet. Do you want me to come over?"

"No, I don't think so. I'd rather do it myself. I'm going to get that doll right now and burn it out back in the fire pit. I want to get it done before she gets out of the bathroom."

"I don't blame you. Just be careful."

"I will. I'll talk to you later."

Martha hung up first. She never heard the soft click as the upstairs phone disconnected.

Martha grabbed some lighter fluid and some matches and went outside. She threw a couple small logs in the metal fire pit she had purchased from Home Depot the previous summer. Overhead, a raven flew past. She watched as its large black wings gracefully caught a thermal and seemed to hover over her looking straight into her eyes. After a few minutes she went upstairs to get the doll.

She was sitting prim and proper on the night table and without emotion Martha grabbed her and was somehow relieved as she was halfway expecting a fight, especially going down the stairs. Isn't that where a lot of ghost story nightmare scenes occur, on the stairs? She continued down and threw Krissy on top of the logs. After squirting lighter fluid on her dress and then lighting a match, she flung it and watched as the flames engulfed the doll. As the plastic face began to melt, Martha took a deep breath and said, "Bye-bye you little bitch. Go back to hell where you belong."

CHAPTER ELEVEN

Martha went back inside feeling emotionally drained and opened the top of a Blue Moon that had been chilling in the ice box along with its five other companions. She took a long pull from the neck of the bottle and then placed it on the counter. She heard Lydia in her room, opening and closing drawers, no doubt looking for her pajamas that Martha had washed the day before.

"I hope you're hungry," she yelled upstairs. "I'm making pork chops."

"Fine, Mom, I'll be down in a sec."

Martha stood over the stove staring at the chops in the frying pan, trying to keep her hand from shaking. She almost dropped the spatula twice and was surprised to find herself looking forward to that second beer.

How was she going to tell Lydia about what happened to Mariah? So much had happened in the last couple days. Life was ruthless. If God was supposed to be so merciful, he surely had a separate agenda for her and those whom she loved and knew.

She went to the fridge and grabbed a head of lettuce and a couple tomatoes from the crisper as she heard Lydia shuffling down the stairs. No more cucumbers; damn she had forgotten to buy some for the salad.

It suddenly got very cold in the kitchen and Martha felt strange as if some kind of ghostly presence entered the room behind her.

She heard Lydia's footsteps as she began walking over to the cutting board, "Hey baby! Hand me that knife over in the rack will ya?"

In an ancient and unnaturally rough voice, she heard, "You bet, Mother. This is the sharpest one I could find."

Hearing that awful voice, Martha spun around and as Lydia plunged the knife deep into her throat and began to twist the blade, she heard her slowly whisper, "Bye-bye YOU little bitch! Burn me in the fire again . . .? Why don't YOU go back to hell where YOU belong?"

*"Weeks passed, and the little Rabbit grew very old and shabby,
But the Boy loved him just as much. He loved him so hard that he
Loved all his whiskers off, and the pink lining to his ears turned
grey,
And his brown spots faded. He even began to lose his shape, and he
Scarcely looked like a rabbit anymore, except to the Boy.*

*To him he was always beautiful, and that was all that the little
Rabbit
Cared about. He didn't mind how he looked to other people,
Because the nursery magic had made him Real, and when you are
Real
Shabbiness doesn't matter."*

Margery Williams (1881 – 1944) ~

THE VOICE IN THE FREEZER

CHAPTER ONE

E mma sat at her typewriter like she always did in the evenings. Attempting to write something interesting. Something that would charm readers into buying her thoughts and give her the reassurance that her life was worth living.

No one knew that on the left side of her keyboard was a long, handwritten note to her next of kin. No one knew that on the right side of her keyboard was a Walthers 25 semi-auto with the safety turned off sitting on a small pillow that she had bought for her little Shih Tzu. Her little Mosely.

That night Emma tried to end her own life with a quick pull of a trigger. She thought she could do it but at the last second the fear penetrated her bones, and she pulled her hand away from her head and let the cold, hard weight of the gun drop downward. She had no idea the gun was so sensitive and when she thought she'd released her grip, it went off. The bullet that was meant for her then went straight for her beloved little Mosely, whom she loved with every essence in her soul.

Emma was a complex person; she always had been. One minute up, the other minute down. No one knew it as she hid this side of her personality very well. If busy and focused, Emma was an extremely accomplished individual with goals and most of all happy thoughts. Her organizational skills were top notch, and she was well spoken in any circumstance. She was intelligent and she always thought before she spoke, which is an exceptional skill these days. All in all, those who knew her enjoyed her company and liked her very much. On the other hand, when left alone for any length of time, or if she had too much idle time on her hands, Emma's life could get away from her. She overthought and dwelled too deeply on inconsequential matters. Even simple issues could prove to be too much for her. Being the strong character that she was, she rarely knew when she needed help and sadly for her, she was always too proud to reach out and ask for it.

When the gun went off and killed her dog, she screamed and cried in helpless rage.

She never got over that. She couldn't get over that. Now the awful deed of suicide was even more important for her to see through to the end. If she didn't do it, then little Mosely would be all alone out there. All alone in the blackness of eternity. She could see lil' Mosely wandering, helpless and miserable, wondering why. Why had he been left all alone in such a dark place? How could my mom have done this to me?

It was morning now. Her little Mosely's blood no doubt beginning to congeal in the soft blanket that she had wrapped him in hours before. Yes, she was sure that rigor most surely had begun settling in by now. Soon she would make herself get up and figure things out.

Trying to clear her head and remove the horrific memory of the past few hours, she began thinking about her book. After all, her book was all she had now. Maybe she would eventually finish writing it and that would be the only thing she would leave behind for the world to remember her by. It would be the only proof she ever existed. Yes. She would try and concentrate on that.

Where did the famous authors get their ideas from? Could anyone be so creative as to actually think up all their storylines by themselves? Surely, those writers had to experience hit or miss situations. Surely, they had to focus on narratives that may work or fail. Emma wondered if life would get easier for her and if Mosely's terrible and untimely death would one day be an inspiration for one of her stories. By hell or high-water Emma Blakestone would come up with a magnificent story that would take her to the top. To the top of what was her only guess, but it would at the very least fulfill her dreams of being a paid writer and her life would at last be fruitful. If she chose to go on that is.

Up until now she has been fed promises by a truly gifted literary agent who seemed to be genuinely fond of her writing . . . or has she just been gullible?

Emma had a hard life, but it hadn't always been difficult. Once upon a time she had a man in her life. He had promised marriage, children and, of course, happily ever after. But things quickly changed, and he wound up leaving her for a young blonde bimbo with huge fake tits, pumped up lips and a suntan that wouldn't quit. That was a long time ago and all Emma could hope for now was that her fabulously tanned skin was wrinkled and pruned in the worst way imaginable. Sometimes that thought, that wish, was what got her through most days.

For the last two months, Emma had been renting a small but comfortable home in the historic district of Humboldt, Arizona on Main Street. She enjoyed the slow-paced lifestyle the small town offered and, in the summertime, close to eighty percent of the traffic on her road consisted of dirt bikes, quads, and other desert type vehicles.

The town was located along the foothills of the Bradshaw Mountain Range and there was a lot of history surrounding the area. Mostly old mining folklore that was very dark and disturbing. She loved the old lore, and it made her stay in Humboldt even more appealing. She supposed she fit right in considering the deep depression she experienced daily.

Her thoughts always returned to Mosely and knowing her lovable and trusting friend was lying dead in a blanket beside her by her own hands certainly didn't make her feel any better.

This thought brought back another horrible realization. She didn't quite know what to do with him. She wanted to bury him in a wonderfully beautiful and special place, but where? She rented her current residence after all so she couldn't bury him on the property, and she didn't want to take him to the animal crematorium at the city dump. She knew there were rules about burying pets and she sure as hell couldn't keep him in her freezer. What would she do? She knew any of the veterinarians would ask questions about Mosely. After all, there was no way she could even begin to hide the huge bullet hole that went through most of his poor little body. Yes. They would ask questions that Emma knew she couldn't answer. The more she thought about it the more the freezer was beginning to look like her only option, at least for now. Maybe he'd fit between the big chuck roast she had been saving for a special occasion and a huge variety of cookies she had baked over a month ago. How long would cookies keep in a freezer? She hadn't a clue. Her mind began to wander but she quickly brought it back. She decided to throw the cookies out. That would give Mosely the extra space he needed to lay more comfortably. Emma knew she couldn't lay him to rest all balled up in a cramped position, that would be horrible. The cookies would simply have to go.

She then stopped and realized she was contemplating suicide when she accidently shot Mosely. How could that have suddenly changed? She knew the answers laid within herself. She needed to simply kill herself and all this drama could end right then and there, yet she could not bring herself to do it. She was too afraid.

Emma wasn't a science major, but she did know the issue would soon need to be addressed. The clock was quickly counting down to the inevitable decomposition stage. She tried to not let herself panic, knowing the freezer would serve well enough for now. She would soon think of something that was socially acceptable as well as both legal and cheap. But let there be no mistake about it, as soon as Mosely was comfortable in his grave, she would make herself a spot right next to him.

Later that night, realizing that writing anything productive wasn't going to happen, at least not that night, her thoughts once again turned to Mosely. She couldn't help it. Why did she have to be in such a hurry to bury him? What was the real urgency? After all, Mosely was small and when, heaven forbid, the smell got too intense, the answer would have to be the freezer. There was plenty of room and although the County Coroner / authorities called it by a different name . . . the mortuary refrigerator, it was still just a refrigerator, right? Okay. The real differences were only semantics. What would it hurt to keep her friend close to her for a little while? It wasn't like she had a *person* on ice in there, right? She could keep Mosely close to her for a little while. Just long enough for her to get her shit back together and figure out what she needed to do next to keep herself sane.

Now she began thinking of ways to keep him well hidden in case she had company or just on the rare occasion of someone unexpectedly stopping in unannounced. It was unbelievable how many ideas came to her mind. Yes, she could pull this off. She even became somewhat enraged because after all, this was Mosely's home. She shouldn't have to apologize for him being here, even in death.

At first Emma thought she was going crazy, but after thinking about it, she decided if crazy meant she could continue to communicate with her best little friend, then she was surely blessed to be crazy. Crazy was fine with her. Welcome to Crazy Town and thank you very much!

Over the next few days Mosely came to her often in many ways. Sometimes it was when she was at her computer and trying to write, but most often it would be when she was lying in bed deep in thought. It was always comforting when Mosely showed up and they always had a lot to talk about. Most times she knew she was imagining things, but other times she wasn't sure. Mosely's visits were so damn real.

Finally, the air had gotten so rich and thick with the smell of death that she had no other choice. She tried and tried to come up with a solution besides the freezer, but in the end she could not.

The first thing Emma did was take all of the freezer's contents out and put them on the kitchen counter. Then she laid down a beautifully crocheted small blanket that she had made specifically for Mosely, which was perfectly measured to the same dimensions as the freezer. She then placed a little pillow on top of the blanket and propped up little pictures of Mosely along the inside of the freezer compartment's walls. It made her feel good knowing that Mosely was still able to be near her in death. The more she thought about it, why couldn't she keep Mosely in there for a longer length of time? Who would really care? She lived alone and certainly didn't need much freezer space anyway.

Emma began to smile and made herself a fresh pot of coffee as she sat at the table talking to Mosely. She had begun to feel like her old self and almost felt as though she was getting back into the groove of her life again. Maybe things were beginning to start looking up for her. Maybe suicide wasn't the solution for her problems after all.

CHAPTER TWO

A few days after Mosely was entombed in Emma's Frigidaire Frost Free Upright freezer, she was amazed at how easy it was to sit down and write. Storylines were coming into her mind's eye every day. In fact, she found herself keeping a little notebook in her purse, so she was able to jot down each new idea as they came to her. She actually began to feel as though her writing was improving!

One day a few weeks later, Emma began to feel very tired. She had decided to call it a day immediately after finishing her dinner, which consisted of a tuna fish sandwich with a ton of Miracle Whip and a can of overcooked Chef Boyardee Ravioli. Overcooked wasn't the right description. She nuked the crap out of it for about fifteen minutes in the microwave which almost turned it into cement, but that was the way she liked it, and nobody could tell her any different. She had discovered this meal idea from a book she had read. Unfortunately, she couldn't remember its name. Probably didn't matter anyway.

As she melted into her clean flannel sheets with her favorite memory foam pillow tucked underneath her head, she took a deep relaxing breath and closed her eyes. This was what she had been waiting for all day and she was relieved to finally relax in the moment.

That night she thought she heard a noise. It had to be her imagination because it sounded like a dog, not just any dog though – it sounded like Mosely.

"What the hell?' she asked herself as she found herself climbing out of bed. She walked over to the window and stared out into the darkness, hoping to see a homeless or lost puppy outside. She saw nothing.

Emma kept hearing whining sounds and finally put on her robe and went downstairs to have a look in the back yard. Nothing.

Giving up, she went into the kitchen to make herself some hot chocolate. As she poured it into her favorite mug and began to reach for the mini marshmallows, she once again heard the noise. Her heart began to race with both fear and excitement, and she realized the noise was coming from the freezer!

Her initial reaction was to run away fast and not look back, but her second reaction was both curiosity as well as hope.

Emma had hoped with all her heart that Mosely was back. Maybe he had been alive the whole time. Maybe she only thought Mosely had been killed by the bullet. It could happen.

After all, she wasn't a doctor; she could have easily been mistaken.

Then another thought crossed her mind. You always hear about ghosts and poltergeists. There are T.V. shows and movies and all kinds of people who believe in the supernatural, right? If so many people believe it, why can't it be real? Famous people, professional people, like doctors and lawyers and even regular people swear they've encountered ghosts, aliens, you name it. Maybe this is real? She began to tell herself that just because she knew she was hearing her dead dog obviously calling to her, it didn't mean she was nuts at all. This was amazing!!!

Emma took a big swallow of hot chocolate, wiped her mouth on the sleeve of her night shirt, and carefully opened the door to the freezer. What she saw didn't surprise her, and it was more of a disappointment that anything.

The shroud that Emma had placed Mosely's body in was still in the same spot and was exactly as she had left it.

Emma smiled with a momentary thought of love for her puppy and closed the door.

"It was how it should be, and how God wants it," she said to herself as her eyes began to fill with tears.

Gathering her hot chocolate and a napkin, she checked the doors to make sure she hadn't forgotten to lock them and made her way back upstairs to the comfort of her room.

CHAPTER THREE

A few days went by, and she had finished the first draft of the book she had been working on for the past two years. She had proofed it, revised it repeatedly, and was in the process of sending it off to her editor for its first round of revisions. This was the part of publishing that any author dislikes the most. Nobody wants to see their hard work get whacked by editors, but it was a necessary evil that all writers need to swallow and the first step to what will hopefully be a good payday.

Emma had a Zoom meeting that afternoon with Wayne Matthews, her long-time editor who was both seductively intense, as well as one of the most valued and professional editors his company could call their own. His familiarity with the publishing industry gained the approval of the men writers, and his good looks and charm gained the approval of the women writers. Emma could frankly care less about his charisma and wasn't about to play games with her love of writing, but Wayne was a genuine good guy, and he liked her writing. He always gave her his best shot in the publishing industry and that made her feel good. She came to trust him and that was all that mattered to her.

Their meeting went great, and he was excited to get to work on her new manuscript.

"How're you doin', Emma?" he asked her.

"Oh, you know, the usual. Just trying to write and do the best I can."

"That's good. You know I love your writing; I always have."

Emma smiled and looked into his huge, dark, puppy-dog eyes. "Well, that's what I'm counting on my dear. Now we just need to tell the rest of the world."

He always loved the fact that she never let him make her feel anxious or intimidated like his other female clients. At least if she was, she never showed it. Emma was honest and true. She wasn't flirty or self-absorbed and Wayne respected that about her. It was a rare find in the publishing community.

"I'll get your manuscript back to you as soon as I can. I'm looking at about four weeks. Is that all right with you?"

"Sure, I'll be at your beck and call. I gave my new number to your secretary."

"Yes, you did, and she told me to say hello."

"She's a sweetheart. You know, you really need to give her a raise or something."

"If it was up to me I certainly would."

"Well maybe you should at least give her a bonus." Emma smiled and detected a slight blush in his face.

"Always lookin' out for the underdog, right?" He smiled and held her gaze.

"Yep. I guess so."

They said their professional good-byes and Emma closed her end of the Zoom meeting, happily.

Later that evening, Emma rethought the conversation and wondered how he took her last statement. Could he have thought she meant "a bonus" in a sexual meaning? She wasn't sure if she should be mortified or not. Then she realized she really didn't care.

One thing about Emma, although she may be privately falling apart at times, she was hell bent on never letting the world know it. Although if she could ever go against her better judgement and open up, even a little to give anyone the chance to get to know her on an honest level, she was desperately afraid that their opinions would quickly and drastically change about her for the worse. Maybe that was why she chose to be so private. She hated herself at times for having so much self-doubt.

CHAPTER FOUR

After meeting with Wayne, she was ecstatic. She felt in her heart that the draft of her book was going to be well read by those that made the decisions to publish it. All she could do now was pray and hope for the best. She couldn't wait to change into her pajamas and tell Mosely all about her day.

That night as she sat in front of the T.V., which she rarely did, with the large margarita she had been promising herself all day, she felt herself succumb to the night and the pleasures of a full moon rising.

She had been so amazed to find that since Mosely had passed, the bond between them seemed to have grown immensely. Although she knew he was dead, she felt that he was nearer to her than he had ever been before.

That night Emma spoke with Mosely out loud, mainly out of habit to make herself feel better, yet hoping he was still with her in some form. Although she knew it had to be only in her mind, it felt as though Mosely was right there with her. It was as if they had spoken together for hours and when it was time to sleep, Emma could have sworn that Mosely begged and begged to sleep on Emma's bed that night. Not sure if it was a dream already beginning in her head, but Emma put Mosely with her dog bed and her favorite blanket on top of the mattress next to her and together they fell asleep. It was late and she was planning to get up early. She set her alarm and figured if she got up in just a few hours Mosely's body would still be ninety percent frozen, and that would be okay.

Emma found herself not sure if she was going crazy, but this became the routine for the next few months and Emma had begun to realize she had been staying home so often that she was officially entering the recluse stage. She had been turning down all offers with the few friends she had to go out and basically didn't want to leave the house at all. On the occasion that someone would visit, most times completely unexpectedly, she avoided inviting them inside and found herself keeping people out of the kitchen at all costs. She had even told Artie Newberry, an old-time friend from high school, that she had just mopped and waxed the floor, and it was still wet and sticky. Emma began realizing that keeping her beloved and dear companion in the freezer wasn't healthy and it was time to make a change. Her life was turning into lies. She had mentioned it to Mosely that evening, and Mosely became enraged and refused to speak with her.

Realizing her selfish mistake and knowing that her love for Mosely would never end, she knew she had to do the right thing, even if it meant Mosely would now be uncooperative.

The next day she drove to a beautiful spot of ground, off a riverbank with views of a valley and with the scent of honeysuckle and lavender in the air, she buried her best friend in a box carved with loving words and sentiments of affection.

When Emma finished, she sat by the grave and wept. She knew she had done wrong by keeping her friend so close when she should have let him rest easy, but some things, she knew she couldn't go back and change. All she could do now was pray for forgiveness and move on.

Upon arriving home Emma walked into the kitchen first as she always did to check her phone messages. She was old-school and still had a land line. In fact, she ordered the phone special from a website that focused on old style novelties. It was a brown rectangular box with a black rotary dial. You couldn't find that style anywhere these days and it fit her tastes perfectly. The phone didn't come cheap, good things never did, and besides, if she loved something, she always talked herself into believing it was worth it, no matter what the price. She also had her parents old message machine from the eighties. It still worked fine after all these years and Emma wasn't about to upgrade unless she absolutely had to.

She had two messages. One was from some guy who asked if she needed lawn services and left his number, the second was a girlfriend asking if she wanted to go see a movie the following week. She was happy to have gotten that message. She had been a ghost in recent weeks, and she was surprised and relieved to find out she had any friends left at all.

As Emma reached toward the phone to hang up the receiver, she heard a soft, but steady noise coming from it. The machine said she only had two messages, so this unexpected noise caught her off guard. She brought the receiver closer to her ear and the sound turned into a high-pitched whining noise that sounded very far away. As she closed her eyes and concentrated on the sound, thinking it would help her hear better, she waited, hoping the sound would come again. But the phone was silent. Emma played back the messages, and waited for the sound, but there was nothing. Shaking her head, she hung up the phone and stood in the kitchen staring at the ice box.

She leaned her head against the freezer door and wept, thinking of her best friend, and missing Mosely again, already.

CHAPTER FIVE

As Emma laid in bed that night in the dark trying to fall asleep, she had never felt so lonely in her life. If anyone found out what she had done, they would think she was walking on crazy and knew she could never, ever tell a soul.

When sleep finally came, her dreams that night were dark and frightening. Mosely was in her room sharing her pillow as he always did. He was making his usual sleep noises, occasionally taking a longer breath, or thumping his foot on the bed as if he were dreaming and couldn't decide whether or not to run after whatever invisible entity may be in his midst. The sounds were loud and not comforting as they always had been prior to his burial.

Emma awoke twice and found herself looking around the room with her covers drawn up around her chin. She was upset and couldn't help but to turn on the night light she had on her bedside table. Usually, the old night light was a comfort to her, and she depended on it, but not that night. For unexpected reasons that night, the light reminded her of being afraid. She lay there remembering every time she needed it. All the monsters and goblins in her dreams seemed to come out of nowhere and she was afraid.

The next morning was sunny and clear, and Emma was looking forward to accomplishing quite a few things she had been putting off for way too long. She already missed Mosely desperately, but knew death was a part of life and she had to get used to him being gone. She had to move on. She kept reminding herself that the first days are always the worst in any sorrowful situation, and she had to be strong. She knew she could be and would be.

After coming home from a long day of errands and appointments, Emma plopped on the living room couch and was too tired to even check her messages.

She awoke after an unexpected power nap, just as the sun was disappearing along the horizon line. "Wow. I can't believe I fell asleep," she said to herself as she stood and stretched.

She walked into the kitchen and stopped as she stared at the refrigerator. Emma made a mental note to go to Home Depot and buy a new one the next day. She was surprised she hadn't thought to do that before. She decided to donate the old one to a secondhand store. It was only a couple years old and in perfect shape. Plus, no one had to know it was temporarily used as a dog mortuary. She brushed that thought off quickly, still becoming severely upset whenever she thought about it. She would disinfect it in the morning and call someone to come and pick it up. Besides, she had always wanted one of those new models with an ice maker in the door and the freezer in the bottom half of the fridge. She found herself excited about the new purchase and was amazed that she was actually looking forward to it, to anything for that matter. She was feeling better about herself and her life. She seemed to have a direction again and she found herself happy to be alive.

Her day was full and peaceful. It had only been a short time since she'd laid dear Mosely into his final resting place, and she found herself sighing in peaceful relief.

She reached for the phone to check her messages and as soon as she picked up the receiver, she heard that same faraway sound she had heard the day before. "What was that?" she thought.

This time it grew louder, so loud, in fact, she had to hold the phone away from her ears.

As she stood in the kitchen, she caught the movement of something in the hallway. She looked toward it and in the semi darkness of the hall, she could have sworn she saw Mosely.

This time instead of Mosely being the lovable ball of fluff that she remembered, what she saw took her breath away.

The small thing she was looking at now had long dull colored fur that was knotted, and matted with blood and frothy, slimy matter that she knew was decomposing flesh.

It slowly came at her making the same whining noise that she had heard on the telephone.

"Is that you Mosely? Mosely! Please, I love you! I have always loved you!"

Emma stepped back too quickly and lost her footing on the tiled floor. She dropped with a thud as she came down on the table and tipped it over. The contents on top crashed to the floor.

"What were you thinking? Did you think you could keep me in the cold, tell me lies of forever, and then bury me in the dirt?"

Emma screamed.

"You gave me hope. You gave me promises."

"Oh my God! Mosely!"

Mosely jumped on Emma, and she could smell Mosely's sour and deceased, rotten breath filling her lungs and breathing passages.

The last thing Emma remembered before she was taken down into a darkness of ghastly terror was being licked in the face. Licked by a tongue that was hard and dry and smelled of death. Sharp, hungry teeth tore at her skin. She could feel them transforming her. Mosely was coming to life within her, and she could not escape.

CHAPTER SIX

It had been days, and no one had called or come to visit Emma. Although she had friends and people who cared about her, she had been so uninvolved in anyone's lives except her own in recent weeks, that no one missed her absence. It wasn't that they didn't care about her, it was more that they thought she didn't care about them. Either way, the outcome remained the same. Emma was dead and no one knew it yet.

Chapter Seven

A few weeks later, Wayne Matthews knocked on Emma's front door. She hadn't been expecting him. But was ready for him, or anyone.

Emma opened the door with a vague, yet somewhat sinister smile on her face and openly invited him inside her home.

She was wearing a beautifully handmade scarf around her neck that would have been appropriate for any occasion on any Dior or other highly rated, mega-profile fashion site and Emma looked exceptionally beautiful. Her eyes were brilliantly blue and her skin radiantly pink. She was careful, however, to wear clothing that would cover the bruises and ripped flesh along her torso, legs, and arms.

Wayne came inside and immediately felt well received and pleased that he made the added effort to come to her rather than have his secretary call and make an appointment for her to come see him. He wanted to take this time to get to know her a little better and possibly ask her out to dinner that night.

Once they sat down on the couch in the enclosed back deck, which overlooked Emma's quaint, although lovely, rented garden, Wayne told her that he had finished the editing and passed her book on to the big guys. It was immediately picked up by one of the top five publishers out of New York and they had offered her one hell of a deal.

Emma smiled and reached for him. He assumed it was for a congratulatory embrace, which would have been well delivered and happily accepted. He innocently and honestly hoped she had further intentions, and as he let her draw him to her, she smiled and her large canine fangs seized him and tore into the soft flesh of his neck. She was strong now and she was fast. He couldn't escape her embrace.

She had been waiting and she was hungry now.

*"I walked to the end of the pier and threw your name into the sea,
And when you flew back to me —
A silver fish — I devoured you,
Cleaned you to the bone,
I was through."*

Nicole Callihan ~

THE BOY ON THE PIER

CHAPTER ONE

Back when I was a kid, I had no fear. Most adults thought I was crazy and too spirited, which impressed the girls and made me quite the catch in their eyes, but to the guys I was competition and there were frequent after school battles, which I oftentimes won with flying colors. The other times, well . . . I won't talk much about them. But I will say that on those occasions I'd return home with blackened eyes and bloody lips. In a family with only boys, my parents grew to accept the confrontations and most times these events went unnoticed with little, or nothing mentioned of them at all.

My parents, whom I tried to impress the most and worshipped most vehemently thought I was just plain stupid and immature. I spent almost my whole childhood trying to prove I was good enough for them. I would do anything I could to gain their favor. If it was sports, I would be determined to win. If it was English or Science, I would get the highest grade in the class. It was a losing battle though, as no matter what I accomplished in school ever rated to a hill of beans in their eyes, but that's okay.

I never complained and even if my wins didn't matter to them, I knew I was still ahead of the game to the rest of the world.

Not everyone was meant to have kids, I knew this. Not everyone who had kids were meant to be good parents. I understood this and it made life easier to deal with knowing that I was strong and the lack of respect they had towards me would only make me stronger as time went on.

Things never used to be that way though. During the good times, when I felt my parents truly had a high regard for me, and I really saw the love in their eyes, was prior to when my older brother died. I was five and Shephard was two years my senior. I also have one other brother named Jacob, and he was younger than I. That was when our family was perfect.

I remember backyard barbeques, trips to the beach, and wonderful holidays. Nights on the couch cuddled together. Life was good. Of course, being only five, I now realize I had little memory of those days. But, when daily life drastically changes for the worse, you always remember there were once good times, no matter what age you are.

Jacob never knew Shep. He died when Jacob was a year old and if you were to have ever spoken with Jacob back in the day, he wouldn't be able to give you any information at all about him and wouldn't have even seemed to care. To Jacob, it was as if Shep never existed. It has always been a strange concept for me to wrap my head around.

One day, Shep was there and the next day he wasn't. All my parents told me was that he had drowned. They told me I was too young to understand and that it didn't matter. He was dead and the family had to go on. I was told he was in a better place, life wasn't fair, and when I was older, they would explain things better. At that point in time, I never felt the need to argue. Trying to get more information didn't cross my mind. They dealt with the loss in a very angry and non-compassionate way. I thought it best to keep my mouth shut, and that was exactly what I did.

CHAPTER TWO

I grew up on the East Coast and loved the Atlantic Ocean. It was my backyard and every moment on the beach overwhelmed me with contentment. The best and most restful, rejuvenating place on Earth for me was Assateague Island, located on the eastern shore of Maryland. Chincoteague is a small town on the island and most famous for its wild ponies that roam the beaches. I remember as a child camping there with my family. I woke up one night, and as I opened my eyes, I saw a large furry head sticking into the window of my tent. I remember screaming, thinking it was a monster that came out of the ocean to kill us all. Once my parents calmed me down and told me it was only one of the wild ponies, I was ecstatic and all I thought of was wanting to see it again.

The year after graduation I rented a house on the beach, much to my parents' strenuous and alarmed objections. Being so fresh out of school and green in the workforce it was a struggle to keep up on the rent payments. I was, in all truth, practically still a kid. After much deliberation, I decided to rent a couple rooms out to friends which helped me get through the early times.

This property had always been my favorite place to fish, spend my evenings, and where I chose to spend most all my free time. It was on a quiet and out of the way stretch of shore that I had visited as a child. The then owners were always friendly and welcoming. I'm not sure what led me there but something in my heart always pulled me to this place. When I found it available for rent, I snapped it up and was happy I did.

I knew the town folk had old stories about shipwrecks and drunken sailors dying just off the back yard shore where the water became deep as it entered the channel, but instead of being frightened by the tales, I loved thinking about the possibilities. The excitement of it all hypnotized me. Maybe in my heart I always knew that someday I'd live there.

The only thing that really got to me after a while were the noises I kept hearing along the edge of the property at night. They weren't terrifying in the beginning, yet only seemed like lonely calls as if a desperate and lost traveler needed someone to help them find their way.

CHAPTER THREE

I was employed at the docks in a local port helping the crane operators that received the ocean containers off the ships. It was very exciting and since I was right out of school at the time, I suppose I was considered fresh meat to the Port Authority. Doing the odds and ends jobs that no one else wanted to do, was a gift from God at my young age. Well, at least it was for me. To them I was probably just a pain in the ass, but since I was so good at taking orders and not giving anyone any lip back, they grew to accept me. I knew the opportunities were endless if I could only do the time, stick with it, and gain the confidence of the management. I had heard the money was fantastic if you were lucky enough to get the position of a crane operator. It would be difficult, and without a doubt challenging, but that was my goal, and I was determined to get there some day sooner than later if I could beat out the competition. I offered to work weekends, nights, and anytime they needed me. I was at their beck and call. I would even show up on my days off at shift changes to see if anyone had called in sick, always willing to work. After a couple of years, it paid off. When the other, mostly older guys would bail for whatever reasons, I started getting calls to fill in for various shifts.

Eventually, I was getting calls to work shifts for positions that I wasn't qualified to do but, was also getting plenty of on-the-job training during my own shift when things were slow. They knew I was dependable, and they also knew I was determined to climb the ladder. I believe that made me invaluable. In a time when so many people didn't want to work, and were counting on government hand-outs, I was always there. I was always ready to learn.

Thanks to the guys I shared my home with for so long, I was able to save a good percentage of my paychecks. My savings account grew quicker than I had expected and within three years I had enough saved to put an offer on the property. The owners knew me and remembered my eagerness to help out when they needed someone to weed whack their yard or spread gravel along their driveway. Although my offer wasn't as high as the other offers, the owners accepted my contract for their own personal reasons. Reasons which I'm hoping were due to knowing me and my love for the property. My life was happy, and I considered myself very lucky.

When I told my parents that I had made an offer on a nearby home and it was accepted, my dad took it as an insult because I didn't consult with him prior to making the offer. He assumed I had made an irrational purchase and my offer had to be inappropriate. Heaven forbid, he be anything but happy for me. Heaven forbid, he be proud of his son. However, instead of being angry or feeling sad, I took the high road and disregarded his response. I knew then that he would never be pleased with me, no matter what I might accomplish in my life.

In hindsight, I realized that any closeness or parental love my parents may have had for me ended when Shep died. It was as though they stopped wanting to know me. I think now they were afraid to love me. Maybe they were just too afraid to open their hearts to the possible loss of another child, whether it be myself, or Jacob.

My brother, Jacob, was just as hard-headed as my dad. However, instead of thinking I would eventually fail, he was green with envy as he had never had much of a work ethic and was among the vast majority these days, or so it seemed, that preferred to count on the government entitlements that were being distributed so readily. He never understood that nothing was for free, yet he was determined to suck the government dry as were so many others, unrealizing and uncaring that the taxpayers ultimately had to pay the price for all of the "easy money". No amount of education will teach a lazy person if they know another method exists which will allow them to continue to be lazy. Stupid is as stupid does. I quickly learned this viewpoint the hard way.

One morning as I was arriving to work, Jacob unexpectedly met me in the parking lot. He approached me hoping that I would be able to help him gain employment and thought that I could get him in to see someone in Personnel on the spot. I was happy he came to me, and I was looking forward to helping him in any way that I could. I explained that the Human Resources Department didn't open until 9:00 A.M. and it was only 6:00 A.M. and there was no one available to speak with until then. I also explained that he would have to fill out an application in advance of meeting with someone. He became outraged and accused me of deliberately holding up his career goals! He stormed out of the parking lot with a major attitude and instead of jumping through the hoops and scheduling a future meeting with H.R. as I had advised, he dogged me and refused to speak to me for about three weeks. Soon after, my dad asked me why I wouldn't help Jacob get a job at the Port Authority. What the hell? Again, I'm the bad guy.

CHAPTER FOUR

A month later escrow finally closed on the property. I decided to keep my renters to help financially but soon they left as one got married and the other was leaving Maryland altogether to find fame and fortune on the West Coast. I wished them the best.

I had begun renovations on the boat house and the garage. The house also needed work but being a single guy, I established my priorities, and unfortunately the house didn't win the toss.

At the time I had no boat, not yet. My goal was to be ready for the day when I could bring her home, knowing she would be tucked safe and sound in a favorable harbor and out of the weather. I knew that keeping the weather off made for a long life on both the inside and the exterior of any machine. This was another thing I learned the hard way. My dad would buy a tool or something nice and leave it outside rather than covering it or putting it inside. He was always too lazy to go the extra mile and make nice things last. Instead, he would gripe and bitch about how quickly things turned to shit, when it was his fault all the time. It was truly amazing that I survived past childhood.

Within six months of purchasing the property I had completely refurbished the boat house and was beginning to start restorations on the house. It would be a very slow process, but one that I anticipated with great desire. I saved a lot of money being able to do most of the work myself and what I couldn't do, friends helped, and tradeoffs were made. I was happy and for the first time in my life I felt my goals were actually within my reach. I also realized hard work really did pay off.

CHAPTER FIVE

One evening as I was pulling up the crab pots that I had left dotting the length of my pier, I happened to notice a loon hovering about three feet over the water as if waiting for that perfect moment in which to dive on its prey. No doubt a blue fish or possibly a striped bass, which I saw often in the waters. Suddenly it flew off as if something were lunging at it. The bird's speed in which it maneuvered away was eerily fast and I thought for a moment whatever had frightened the bird would surely break through the surface, reach up, and drag it under the waves. Nothing did, of course, but I waited just the same.

It was then that I heard the voices. Sounds carry a great distance over the water. Up until that moment I always told myself that very thing. However, this time was different. The voices were calling out as if whomever was trying to communicate was short of breath and desperately needed help.

I ran to the end of the pier and looked down into the blue water.

The waves rolled solemnly.

The voices quieted. Once again, I found myself standing in that same spot, as I had stood so many times before, listening. But, listening for what? Voices? I felt as though my mind was remembering something, or at least trying to. Was it voices or the sounds of the wind or the surf? If, in fact, I had been hearing voices, I thought very much how I wanted to learn the reason for their need to communicate. Could they be the voices of those who died in the stories I'd heard as a child?

Giving up, I began to turn away when an unexpected rush of gloom swept through me. All at once I felt total desolation and complete loneliness. I had to sit down or else I feared falling. As I sat, slumped, cradling my head in my hands, I looked into the water.

The swell of the tide made what lay beneath the water move but also distorted my vision. I couldn't make out what it was, but that doomed feeling never left me and I couldn't shake it. The need to leave the pier became very strong and I couldn't shake that feeling either.

The sun had begun to set, and the shadows were inching their way over the water. I knew I was just imagining the worst. I had been in the sun all day and had little to drink. I knew I had to get into the house to sit down, get my head together and relax.

CHAPTER SIX

The next morning, I stood on the scale and saw that I had lost five pounds since the week before. I felt weak and dehydrated. Thank God it was Sunday. I would stay home and take it easy. I obviously did too much the day before and my body was turning on me. When you're in your prime and physically fit, you never stop to think about the power of the sun and the after-effects of hard work. Mix both and you can potentially invite disaster.

After fixing a breakfast of good ol' shit on a shingle on toast with a few pieces of bacon, I remembered what I felt the day before and the need to see what lay under the water. The intensity of it being so strong I couldn't get it out of my head.

I suppose that had been the reason for the dreams. They were dark ones. When I awoke, I knew I had to go back out there and see for myself. Something told me not to ignore how I felt.

We've all heard stories about pirates, bad storms, and shipwrecks. We've all heard the rumors and folklore about horrendous deaths and battles that occurred in the waters offshore of various beaches that are so popular with millions of people today. I still couldn't shake the thought. I was cold with it.

Before I went out to the pier again, I felt the immediate need to talk with the people that owned the property before I did. I hadn't spoken with them since I was a child. When I purchased the home, I did it via attorneys and realtors, so I never spoke with them during escrow. They were good folk and always kind and easy-going to me when I visited them so long ago. All I really knew was that they were taken to an old folk's home a few years before I graduated high school. Looking back, I should have made a point to speak with them. After all, out of the other offers they chose mine since they knew me. I really owed them a visit. I immediately felt guilty I hadn't tried to contact them to say hello until now.

That afternoon I drove across the bridge to Haynesville, where I was told they were living in an assisted living community not far from town. The drive would have been a lot more peaceful if I hadn't been so geared up for what I feared they would tell me. In my heart, I knew they had heard voices on the shore, too. In my heart I knew I probably wouldn't like what they were going to tell me at all.

When I knocked on their door, they smiled and greeted me warmly. They invited me out on the balcony and within a few minutes Mrs. Smoyer returned and gracefully offered me a Tom Collins. When she served it to me it was in a fancy glass with a wedge of orange and a cherry held together with a multicolored toothpick. I had never had a Tom Collins but was pretty sure that most everyone who loved Dean Martin and Old Blue Eyes, surely had, and I had to admit that it was pretty good, coconutty. I enjoyed the fact they were so happy to see me and that they remembered me to the extent that they did. In all honesty I would have loved the drink even if it tasted like dog shit.

They were both very delighted that they were able to sell me their home and I apologized for not making the drive to see them earlier.

"We were just so happy to learn that you made the offer," Mrs. Smoyer said. "We always thought so fondly of you. I remember looking out the back window and watching you trying to set the hook when a fish would bite and laughing at your intense expressions. Of course, you had no idea I was watching, but you never gave up. I could always see your grief when you didn't catch one, and your happiness when you did. You were the cutest boy."

"Mrs. Smoyer,"

"No, now you're an adult, you call me Beth. I won't have it any other way."

"Okay, Beth. Wow that sounds weird and borderline disrespectful, calling you Beth," I said.

"Yeah, well, old people are people, too, and it's cool with me if it's cool with you."

I laughed out loud when she said that. I think I'll remember that til I die.

Mr. Smoyer left the room and Beth looked at me with caring, yet hard eyes.

"Honey, what made you come out here today? I know you didn't just want to visit out of the blue. And please forgive my husband for leaving the room. It's not you dear, he just has a hard time dealing with certain things, and he isn't good at making small talk. He knows he should try harder. Some things he just can't forget."

Assuming she was referring to them having to move out of the home he loved and the property that he enjoyed for so many years, I nodded with understanding. It must really suck getting old. I hope when my time comes, I get hit by a truck or shot in the head. Something quick. Losing your strength and dignity as you age scares the shit out of me, it always has.

"Well, I . . ."

"I know. You don't even have to tell me. You've heard them, too, am I right? I can tell," she interrupted. Her voice was very soothing and steady. It was as if she was trying to be very quiet as though we were in a library instead of her living room. "There is something you need to know. My husband never heard the voices. If he did, he never admitted to it, and I've asked him a million times. You see, I used to sit out on that pier and listen to the voices often. I even tried to respond to them. In a way, I grew to like them. They weren't always sad and hopeless. I tried to ease their pain."

"I knew it," I said in a tired, emotional whisper as I ran my fingers through my hair. "Yes. I hear them, too. I think I've always heard them. Maybe that's why I wanted to buy the property in the first place. I remember hearing them as a kid, but thought it was just voices being carried by the wind. In fact, I think I forgot about them until now."

"The day we put the house up for sale I heard a child screaming in my head. He was telling me to help him. The waves were building, and I jumped into the water. I was convinced someone was under the waves dying. I was sure that someone needed my help. That was the last day I heard the voice."

"Oh my God, you jumped in the water? What happened then?"

"I'm not sure. I remember jumping, and I remember trying to swim deep, searching for something. The next thing I remember I was waking up in intensive care. They told me I was dead when they pulled me out of the water. I was lucky they were able to bring me back."

"That's quite a story," I said.

"Yep. The only thing I can tell you, is don't believe what you hear. I think if you listen to the voices long enough, they will get you, too. That's why we left. My husband is in denial. He's a Christian and he doesn't believe in voices. But I do. I'm also a Christian, but I can tell you that I'm afraid of them because I know in my heart that I heard them. They can't be good. If I had fully listened to them, I'd be dead right now."

"Thank you, Mrs. Smoyer, Beth. I appreciate all your honesty. I need to go home and think. You know, get my head together."

"Yep. I bet you do. Please remember, voices don't always tell the truth. You never know what side of the fence they're sittin' on."

As I got up to leave, Beth gave me a hug and told me to be careful. She said to call on her again and that she would pray for my good health and long life. I gently folded my hand around hers and looked into her eyes. I saw goodness and genuine affection.

"I wish I could be with you to help solve the mystery. I spent my life on that shore. I would have surely died to protect it."

"I know," I said.

As I left their home, I thought of all the memories of my childhood on their pier, my pier now. I am, and always will be grateful to have known them. I often wish I would have spoken with them more often. Instead of sneaking onto the property, I realize now I should have asked and done it proper. Old people scared me as a child. I always thought they were different, but thanks to reconnecting that day, I've learned that they aren't scary. They are exactly like young people, only a little more brittle.

CHAPTER SEVEN

As I returned home and started the grill for a couple of cheeseburgers, I couldn't help but stare out at the pier remembering what Beth had said.

Later, as I got ready for bed and looked out the window, seeing the moon shimmering off the water, for an instant I thought I saw a boy on the pier. He was sitting in the same spot where I had fished so many times before.

I decided to put on my boots, grab a jacket, and run out there to see if it was my imagination or if my vision was real.

When I got to the pier he was still there. I walked up slowly and was determined to confront him. As I approached him, I introduced myself. I thought it strange that he didn't turn around or acknowledge my greeting in any way.

I kept walking towards the pier.

"Don't come out here," he said.

My first thought was *that was a helluva thing. The little fucker sure is full of himself. Telling me not to go out on my own pier.*

"What are you doing out here?" the kid asked.

"I'm asking you the same thing. This is private property and you're too young to be out here this time of night by yourself. Where are your parents?"

The kid totally ignored my question and didn't move.

Finally, he stood. However, he didn't turn around. Instead, he kept facing the breakers and began to speak again.

"Don't ever come out here at night and swim. Don't ever trust what you see. This place is bad."

His last sentence was a whisper.

I wiped my eyes and truth be told; I began to feel unsteady on my feet again. I looked down and adjusted my footing. When I looked up, he was gone.

Not sure of what to do next, I stood for a moment. About to walk out on the pier, I remembered his words of warning, and turned back towards the house.

Chapter Eight

The following morning, I drove to the public library and did a little research on occurrences that had happened in our town over the years. I discovered that there were, in fact, ships that had sunk off the inlet and, as it turned out, many events were documented, but not finalized or confirmed in the town records due to insufficient information or other unknown details that were needed to authenticate certain incidents.

Since I had purchased the property of my dreams, and this particular property was substantially holding my own personal peace of mind, let alone sanity, I decided to do whatever I could to find out if Mrs. Smoyer's vision, and my own, could be substantiated.

I decided to hire a couple of divers as well as anyone else I needed, to end this drama. It would set the renovations back on the house, but during my time working at the Port Authority I had made quite a few connections and knew I could pull it off without losing my shirt too badly. I had to know exactly what I was up against and how to end it. Living in fear and doubt was not going to happen. This property was my dream home, and I wanted to live happily without fear. I decided to do anything I could to achieve that goal and I needed to know what was under the water.

The divers were scheduled to show up at the property a week later, and they would bring underwater video equipment to capture anything that needed to be noted.

I happily awaited their arrival and had planned to take a couple days off work if necessary to be there in case they found anything out of the ordinary.

The next morning, I drove back to see Beth Smoyer and her husband.

CHAPTER NINE

I t had been quite some time since I had visited my folks, and on one particular evening prior to the diver's coming, I decided to go over, see how they were doing, and join them for dinner. Ever since I had told them about my intentions of buying a house, which had been promptly disregarded by the entire family, without so much as a congratulatory word or even to find out where it was located, I realized my aspirations of being a homeowner, or well anything, was of no matter of consequence to them at all. I was determined not to bring up anything in my life and tried to concentrate on other issues.

It seemed my brother's sole intentions were to make everyone around him miserable and me in particular. Where his mistrust and hatred for me came from, I had no idea. Maybe it stemmed from jealousy and over the years it grew into a menacing, all empowering desire for revenge. Evidently, he had gotten himself into a lot of trouble with the law and Mom and Dad had been unable to help him or, for that matter, whenever they mentioned hiring a lawyer for him, Jacob went from his usual obnoxious self into teetering on the edge of hysterics.

By the time dinner was finished and dishes had been cleared, there had been no questions about my home purchase, or any other subject that I showed any interest in. They had been swiftly swept under the rug. I graciously thanked Mom for the meal and let myself out.

Now it had been weeks and I'd done my best to keep on my side of the inlet, far enough away from any accidental contact with them that might creep my way. I had heard nothing from any of them since that evening, including Jacob, who's interest in employment with the Port Authority was obviously nothing more than just another attempt to jerk my chain. All of this didn't stop me from worrying about my brother though. I knew he had one foot on the crazy train and in my heart, I didn't put anything past him.

CHAPTER TEN

As I pulled into the parking lot of the Smoyer's complex, I parked my old Dodge in the closest space handy and began to walk towards their building. I was surprised that I hadn't noticed how nicely the grounds were maintained. The garden areas had plenty of shade and the variety of flora was beautiful. As I rounded a corner on the footpath towards their building, I noticed Beth sitting on a bench reading a book. I announced myself, and once again she seemed happy and eager to speak with me.

"Again, so soon! I wasn't expecting you to come back, although I knew you would. We have a connection now, don't we?" she asked.

"I suppose we do, Mrs. Smoyer, I mean, Beth."

She smiled.

I attempted meaningless conversation about the weather and current events, but she saw right through me. The look she gave me was one of anticipation and well, maybe a little fear.

"When I got home the other night, I saw someone on the pier."

She made no attempt to interrupt me or stop me. I could tell that she was frightened but none the less interested and wanted me to continue.

"It was a kid. He told me never swim at night or trust anything I see. Then he disappeared."

"I'm not surprised," she said coolly, but added nothing and waited for me to continue.

"I've hired a couple divers and they are scheduled to come out to the house in a week if you and your husband would like to be there. You both have a special interest in all of this, and I thought I would ask you. Also, if anything is found, I have a crew scheduled to come out after and see what is under the water. They will be bringing whatever equipment is necessary to give us answers. It will cost a lot, but I have some connections with the Port Authority."

"Thank you, dear. We both are very interested in your quest for answers. But I need to tell you something," Beth said as she looked down at the tissue she was holding in her hand.

"My husband died the night you visited us. He never handled any of this well, and I suppose his heart just couldn't process it. He is at peace now; of that I have no doubt."

"Oh my God, Mrs. Smoyer, I had no idea. I am so . . ." she cut me off.

"Please, let me know how things turn out after your people search the water. I am in no shape to go out there. Truthfully, I don't think I would handle it much better than my husband did. Although, it is in my heart to know. I love that place and I will always have it with me."

I kissed her on the cheek and took hold of her hand.

"I will see you next week. Is there anything I can do for you now?"

"One thing," she said as she grabbed my hand. "Don't ever go out there at night and swim and don't ever trust what you see."

Hearing her whisper those words chilled me to the bone.

Walking away from her that night was a very hard thing for me to do. She had always been good to me growing up, as I mentioned earlier. But that night I felt a fondness for her that I will never forget.

After I got home, I ate some dinner, which I basically picked at more than anything else. I changed into some pajamas, grabbed a beer, and an old book I was trying to get into and went out back to sit on the porch. Although the moon was full and bright and reading should have been easy, no matter how hard I tried to focus on it, I couldn't get the death of Beth's husband out of my mind. What a kind man. His life held substance. It held family, and that is never an easy thing to let go of. I don't think I'll ever get over him; I know I'll never forget him and only wish I would have spent more time getting to know him.

I looked up and noticed once again, the boy was on the pier. He sat, fishing pole in hand, and made no attempt to speak to me.

I thought I was going crazy when I noticed that the moon, although big and bright, seemed to go right through him as if he wasn't there at all. I knew I saw him. I knew he was there, but it was as if he wasn't solid. The rays of light seemed to illuminate him, yet also throw light upon the pier without leaving his shadow.

When I left the porch and began walking toward him, he abruptly stood and held up a hand. He always looked away from me as if he didn't want me to see his face. Again, he told me to not go into the water at night and never trust what I see.

I thought it best not to dispute him and although he refused to speak further, I respected his intentions and did not try to approach him. This happened every night for five nights.

CHAPTER ELEVEN

The following week the team of divers arrived. As I walked them to the end of the pier, I noticed they brought all the necessary gear to accomplish the job I had requested. Two separate divers came along with them to film the entire event. I was happy about that as I had no idea what to expect and due to the sensitivity surrounding the dive,

I was looking forward to viewing whatever they would be able to uncover while under the water.

I never requested time off, even when I had it coming, so the company approved the personal time without question.

The divers were under the water at the end of the pier for less than half an hour when they abruptly surfaced and seemed both excited as well as distressed.

"We found something!" the lead diver yelled as he quickly yanked out his mouthpiece.

Within minutes the divers, as well as the photographers, were out of the water and coming towards me.

They explained they had found part of a ship. It looked to them as if it was a piece of a hull and attached to it were cages. They said the cages were welded to the framework of the ship and they could not pull them up.

"Bones, I saw skeletons of humans in those cages!" the first diver said gasping for breath. "As soon as I shined my light on them, I swear I saw movement. I can't explain it, but the movement was not ocean currents. It was as if heads had raised, all at once and stared at me." The diver shook his head and followed by saying, "I know what I saw and I'm not going back down. You can find another diver; this just isn't natural. Not natural at all."

The lead diver walked up and excused himself and then grabbed the first diver's arm and walked away from me. He tried to be discreet, but I heard him speak.

"Do you have any idea what you're fucking saying? We are a professional outfit. If you start talking shit like that in front of the customer before we even have a chance to check tape, I'll black ball you in this business faster than shit. You got that straight?"

The diver nodded and began gathering his equipment.

Within minutes the police showed up with investigators, along with Coast Guard divers and all their equipment for further exploration of what they had found under the water.

Chapter Twelve

That afternoon my cell phone rang. I looked down and saw that it was my mother. I answered the call, and she immediately began pleading for me to come out to the house. She said she needed to speak with me right away and that she thought I was in danger. Seconds later my father took the phone away from her. I heard him yell and the phone went silent. I tried calling back but there was no answer.

I grabbed my keys and left for their home. I arrived quickly and my father opened the door before I had time to knock. I didn't think he'd allow me inside, but after a brief pause, he waved me in and pointed down the hallway. He never said a word. I found my mother pacing in Jacob's room.

She looked up with tearful eyes and held an outstretched arm toward me. In her frail hand she held a small notebook. As I took hold of it, I realized it was a journal. I noticed some of the pages felt moist and I knew it was wet from her tears. The pages were old and dog-eared, and the handwriting was sloppy and at times jerky, but there was no mistake, it was written by Jacob's hand. He'd obviously had it for a long time and had written in it often.

"Your father thinks I'm wrong. He thinks I'm delusional. But I'm not and I can prove it," she said. Her eyes were deep, so haunted and so tired that all I could do was sit on the bed, head down, and read as I held her shaking hand.

Jacob's entries were deviant. He wrote about family and dark things. Shep, the brother he had never met was mentioned often. Jacob blamed him for our parent's hostility towards he and I while we were growing up. He blamed me for letting it all happen. I believe he had gone mad. He had so much blame, so much hate. He was writing an incredibly elaborate scheme in which murder was the final chapter. My final chapter.

She hadn't seen Jacob in over a week.

CHAPTER THIRTEEN

I drove back home dumbstruck. All these years there had been so much going on that I never knew. It seemed each one of us had been haunted in ways that neither one of us could comprehend. There had always been so much silence. So much misunderstanding which had led to neglect in all our communications. So much had been ruined. So much love denied.

When I returned home it was night. The divers had all gone, yet the water surrounding the pier had been roped off and "Unlawful Entry" signs had been posted on the pier ramp.

I quickened my pace to the back door as I heard the kitchen phone ringing off the hook. I make it a rule to turn off my cell phone often, and usually by 8:00 p.m., as I am not what you would call a very talkative person. In fact, if cell phones where never invented, I wouldn't miss them one bit. However, one can't turn off a landline as easily. I answered it reluctantly.

It was the Coast Guard office letting me know they were waiting on a crane, and at first light they would be arriving to bring up their findings at the end of the pier. They felt the sensitivity of the find required the area being roped off as any unnecessary activity may be hazardous. I agreed.

I knew what was under the water now. Jacob's elaborate description of his plan was dramatically evident in his entries.

I couldn't stop thinking of my mother, and I phoned home moments later to check on her. She had just settled in front of the fireplace into her cavernous armchair with a hot chocolate and her current knitting project. I was relieved.

I told her about the recent sightings of the boy and filled her in on the divers, etc. I also told her about the Coast Guard coming out in the morning and asked her if she wanted to be there.

She said she felt so ashamed that she never showed an interest to visit or take part in helping with the purchase of my new home or to help with the move. Her voice began breaking down as she said she knew it was wrong and apologized.

Remembering my anger concerning this subject during the past recent months, I was still able to easily forgive her as I understood her sorrow. I thought to myself that after reading Jacob's journal, as horrible as it was, it brought so many things to light that needed to be said. The only one still in the dark was my father.

My mother asked me for my address and said she would be there if she could.

I waited for her to grab a pen and a piece of paper and could hear her slippers shuffling across the wooden floor. When she came back on the line, I slowly gave my address to her and asked if she needed directions.

I heard a weak gasp of realization as she dropped the telephone onto the cold, hard floor.

CHAPTER FOURTEEN

That night I knew I wouldn't be able to sleep with all that was happening. I grabbed my jean jacket and a Corona and wandered outside. Without thinking I found myself walking out to the pier. I ignored the signage and stepped over the ropes, which blocked my entry.

The boy was on the pier again, as I knew he would be. I felt it.

This time he spoke.

"It was going to happen two nights ago. I stopped it. You won't like what you see here tomorrow," the boy said with his back turned towards me, as usual.

"Why won't you look at me? Who are you?" I asked him.

Once again, he didn't respond. I waited, hoping.

"He wouldn't have stopped you know. I couldn't let it happen. Not here. Not again."

"What are you talking about, kid?"

But, as I finished asking him, he melted out of my vision and was gone.

CHAPTER FIFTEEN

The next morning the crane and divers arrived promptly by sun-up.

Within the hour they were ready to hook up lines to pull whatever was down there up and out of its dark tomb. As the large chains began to tighten with the resistance of its cargo, everyone waited with excitement to see what exactly was going to be brought up.

It was about twenty-five feet below the water. Although exciting, the process seemed to take forever as the anticipation was intense.

As the hull began to breach the surface, we saw that the divers were correct. There was what looked like iron cages placed on the deck. Sadly, there were also numerous skeletal remains inside the cages. How long had they been there? Why cages? Could the people have been destined for the slave trade? Human trafficking? So many questions. Some of the fingers still curled around the bars.

The crane operator slowly rotated the hull toward dry land. This part of the ship must have broken apart over the years. It wasn't clear if the rest of the ship was also down there, or if only this section remained intact.

As it was laid on the shoreline, we were able to get closer. As we did, we noticed the other body. This body hadn't yet decomposed, and the clothing was still intact and modern.

Within moments I was told to get back and stand away from the area. Unfortunately, it was too late. I saw the body behind the bars of the cage. It was my brother, Jacob.

What was left of his cloudy, muddy eyes stared blankly into nothing. His body had begun to bloat, but the fear in his face was blatant and direct. It looked like he had been screaming when his death occurred, and his face never relaxed from it. One arm reached through the bars as if hopeful to grab onto something that would help him. Help that would never come.

The investigators said that somehow Jacob must have been on the pier and fell in. Maybe he had been drinking or maybe he couldn't fight to stay above water due to the weight of his clothing. When he sunk down onto the cages a door could have fallen inward, thus locking, and blocking his escape. Details were still too early to be sure, but they would know in time.

CHAPTER SIXTEEN

Thank God my mother never showed up that morning. It would have been awful for her.

If Jacob was determined to kill me, it made sense that he knew where I lived. I never told him, but it's a small town. Anyone can find anyone if they look hard enough.

Was one of those enclosures meant for me? I believe it was. Jacob must have gone out there in preparation, to make sure his plan would work. He must have gone out there to make sure he could open and close the cage door. It would make no sense for him to knock me over the head or shoot me and if he couldn't hide my body, then what?

I stood in silence. Legs weak and wobbling, a bottle of bourbon in one hand and a cigarette in the other watching the waves break on the shore as the sun set over the horizon. I still couldn't believe what had just happened.

"I knew one day I would be standing here again."

I turned around as my mother walked through the yard and joined me on the pier.

"I'm so sorry, Mom."

"Yes. I am, too."

There was a long silence. Then she spoke.

"We had a wonderful family once. Long ago."

"I know this is going to sound crazy . . ." I couldn't decide if I should tell her about how I knew to stay away from the pier and how I knew to hire divers in the first place. In the end

I felt it mattered, so I began, "I was told to never come out here at night to swim, or trust what I see. I think it was a ghost."

She smiled and said, "I've been having dreams."

"Dreams?" I asked.

"We kept a lot of things quiet while you boys were growing up because we wanted to keep you safe. I know that was wrong now and we should have told you. We should have been honest."

"Mom?" I could only look at her.

"Your brother, Shep, died here." Her eyes filled with tears. "There was a storm, and he was on the pier fishing. We told him not to go outside or to leave the yard, but he didn't listen. He came here. I couldn't face it, and neither could your father. We had no idea this is where you moved, we were too hardheaded to move on with our lives and instead have been living in the past with sadness and hate."

"You mean, the boy I've been seeing on the pier?"

"Yes, son. The boy on the pier was your brother." Suddenly things began to make sense.

"How did you know?" I asked.

"It was all in my dreams. Jacob was going to trap you into one of those cages. He was going to trick you. He knew you trusted him. Shep didn't tell me this until today. I wasn't to interfere. I knew Shep was going to help you. He told me he would."

As we looked up and out towards the end of the pier, there he stood, fishing rod in hand. My mom grabbed my wrist and held on to me. As he turned around and finally held his face that I may see him, I saw him smile. He looked exactly as he had the last time I saw him. His free hand rose upward and waved.

Mother and I waved in return.

Then he was gone.

"Where the wave of moonlight glosses
The dim grey sands with light,

Far off by furthest Roses
We foot it all the night,

Weaving olden dances
Mingling hands and mingling glances
Till the moon has taken flight;

To and fro we leap
And chase the frothy bubbles,
While the world is full of troubles."

W.B. Yeats (1865 – 1939) ~

HOT TUB SALLY

CHAPTER ONE

Sally Federline was a happy, single woman at the tender age of thirty-two. She was a professional, established in a lucrative career, and often referred to marriage as walking the plank, or some other type of disparaging sentiment.

Sally never dated much and for that matter never really took marriage all that seriously. She had friends who, from a very early age, couldn't wait to find that perfect someone and devote their lives to them.

Sally, however, just didn't see things that way.

She was a hard-working woman; she always had been. She had a lot of hopes and dreams and for the most part managed to achieve her goals unceremoniously. But the fact remained, she did achieve her goals, and she did it on her own terms.

This story begins when Sally ran into a few girls she knew from her early years and felt practically hog-tied to sit and listen to all their stories about marrying into money and having all the things they ever dreamed of while putting in little effort. It made Sally sick to her stomach, and she quickly determined that they were all nothing but takers, basically whores with a marriage license, which legally made it all "okay".

During her drive home, and after a little time to ponder, she began to question herself. "Two incomes, are most always better than one . . ." Sally realized that although she had been able to treat herself to the things she always wanted, there were still quite a lot of things that as of yet, weren't attainable. Sally began to dwell on this thought.

At thirty-two with gray hair and stiff joints quickly looming in front of her, she found herself asking if marriage might be a consideration in her future after all. She was attractive and often turned down invitations by men who wanted her company for dinner and parties. These men were mostly affluent and good-looking to boot. There was no reason for her to decline the invites other than she just enjoyed being by herself most evenings.

Sally worked hard, played hard, and at night she mostly enjoyed cuddling with her cat and watching Sci-Fi movies with a glass, or three, of a nice Cabernet Sauvignon. What was wrong with that?

After visiting with her old school chums, she found herself debating the whole marriage *thing* in her mind. She decided that maybe she should settle down, or, well at least not zero it out entirely. There was bound to be a suitor for her out in the world somewhere. Besides, at thirty-two she wasn't quite halfway through her "Want List" yet and before she physically started slowing down, she knew she damn well had to do something to speed the process up of getting what she wanted. She decided to start thinking like *them*.

Sally knew she was a little materialistic, but who wasn't these days? Materialistic? Yes. Greedy? No. There was a big difference. Sally was also humble in many ways. Well, humble to a point that is. She would never flaunt her possessions like a lot of her friends did, and she certainly would never attempt to trick a man into wanting her. She was honest as the day was long, as the saying goes, and knowing that made her feel good about herself. Sally also began to realize that if she did find someone she could care for, it wouldn't mean she'd necessarily have to throw away her power or independence. That was very important to her and almost made her want to take a step back from the entire idea. Maybe, she thought, she could find an older man. Someone who wanted more of a relationship based on security and respect versus love and all the needy emotional drama. This Sally knew would be an honest way for both sides to accomplish their goals. Yeah, one day at a time. She wouldn't rule it out quite yet.

CHAPTER TWO

During the next few days, she did a little shopping to spruce up her wardrobe. She bought some new jewelry and had her hair done. A little color and highlights around her face would make her eyes pop in a more youthful way. Sally also joined a couple of Facebook groups for singles and before long, men began to send her "friend" requests and her calendar quickly began to fill up.

"This is easy," she thought to herself. "I could be married in a year!"

Sally wasn't sure if she particularly enjoyed this realization, but it was part of the new experimental plan, and she was going to see it through come hell or high water and get her feet wet. Yes, indeed, the next time she saw her old girlfriends she'd be able to chime right in and put them all to shame. As I had mentioned before, Sally was humble. Although, to a select few girls that deserved it, she would have no problem giving it right back to them. She smiled at the thought.

Within three months she had found a very attractive and fit man who was her senior by ten years. He was a businessman who enjoyed most all the things she did, and she found herself falling head over heels in . . . in what, she thought? She found that although falling in love wasn't necessarily part of her plan, she wasn't complaining by any means. Besides, it couldn't be love that she felt, but she did enjoy his company and his wit. He was sweet and warm and treated her like no one else ever had. He was incredibly thoughtful and seemed sincere. She truly enjoyed being with him and when he wasn't around, she actually found herself missing him.

Sally enjoyed his spontaneity as well as his kind nature. He enjoyed sailing and other outdoor activities, and he pushed her to try those she had never done. Life was exciting with him, and she soon began to see another side of life that she had never experienced before.

Before long she realized that she wanted to get married, maybe.

After about three months, Dillon came to her and asked her to sit down. He had something important that he needed to discuss with her. Without hesitation she sat, and he pulled up a kitchen chair and looked at her. She found herself nervous and wasn't quite sure how to handle the feeling. Nervousness wasn't part of her nature, at least it never had been until that moment.

"I have a surprise for you and before I plan it, I'd like to see what your calendar looks like for the first two weeks in August," he said.

"Well, that depends on how much it will cost me and if I'm going to need to pack for a trip to the moon," she said smiling.

"It won't cost you a cent and this is a trip to where I grew up. I go every year. I've never spoken much, or at all, about my family. In fact, I find it odd that you have never asked."

"I suppose I haven't. I don't think either one of us has talked about family."

"No, we haven't. Well, mine is unconventional. I don't talk about them because they are dead."

"Oh, Dillon . . . I had no idea. I'm so sorry."

"Don't be. It was all a long time ago. As I don't have a brother or sister, I'm the sole heir to the family homestead. I'm only bringing it up because in case you haven't realized it, I've fallen in love with you, Sally. I've never met anyone like you, and before our relationship progresses any further, there are some things you need to know about me."

"Is this where I should run away as fast as I can? In case you are wondering, I'm not going anywhere."

She questioned her words as soon as she heard herself say them. Things were happening fast, and she quickly became unsure of her feelings. She thought she could love him; she knew she was happy. But this was all so new to her, she began thinking she needed a little time to digest things. Probably because she never felt these feelings before. At this moment, she was almost sick. She almost felt like she needed to run, but her heart wouldn't let her.

Dillon smiled and sat looking at her. He didn't say anything right away. Instead, he thought about how to say what he knew he needed to.

She waited.

"I'd like to take you to visit my parents."

"Didn't you just say they had passed?"

"I did. But I need to take you there."

All Sally could say was, "Okay."

CHAPTER THREE

They left at 10:00 a.m. the following Saturday and by noon Dillon pulled onto the private road that met the property. Soon they turned onto the front driveway of Dillon's family estate. The heavy iron gates slowly swung open and allowed them to enter. The place was huge. The property had to be at least five-hundred acres and the house was equally as big.

She gasped at the enormity of it.

"Ja-ja-ja- JACKPOT!" she thought trying desperately to hide her grin. She decided to herself at that very moment she would do whatever it took to keep Dillon's favor. Hook, line, and sinker. He was the only heir and she wanted to, needed to, grab up this chance no matter what the cost. Her plan was working spot on, and she could almost smell the money.

She somehow managed to collect herself and drily remarked, "I thought you said this was your family homestead. In case you didn't know it, this is a whole lot bigger than a homestead."

Dillon stopped the car and walked around to help Sally out, and together they walked up to the front entrance. Sally fought an urge to cover her face and turn away as a rush of stale, cold air hit her the moment Dillon opened the creaking doors. Trying to keep her composure, and determined to think nothing more about it, she followed Dillon into the entrance hall.

Although she cared for him deeply, she couldn't help but remember her "Want List" and the promise she'd made to herself to make sure the next man in her life could fulfill her dreams. If she didn't really love him, it wouldn't matter. She knew she could fake it well enough to keep him for a while. At least until she could legally accomplish her goal. She was obviously torn between doing the right thing and doing the ambitious thing.

Sally wouldn't think about all of that right then. Dillon was a great catch, and she knew he cared about her, and she knew he was genuine. The only sad reality was that even though he was genuine, it was a shame that she was not. Or was she? She sure wished her heart would hurry up and tell her something.

She kept going over the plan in her mind, trying to stick to it. Trying to ignore the love that had been building in her heart for him, and the good in her began to feel truly guilty.

Once they entered the home, Dillon gave Sally the grand tour. There were four levels and many rooms: two kitchens, one for the family and one for the servants; pantries, a library, and many other wonderful amenities. He mentioned that after they settled in, he would give her a tour of the grounds which included gardens and the pool that was heated in the colder months. It was all Sally could do to not grab him by the wrist and yank him outside.

The first night they stayed together in Dillon's old bedroom. It was very large and clearly decorated by the hand of a small boy. Sally found Dillon very charming and fun. She noticed his enthusiasm as he shared childhood stories with her. She found it priceless that he was able to share so much love.

While she was sleeping, she never knew or saw the cold, cloudy haze that entered the bedroom and caused her to pull the covers up and around her neck.

The first morning she and Dillon were awakened by breakfast in bed. One of the house servants cheerily greeted them with two trays covered with French toast surrounded by four silver decanters of various flavors of syrup, crepes, sausage links and two small bowls of fruit. There were fresh flowers in a small vase and a large pot of hot coffee.

Sally was officially both stunned and impressed to a degree she never would have imagined.

Dillon thanked the server and as she left the room and gently closed the door behind her, Sally burst out in soft laughter.

"Okay, Okay! I get it! I know it's a little over the top, but it's just how things are done around here," Dillon said.

"What would she have done if I told her I wanted pizza instead?"

"She would have given this shit to the cats and started making pizza. What do you think she would have done?"

They both laughed.

"Baby, I have a question . . ." she hesitated, "this may be inappropriate, but . . ."

"Go ahead darlin. Nothin' you want to ask is inappropriate. Honest."

"Well, no one lives here any longer, right? How is it that there are servants here?"

"To be honest it was in my parents' will." Dillon looked as though he was either lying or unaware of how to be truthful in his answer.

"This is something that I've been wanting to discuss with you. Why don't we enjoy the day, and then we can talk about more important matters after dinner?"

Unaware of the suspicions she should feel, she smiled and leaned into Dillon's arms and kissed him passionately. He grabbed her and returned her embrace.

The two of them had a wonderful day exploring the grounds and hidden recesses of the eerily huge mansion, and Sally listened intently to the stories he told her of his youth. She remembered thinking that the home wasn't what she originally thought it was. It wasn't full of happy memories, not entirely. She saw darkness and loneliness in a lot of his stories, and it bothered her.

At one point he had run ahead of her, and she found herself alone; it didn't take long for her to become frightened. She had the feeling as though someone, or something had walked up behind her. Sally noticed the air turning cold and for a moment she even saw her breath. Then Dillon walked up to her. "Come on slow poke, I thought you got lost for a moment."

"I think I did," Sally said quietly, never mentioning the cold air or seeing her breath. She wanted to forget about it as soon as she could. He would probably think she was being ridiculous, so once again she blew it off.

After they ate lunch, Dillon introduced her to the Olympic-sized pool, where they swam nude most of the afternoon. Afterwards they laid out in the bright sunlight drinking frozen banana daiquiris and enjoying their quiet escape from the city.

"Come on, let's go over there," he pointed to an area off the pool that was surrounded by rose bushes.

"Sure. What's up your sleeve this time, Houdini?"

"You'll see. I think once I take you there, you'll never want to leave. In fact, it's my favorite area of the property."

"Well, how can I say no? Dillon, you are spoiling me, you know that don't you?"

They stood up and began walking over to a path between the rose bushes.

"Now close your eyes," he told her.

"Okay, they're closed."

He walked her to the entrance and told her to open her eyes.

What she saw was perfect. It was a huge spa with pink cement and gorgeous tiles surrounding the water line that matched the stonework on the ground. Cherub statues stood at the base of the rose bushes and an elaborate gas firepit had been constructed for chilly nights under the stars.

"This is all so breathtaking. Oh my God, it's absolutely beautiful," she whispered. "Whomever planned this area did a fantastic job. It's gorgeous!"

"I knew you'd approve. Let's get in. Be careful on that first step, it's a little steep." He stepped ahead of her and reached for her hand.

As they climbed into the water, she stepped on something. It moved as she touched it, and Sally noticed it was not a stone as she first thought. "There's something in here; I can't tell what it is," she told him.

"Here, let me see." He quickly disappeared under the water and when he surfaced, he had the object in his hand.

"What is it? Is it a stone?"

He smiled and handed her a small, wet black velvet box. "Sort of . . ."

She looked at him and her eyes began to tear up. She secretly hoped he wouldn't notice.

"Are you going to open it, or just stare at it?" He smiled and reached for her. "In case you can't see through the water, I'm on my knees."

"Oh my God, Dillon, are you really?"

"I believe I am. I also believe that I'd like you to be my wife. I love everything about you, and every day, I discover more things about you that I love even more. I'll try to make you happy. I promise. Sally, will you marry me?"

In a weird, selfish way she knew the "old" Sally would have opened the box before answering, but at that moment she couldn't have cared less about the ring. All she wanted to do was answer Dillon's question.

She brought her face to his and slid down onto the next step into his arms.

"Yes. I will," she said as her tears flowed freely.

He opened the box himself and took her left hand in his. The ring was old, clearly a family heirloom. It was fancy, yet tactful, and beautiful in every way. He looked into her eyes and slowly slid the ring onto Sally's finger.

As they made slow and passionate love in the spa Sally barely noticed that the firepit had come on, the flames reaching high into the darkening sky.

CHAPTER FOUR

As they both enjoyed the brilliant colors in that evening's sunset from the warm and bubbling waters, Sally looked at her engagement ring and told him she loved him for the first time. She knew she meant it and knew she would do her very best to make him happy for the rest of her life. To hell with that ridiculous plan, she thought as she found herself happier than she had ever been before.

They gathered their towels and walked into the house to get dressed for dinner. It felt weird to Sally that although she knew they weren't alone in the house, she never ran into any of the servants. The entire time they had been there, the only person she saw was the woman who had brought them their breakfast that first morning and she only saw her once and never even got a good look at her face. She pushed the cart into the room and disappeared without speaking a single word. Also, in a house this size there must be some kind of staff to have everything so clean and maintained. Maybe she should stop over-thinking the issue and just enjoy the space and what lay ahead.

She decided to wear a floor length, black gown with a neckline that plunged almost to her navel. It was very slimming and showed off her petite figure beautifully. She had owned the dress for a couple of years, but never had the nerve or opportunity to wear it. Sally considered herself fairly conservative and as such, the dress made her feel awkward and a bit out of place for her taste. She had bought it on a whim. But this night she felt seductive in it and was happy she was finally able to wear it without feeling bashful.

The ambiance of the house had gotten the best of her, and she was enjoying every minute. As she slowly walked from the bedroom, down the great stairs, and through the entry into the dining room, which was large enough to entertain a soccer team, she never saw the shattered and misshapen faces of his family looming just below the ceiling. As she walked, they followed her with miserably deranged expressions of both queer anticipation and uncaring empathy. As she stopped at the entryway, she looked at Dillon. He stood by the enormous fireplace, a fragrant cigar in one hand and a tall brandy in the other and turned and gazed at her affectionately.

"You look amazing, Sally. All I can say is, 'Wow!' Please, come in. Do you remember me mentioning that I wanted to tell you a little about my family?"

"Of course, I remember. I didn't want to pry; I knew you'd get around to it in time and I didn't want to pressure you."

"I appreciate that. Thank you. I hope I didn't lead you to believe my family is mysterious or secretive. It's just a hard subject for me to talk about openly. Come in, relax. I poured you a brandy. Our dinner will be ready momentarily." He walked her to her seat, pulled out her chair then handed her the glass. "Sorry about the elaborate table. I know it's kind of enormous, isn't it?" He laughed and rolled his eyes.

"It's wonderful, Dillon, everything's wonderful. Pardon me, all of this is so overwhelming, but wonderful!" Sally laughed and as she took a sip of her brandy, she spilled a little bit on the table. She laughed again, as did he, and together their eyes met. It immediately calmed her and brought her back to the moment.

"My family has passed on, as you know. This house, the memories . . . as I had mentioned, I am the only surviving heir to all of this and in my parent's will, I am to live here until I die. If I do not, the estate will be sold, and I will get nothing. I have been struggling with this as although I love the house, I also love my life in the city. The commute is easier, and I don't have to tell you that this place is so isolated, sometimes too isolated. Sometimes it's hard to adjust to all the quiet."

"What are you trying to tell me, honey? I feel like there is something more in what you've said. Something else."

"My family is still here, and I know they want us to join them. Are you willing to stay and love me forever?"

Despite his odd statement about his family, Sally didn't have to think long. She knew she loved Dillon and wanted to spend the rest of her life with him.

"I want to be with you and spend my life with you. Whether we live in the city or out here, I'm sure we can be happy. My choice is with you."

Dillon smiled. That cold air came through the room again. It made Sally shiver and she wished she had a shawl. Outside a loon cried. It was a lengthy and forlorn sound. Somehow it made Sally even colder.

"Dillon," she asked, "tell me about your family. You mentioned they want us to join them. What does that mean exactly, and would it upset you to tell me how they died?"

He took a slow, deep breath and poured more brandy into both their snifters. Then he looked into Sally's eyes.

"You wouldn't be the woman I fell in love with if you didn't ask me that question. I knew it was inevitable. You see, my parents were told they could never have children. I was completely unexpected and came late in their lives. The doctors told them that my mother would surely die if she proceeded with the pregnancy, but she wouldn't listen. My father tried to make her understand, but she wouldn't have any more talk about it. I arrived a few months later, ten fingers and ten toes and healthy. They said it was a miracle birth."

He paused.

"I know that's not entirely the answer to your question. You want to know about my parents."

Sally patiently nodded and smiled.

"I would like to offer that my father was an honest man. He worked as a field hand originally on this property and later, when he was in his twenties, won the entire estate in a poker game. No one ever challenged the legitimacy of the game as the owner was, for lack of a better phrase, a cocky son of a bitch who didn't know his limitations or, for that matter, how to drink. Unfortunately, for him, the other players held him to his bet, and he learned the hard way.

"My dad, having worked so many years under him, knew how to work the land and run things. He built the place up bigger and better than it ever was. He even let the man and his family live on the property until they died. They're buried on the eastern property line. Their markers remain until this day. To that end, I feel that showed honor in my father."

She had made her decision to marry Dillon, and she knew she was truly blessed. She didn't need a huge mansion; she didn't need those fabulous gardens or that glorious pool. In her entire life, she couldn't imagine a better hot tub, and Lord knows she'd dreamt of having one her entire life. But even that paled in comparison to her feelings for Dillon. He was what she wanted now, and she knew it in her heart. Sally, for the first time in her life, knew what love was. In the beginning her intention had been purely selfish. Now, well, now everything was different.

They had braised lamb for dinner and Sally couldn't remember when she had been so happy. She loved him and knew that they would have a perfect life together.

CHAPTER FIVE

After they enjoyed dinner, and after a few more cocktails, he suggested they change and go back out for a midnight soak in the hot tub. He would meet her there and told her he would have another surprise waiting for her. Sally loved the spur of the moment impulse to meet out there as she loved being in the warm bubbling water. Considering all the amenities the estate had to offer, the hot tub was her favorite area and Dillon knew it. She wondered if she should show up naked or in the new bathing suit she had purchased before their arrival.

Dillon went to his room and after carefully going over the documents for his Last Will and Testament one last time, he signed them, scanned them, and emailed them to his attorney. He then cleaned himself and stood naked as he watched Sally from his bedroom window as she walked along the path through the roses to meet him. Then he said out loud to himself, "I will be there shortly, my dear, and my parents can't wait to meet you."

The home and property would soon be taken by the state due to unpaid taxes and unpaid second and third mortgage loans that Dillon struggled to pay but could not. He did his best but with the high interest rates it was impossible. As of late, a short sale on the property had not presented any buyers and he had been told by his attorney that the beautiful home would be sold and most likely be renovated into a hotel or other type of resort complex. It would still stand, as it was far too elaborate, and beautiful. Not to mention the estate's history was far too rich to ever be demolished. Yes, his family, Dillon, and Sally would always be there, forever.

With the blue nylon rope Dillon had purchased three days earlier, just before he picked up Sally from her apartment, Dillon hung himself abruptly without any last words or prayers of forgiveness. He had brought the rope in with his luggage and Sally never took notice of it. He knew his parents would be proud of him for fulfilling their wishes by keeping the family together in their family estate. He was so glad he'd made the right decision. Everything was turning out just as he had hoped, and he knew he and Sally were destined to be together forever.

Chapter Six

Sally arrived at the hot tub and was happily surprised to see the fire pit blast into life as soon as she entered the area. The flames were high. Soft music began playing from unseen speakers, and the aroma of flowers filled the air. This was after all, their first night since promising to spend the rest of their lives together, and she was amazed at how creative and thoughtful Dillon was to provide such a romantic atmosphere.

As she stepped into the hot tub, remembering that the first step was deeper than the rest, she gripped the railing and effortlessly slid into the water. She let the warmth cover her body and closed her eyes as she allowed the water to consume her. Moments later she felt something tighten around her ankle and it began to quickly drag her under the water. It held her down. Sally fought it and kicked at it and yet she still felt herself being pulled under the water.

Once underwater, she opened her eyes to see what had grabbed her. She saw Dillon and noticed his hungry appearance. His eyes were blood-red, and he had what looked like burns and ripped flesh around his neck. At first, she thought he was only playing around and tried to push him away. He grinned as he looked into her eyes and pulled her close. With her last breath held tight in her throat, she realized he was not going to save her. Instead, he was going to kill her. As he held onto her shoulders and smiled as she struggled to breathe, she read his lips as he said, "Welcome to the family, my dear."

"Though my soul may set in darkness,
It will rise in perfect light;
I have loved the stars too fondly to be fearful of the night."

Sarah Williams (1837 – 1868) ~

BUCKY'S BEST

CHAPTER ONE

B ucky's Casino in Prescott, Arizona always brought in a lot of crowds. Especially on Friday nights after most of its customer's direct deposit paychecks have landed in their accounts.

I've never been much of a gambler and the thought of blowing my hard-earned money on a stupid bet or chance was just, well, stupid. I've known a lot of people who can't say that, and most of them have lost more than just their paychecks from time to time. You'd think people would learn a thing or two after getting hit in their wallet enough times, but evidently not.

One of these poor individuals was a guy I used to work with named Tom Grayson. Nice guy, good looking, and relatively intelligent. He was above me in the company and supervised his own department. He had about twenty-five people under him. He knew how to graciously delegate authority, was respected, and most of all he was fair; three key traits to being a good supervisor. It was a shame that he wasn't so smart about managing his money.

One Friday night while Tom was walking from his car to the casino a woman approached him and began to engage him in conversation. She was tall, slim, and had incredibly striking slate grey eyes. Tom thought she was gorgeous and maybe she was. He had told a friend later that evening she was completely captivating.

The woman called herself Maribelle and when she said her name, she emphasized the "L" by slowly showing her tongue and moving it in a leisurely downward thrust.

Catching Tom off-guard, yet quickly bouncing back from her mesmerizing eyes, he asked her if she would like to come inside the casino with him and have a cocktail. Her response had been strange, Tom thought, as she informed him, she was meeting a friend and could not. She then handed him a chip, said she would be back later, and if the chip paid off, he had to give her a kiss.

Somewhat enchanted and completely taken by her, Tom agreed.

"When will you be back? How will I find you?" Tom asked.

"Don't you worry, I'll be around." She smiled and walked away.

She was wearing a long dress with a tightly cinched waist and the neckline pronounced her breasts in such a way that reminded Tom of something Kitty would wear on Gun Smoke. Her long hair was curled and delicately lifted high, so it flowed down her back, yet showed every curve of her neck and shoulders. Although her dress was outdated, she was enthralling.

Tom watched her as she walked across the parking lot, her dress streaming behind her in the wind. His cell phone vibrated in his pocket, and he dropped his eyes for a moment, annoyed to find it was only a scam caller. He quickly declined the call and when he looked back up, she was gone. "Where did she go?" Tom thought. He had only looked away for a moment. He scanned the lot, but she was nowhere. Tom wondered how she could have disappeared so quickly. He shrugged his shoulders, turned around, and headed toward the casino's entrance.

CHAPTER TWO

Tom didn't have a whole lot of luck at the poker table that night. He had been there for almost three hours and was down about four-hundred bucks. In his mind he was going over the bills he had due, deciding which ones could wait until his next paycheck and which ones could not. Finally, he decided to wander over to the Blackjack tables. Carefully eyeing the dealers and watching how they were running their tables, Tom chose a table and sat down. Blackjack wasn't his game of choice, but he enjoyed it all the same.

His luck had run out as it almost always did about midnight and after a few drinks. He was out of money and told himself he would not hit the ATM machine again. He fished around in his pockets and felt the chip that Maribelle had given him in the parking lot. He found himself smiling as his fingers closed around it. He drew it out and looked at it for a moment. It looked old and discolored. He handed it to the dealer and halfway waited for him to question its authenticity.

The dealer took a long look at it and held it up to the light.

"Where did you get this chip, Sir?"

"A friend gave it to me earlier tonight. Is it real?"

"I need to call the floor supervisor and have him take a look. If it's what I think it is, it's worth a lot more than you might think."

Tom sat and waited for the floor boss to come check out the chip. "I can't believe that chick gave me a fake chip. I should have known," he said to himself.

Moments later the man showed up and examined the chip Tom had handed to the dealer. His smile was contagious as he looked at Tom and said the chip was one of the original chips from when the casino was first built. As far as he had known, there weren't any of them left. Certainly no one used them anymore. Long story short, he offered to buy the chip from Tom, and that night Tom walked away with over three-hundred dollars in his pocket.

As he walked back to his car later that night, fairly inebriated, Maribelle greeted him as he slid his key into the driver's door of his car. He knew she was there before he even saw her. The air seemed to turn cold, and he felt her presence even before she spoke.

"So, how'd you do in there? Did you win big?"

"Not particularly, but your chip sure did."

"Does that mean I get a kiss?"

She walked up to Tom and stood close. He could feel the cold as she approached him, but he ignored it; he liked it. He wanted her. From his winnings at the casino, he could get a room; to hell with his bills. He knew she'd be worth it. Her smile, those piercing eyes . . .

"Come with me," he said. "Is there anywhere else you need to be?"

"No. Not tonight. I can't go inside. Maybe you'd like to come with me?" Her eyes were wide and appealing and although she was very cold, he felt heat. He wanted to go with her, it was hard for him to say no. Suddenly a part of him became uneasy. He thought it was strange for him to feel the lust so quickly, but then thought it was probably just the beer talkin'.

"I'll be here tomorrow night. Would you like to meet me for dinner?"

Disappointment in her face, she only smiled. "I'll be here. I'll look for you. Maybe we can take a walk up to the butte or through the Dells instead. The walk is spectacular at night. It's quiet and we'd be all alone. It feels as though I haven't been there in years."

He was happy with her response, although he hadn't expected it. No one goes there at night.

As he said goodnight and watched her turn away, he also turned and continued unlocking his car door. Seconds later he felt a cool sensation along his forearm. It felt erotic and the pleasure pulsed through him again. He realized Maribelle had returned and was standing beside him. Her eyes where captivating and wanting.

"I want you to have these. I want you to tell me if they bring you luck, if they bring you happiness like they brought me."

Tom looked down to see what Maribelle had placed in his hand. It wasn't just another chip; in fact, it was a few chips. Part of him was extremely happy. Being the gambling man, he accepted the gift easily enough and was happy to do so. But Tom knew something was off. As he watched her walk away, he held the chips in his hand, and realized they were freezing cold. He might as well have been holding ice.

The next night he won over fifty-thousand dollars.

For the first time in Tom's life, he paid cash for the finest suite the hotel had available. But before he went upstairs, he walked down to the parking lot and began looking around, hoping to see Maribelle. She hadn't met him at the casino that evening, and he had been waiting for her eagerly. After a few minutes had passed, Tom turned to go back to the lobby, and once again, he felt a cold chill overcome him, and there she was.

He told her about winning the money and even about the house paying for the chips. He asked her where she got them and if she knew they were worth so much money. She only grinned at him.

"Come upstairs with me."

Maribelle stepped toward him. "I would love to. You go on up and I'll be there in a few minutes." Without waiting for him to respond, she turned and began walking away.

"Wait, you don't even know what room I'm in. Where are you going? I can wait for you. I want to."

"You're in room thirty-eight."

"Yes, I am. But how could you possibly know that?"

She smiled, turned, and continued to walk away.

Tom decided that this chick was by far the most bizarre and mysterious woman he'd ever met. On one hand he enjoyed it, but on the other hand she kind of scared the shit out of him and he wasn't too proud to admit it. Realizing that made him feel better in a weird way, and he knew it would make for a more exciting night.

He decided to let her continue to walk away and found his eyes watching her slow, seductive gait as she moved gracefully across the parking lot. Her body was beautiful, and her long blonde hair flowed behind her in the soft wind like silk. He knew a woman like that, so fascinating and attractive, could have any man she wanted. He decided if he wanted to win, he would not push her or act overly greedy. He would let her call the shots and roll with her pace. He could do that. He knew he had a gentleman inside him somewhere. It was finally time to let him out of the box. He wasn't sure he liked it, but if it would get that woman into his bed, he'd surely give it a try.

CHAPTER THREE

Tom visited the lobby store and not knowing what Maribelle would like, he bought a bottle of champagne, a bottle of Jack Daniels, and some mixers. He figured that ought to cover the bases nicely. Then he went up to room thirty-eight and let himself in with the little plastic card that, to his amazement, worked on the very first try. Usually, he had to stick the fucker in four or five times before he got it right. Room service was twenty-four hours a day, which was pure heaven as far as he was concerned, and he planned to take advantage of that before morning with or without Maribelle.

He waited and waited and eventually realized she probably wasn't coming. He couldn't believe she had stood him up. Even with the strange, coldness that seemed to surround her, he had gotten such good vibes from her that night. Not wanting to waste the room's excellent amenities, he started a bath in the huge jacuzzi tub that was encircled by mirrors in the spacious bathroom.

He was on his second J.D. & Coke when he set the television's cable to a good blues station and climbed into the tub. He laid back in the hot bubbling water listening to his favorite tunes and after drinking almost half the bottle of Jack, decided he'd better get out before he drowned.

When Tom woke the next morning there were casino chips lying next to him on the bed in a beautifully hand embroidered bag. There must have been hundreds of dollars' worth of chips in there. Old ones.

He knew she had been in his room. But how? Why didn't she wake him?

What the hell was going on and how could she have entered the room without his knowing? He was a relatively light sleeper, especially when he was out of his element and in a strange place. There was no way she could have gotten in without a key. There was no way she could have opened that door and come in without him waking, no matter how much alcohol he drank. He knew his limit and knew when it was time to quit. Now he was just plain pissed. Being beautiful and desirable didn't excuse her for standing him up, then entering his room unannounced. It was just too fucked up.

Although he wanted to play her game, and was tremendously thankful for those chips, he also wanted to know her on another level. He still wanted to be with her. However, he was seriously considering pulling the plug on this thing, he didn't even know what to call it. It wasn't anything except a parking lot connection. Thinking of this almost made him laugh out loud.

Tom was going to gather his clothes, make sure there was nothing left behind in his room and hit the breakfast buffet. He would come back later and use those chips. That anticipation hadn't changed in the slightest.

Chapter Four

Arriving at the front desk, Tom smiled at the attendant. "I'm Tom Grayson and I'd like to check out and get a receipt please. I was in room thirty-eight. I forgot to bring it down, but I left the plastic door card on the dresser."

"That's fine, a lot of people do. The maid will bring it down," the gal at the front desk said.

"How was your stay, sir? Hope everything was okay."

"Yep, it was all good, especially that spa."

"I bet, I've never stayed in that suite, but I hear it's really great. Here's your receipt and thanks for visiting us. Oh, I forgot to mention it, but behind you there is a book for our guests to sign if you'd like to add anything to it. You were in one of our most popular rooms for seeing strange happenings."

"Strange happenings . . . like seeing ghosts or dead cats or something?" Tom asked.

"Well, this hotel is known for lots of weird happenings that our guests can't explain. It's probably why we are always so busy. Lots of our guests have seen things they don't understand and if you don't mind me saying, you stayed in the most haunted room in the hotel. Anyway, people write down any paranormal events that they may have experienced during their stay. A lot of people enjoy reading through it."

Tom loved the idea of a haunted hotel and was immediately drawn to the excitement of it all. After he thought about it, he asked the front desk clerk what the history of room thirty-eight held.

The desk clerk told him room thirty-eight was originally rented by a beautiful young woman who loved to gamble. "Her name was Maribelle Softner."

Tom's eyebrows dropped down into kind of a squint.

"She came to town as part of a wagon train headed for California and decided to stay in Prescott. No one knows why but two weeks after she decided to stay in town, she shot herself in the head outside in what is now the first parking lot;

the one right next to the casino. The stories I read about her death were awful," the clerk told him. "I thought the creepiest part of her suicide was the fact that she was in room thirty-eight and the gun she shot herself with was a thirty-eight. Do you think that's coincidence or fate Mr. Grayson?"

Tom couldn't respond to the question. His heart was in serious "information overload" and he just needed to leave. At that moment, all he wanted to do was get outside to the fresh air and let it clear his head.

He thanked the clerk and began reaching for his bag which he had set down next to his feet. He tried to remain emotionless but as he bent over to grab the bag's handles the recent knowledge of Maribelle got the best of him. As he stood up, he nearly hit his head on the countertop and tried to regain his composure.

"Sir, are you alright?"

"Oh yes, I'm fine. I just got a little lightheaded. I spent too much time with Jack Daniels last night I suppose." Tom smiled weakly and began walking out of the lobby, caring less if the girl understood what he meant.

The clerk hollered after him, "Did you want your receipt?"

Tom ignored her and continued towards the doors which led outside. He prayed that he could walk the thirty or forty paces out of the lobby without barfing. He dropped his bag and sat down hard on the first bench he came to. It was intended for people waiting on busses or rides to and from their eagerly anticipated sightseeing tours, and he thanked God it was tourist free, so he had a little privacy to get his act together.

He sat and tried to make sense of what he'd just learned. Maribelle was real, she had to be. Things soon came to him in bits and pieces. Her coldness, the way she dressed was so old fashioned yet beautifully seductive, the way she spoke, the old, outdated chips she gave him, her eyes, those wonderfully hypnotic eyes. She couldn't have been a ghost.

Every night for weeks when he got off work, Tom visited the parking lot where he had seen Maribelle. He wanted so much to see her again, to talk to her. He wanted to ask her if what he had heard was true about her life, and especially about her death. In his heart he knew it was.

Unfortunately, he never saw her again, but from time to time he could feel her near. Especially when he was rolling the dice.

The Following Story
Is A Gift From The Author.
It Is From
"When Hearts Bleed",
Her First Book

THE INDIAN

CHAPTER ONE

L ife in Prescott, Arizona was everything Maureen-Ann and Bobby Butler had hoped it would be. Big blue skies, rolling hills, and the heavy scent of pine that hung in the air made them want to throw down a blanket, grab a good book, and get lost in the moment.

The couple had recently transitioned from northern Maryland where they had been taking care of Maureen's mother, Adeline, who had been dying of brain cancer. She fought it bravely for two long years, but as with any debilitating disease, it finally had its way.

Maureen had never been around someone dying before and although it was extremely hard emotionally, when the end finally came, it seemed to be swift and nothing like the horror stories her friends and hospice nurses had been preparing her for. Her mother simply closed her eyes, breathed deeply, and they watched as her chest slowly fell, and remained still. There were no sudden jerks or harsh cries of pain. Her mother never sat up blindly reaching for some imaginary entity who had finally come to take her into the next world. She simply died. No tears or drama. During her moment of death, Maureen and Bobby looked stupefied at one another. They both knew what the other was thinking and looked into each other's eyes with the same inquisitive expression. "That's it?"

The nurses gave Maureen and Bobby plenty of time to sit with Adeline alone. Then they came back into the room to perform their final duties for the deceased. Maureen thought to herself if she heard the horrible term "expired" one more time she would hit someone.

Originally, the family had decided to put off a memorial service for Adeline until a future date, most likely in the spring of the following year, to give out of town friends and family time to make their travel arrangements. They were thankful times had changed, since funerals were traditionally scheduled within only days following someone's death. Maureen felt having the option to delay relieved the emotional pressure of having to think about funeral services, and all the hotel decisions for friends and relatives so soon after losing a loved one when the family only wanted some personal time to heal.

Her mother had thought about cremation, but in the end, Adeline and her family had decided that a traditional burial in the family plot would be the best thing. She was to be laid to rest next to her husband, Maureen's father, who had passed after a quick and massive brain stem stroke ten years prior. The plots had been purchased jointly thirty years before and everyone decided it was best not to change the plan this late in the game.

Maureen finally agreed and was amazed at how quickly all the details were tended to. Wrapping her mind around the fact that her poor mom was gone and soon to be interred in a dark box under the cold ground, made her both very sad and very angry. She quietly sat in the funeral director's office long enough for Bobby to write the check for the services and then, as soon as their good-byes were whispered, they left the facility hand in hand. Maureen kept her dignity intact without a display of tears.

As they exited the building and walked to their SUV, Maureen thought how proud her mother would have been of her for handling all the details so well. She smiled as Bobby closed the passenger door for her while she got settled, happy in thought that this whole ordeal was finally over.

Now that Adeline's house was up for sale, it was time for Maureen and Bobby to get on with their lives. They both wanted to get away from the East Coast and find a little place where the pace was slower, and the winters were more forgiving. Prescott, Arizona was the answer, and they would soon head west before the snow started falling.

CHAPTER TWO

The house was built back in 1864 when the town was founded as the Territorial Capital of Arizona. It was one of the first homes ever built by the settlers and, therefore, had seen many changes. The land originally belonged to the Yavapai Indians and was said to have had many battles fought in the surrounding mountains over the years.

As both soldiers and Indian warriors fell, cemeteries were established to hold the dead. Eventually, pits were dug for burning and disposing of the bodies that were either so badly decomposed or torn up beyond recognition for proper distribution to the surviving family members. In fact, one of the "Death Pits", as the settlers began to refer to them, was located on the southwest corner of the property they had purchased. There had been some stigma pertaining to building a home so close to the Pit due to accusations of disrespect for the dead, but as time went on, and since the house had been situated so far out in the woods, the issue was eventually forgotten, and it never resurfaced in later years.

The house had been renovated a few years before Maureen and Bobby bought it and as far as they were concerned, it was the perfect retreat and a great place to raise a family; quiet, clean, and remote. It was exactly the home they had been searching for.

They celebrated their first night with a roaring fire and a couple bottles of wine, and without a care in the world they spoke of their hopes, dreams and future plans, as any young couple in love would in their new home.

The place smelled of old wood and aged, organic sweetness.

The electricity hadn't been turned on yet. An oversight by Bobby, but one that would make the night more memorable in every way possible. Candles and lanterns were on the itinerary that night, and it was perfect.

The fireplace was so large you could almost stand in it and there were rails in the stonework for hanging pots for cooking. The place was magical, and they had everything they needed.

At about 10:00 that night, Bobby went out to the side yard where the grass ended, and the woods began, and watered the ground. He stood looking up into the night. They'd had a big day, and he was looking forward to laying down soon.

As Bobby stood there, he felt what he thought was a spider web brush his arm. He looked down to brush it away as it somewhat tickled him. He was surprised to see a very thin, very old, piece of silk on the ground by his right foot. He assumed it was something that belonged to Maureen that must have fallen out of a packing box during the move. Picking it up, Bobby put it in his pocket to return to her once he got back in the house.

That night they made love for hours. Neither of them ever knew they could be so happy. They were finally living their lives for themselves in their own little world.

Chapter Three

The next morning, they awoke fully rested and ready to begin the job of unpacking everything.

When they entered the living room, they noticed one of the boxes with pictures and knick-knacks had been opened. Its contents lay neatly on the floor around the box, as if purposely and thoughtfully arranged. Neither asked about it, assuming the other had woken earlier to begin going through it.

As Maureen looked around the clutter, she said "This is going to be one hell of a job. You know that don't you?"

Bobby came back with, "I sure do, but don't worry, I won't rush you."

"Ha ha ha, you are a nut bag! I'm still not sure why I married you," Maureen responded with a grin.

"I'm fairly confident it was because of my nut bags, honey."

"Oh gaaawd!" She threw him somewhat of an embarrassed glare as she covered her face.

Maureen began breakfast and shortly thereafter they were outside on the porch with hot coffee, orange juice, sausage, fried eggs, toast, and home fries.

"Yep. Kill me slowly, baby. I love it," Bobby said. It was going to be a good day.

The first item on their agenda was to jump in Bobby's old Chevelle and head into town. He wanted to see about getting information on applying for a building permit for a garage he was planning to build to store the car, which had been his pride and joy for better than ten years now. Then they'd head to the grocery store to get some meat for the barbeque. Maureen was also dying to visit the nearest hardware store to pick up a few things for a garden she'd been wanting to hoe ever since they first decided to buy a home. Maybe if they didn't purchase any frozen items, they'd let the Chevelle steer them around town a bit on the way home so they could take in a few sites. She and Bobby both were dying to get acquainted with their new little western town. But then it was their first day, after all, and they could always plan to sightsee another time.

Maureen hit the shops, while Bobby went to the Planning and Zoning office for the building permit. The friendly man behind the counter asked Bobby if they were enjoying Prescott so far and asked about their property. The conversation that followed was a bit strange and Bobby felt the hairs on his neck begin to stand up.

"I know you've heard all the history about the property," the man told him. "It's something the town folk and, to be honest, myself included, have often spoken about. In fact, your property and that house have been kind of a town legend so to speak." The man looked into Bobby's eyes as he spoke as if he were trying to gain insight into his personal thoughts and uncertainties. Bobby didn't like it. He didn't like it one bit.

Bobby looked at him thoughtfully, grinned, and said, "Why don't you just go ahead and ask me whatever it is you want to know?" He was congenial and friendly, not wanting to put the man at unease. He was, after all, too new to the small town to want to burn any bridges on the first day.

"I'm sorry. I guess I've just always had a passion for this town and the old ways," he said. "My name's Sylvester Hampton. People call me Hamp; I prefer it that way. The other sounds too much like that asshole in the movies," he smiled.

Bobby couldn't help but laugh at the guy's honesty. On second thought, Bobby immediately knew they could become friends.

"Ya know, there are a lot of stories about that place where you are—people talk. I've always considered it mostly bullshit and I for one, never believe anything I don't see first-hand. The land up there is beautiful, and I know you and your family have only been there . . . what? One night?"

"Yep. So far," Bobby threw back.

"Well, I'll tell ya what, once you get settled, and if you ever want to cook up some burgers or hit the famous Prescott night life on Whiskey Row, give me a holler. My wife makes the best brisket in town and her martinis aren't bad either. You know where I am during the day, and it'd be a pleasure to get to know you and meet the Mrs."

"Well, shit," Bobby responded. "So far, you're the first person I've met in this town, and I must admit you've got me curious. How can I refuse?"

They both had a laugh. Bobby paid for the building permit, got the regs and headed to the town square to meet Maureen for lunch.

"So, how'd it go? Did you get what you needed?"

"Yep. If we keep it no taller than 12 feet high and no bigger than 400 square feet, we can get away with just a permit and no inspections."

"Is that big enough for your manly ambitions?" Maureen asked.

"Barely, but we can always add to it later if my testosterone kicks in." They laughed. He loved her sense of humor. It was the first thing that attracted him to her when they met.

CHAPTER FOUR

"It's so beautiful. I'm so glad we came here. I've never felt more at home anywhere in my life," Maureen said as she stared up at the stars and held Bobby close. He agreed as they re-entered the house and locked the front door for the night.

Later, as they lay in bed, they heard a noise outside. It wasn't particularly loud or threatening, it was more of a sound as if someone was simply walking through the leaves by the house. In fact, they never would have heard it if the windows weren't up. Bobby thought it may have been a bear or a deer. They both got up and went out on the front stoop. The night was cool, but comfortable, and the sky was crystal clear.

Maureen's gaze immediately left the sky, and she gasped as she saw what was approaching through the trees. She thought she was hallucinating when she saw what looked like an Indian standing by a tree. He looked as if he was hiding, yet his shadow seemed to be getting closer.

Bobby saw the Indian at the same time and immediately grabbed Maureen and pulled her behind him to protect her. In that same moment, the Indian disappeared.

"Oh my God, did you see that? I can't be crazy; I know I saw that. Did you . . ." Maureen's breath caught in her throat as she could barely finish the question.

"Let's get in the house, baby. It's late and we need to get some sleep," he said, trying to keep his voice sounding natural.

Once inside, Maureen ran to the window. She couldn't see anything outside with the light reflecting off the panes, so she hollered to Bobby to turn the living room light off.

No one was out there.

They both knew they hadn't imagined it. It was as if the Indian was walking straight toward them but didn't notice them at all. If he really was there, he had to have seen them. He had to have seen the lights from the house, hear the TV, and for Christ's sake, he had to have heard them talking. Bobby didn't want to add any more drama to the situation. In hindsight, he was trying to protect Maureen, but he realized he was more worried about how he was going to deal with this. Weird happenings weren't exactly his thing.

In an instant Bobby remembered what Hamp had said about the old town stories regarding their property and made a mental note to give him a call. This was something he knew he couldn't let go of. He and Maureen were going to get to know Hamp and his wife a lot sooner than he had originally intended.

Chapter Five

The next few days were peaceful, and they managed to accomplish a lot of homeowner tasks that most people tend to put off. Things were coming along nicely and both Bobby and Maureen were happy about their progress.

Just after sun-down, as Bobby was throwing some trash into the back of his old pickup truck for a run to the dump the next day, he saw the shadow of someone quickly coming up behind him. He spun around and the Indian was almost right on top of him. The Indian looked at him and made no attempt to walk away this time.

Bobby held his ground, although later, he couldn't believe he didn't run like a baby into the house.

The Indian was dressed in skins and wore makeshift sandals with red feathers attached to them. Bobby saw black paint on his face and feathers in his long dark hair. He was silent, and as he moved he made no noise at all. If it hadn't been for the porch light being thrown onto his truck, Bobby would never have seen the shadow he cast. It was clear the Indian was only an apparition and didn't hold any real form. He was no more alive or physical than the faces one can see inside a campfire flame if you look close enough, yet he did cast a shadow.

Bobby spoke to him in a frightened, but strong whisper. "Who are you?"

No reply.

"Why are you here?"

Again, no reply. The Indian just stared at Bobby with eyes as deep as the ocean and black as midnight. His expression was that of confusion and deep concern.

After what seemed like forever, the Indian turned his head and began walking away. He looked back at Bobby once then disappeared among the trees.

At that moment, Maureen walked outside and asked if he planned on staying out there all night.

He forced a laugh and told her he was coming and to keep her pants on.

He decided to keep this incident to himself until he had time to think. Until he could figure out the Indian's intent, he didn't want to alarm Maureen. After all, if there had been any violent intent, the Indian had the perfect opportunity to carry out whatever he wanted but had done nothing.

As he walked back to the house, he happened to look down and noticed there was another piece of that thin cloth he had found on their first night at the house when he was outside taking a piss. It was old and worn and had a smell to it. As Bobby held it up to his face, he noticed it was the smell of campfire and gun powder.

CHAPTER SIX

The following day was warm and breezy, and after Bobby went to the dump, he drove over to the Planning and Zoning Commission to pick up another copy of the building permit. While he was there, he asked Hamp if he felt like going to lunch. They met at noon at a local burger joint right off the Town Square.

After trying to figure out just how to bring the subject up about the stories Hamp had mentioned during their first meeting, Hamp saved him the trouble and brought them up himself.

Hamp simply asked, "So tell me, have you or Maureen seen or heard anything kinda weird after sundown yet?"

Bobby felt the hairs on his wrists stand up but recovered quickly and didn't know how to respond. He could have been honest and mentioned the Indian, which would have led to Hamp immediately thinking he was nuts, or he could have lied and laughed it off. Instead, he tried to reach a happy medium.

"Oh yeah, the old stories. Are you trying to find out if they are true?"

"Well, I suppose I am. You know, I grew up in Prescott and I've heard a shitload of things about those woods. I've always kinda thought they must be somewhat true, considering the history of the place. Plus, when you hear a thing or two, it's easy to forget, but when you hear considerably more, you tend to believe it. When I was a young kid, my friends and I used to dare each other to go into your woods. How's that for a head trip?"

Bobby thought before he spoke and said, "I can't deny that you've got my curiosity up at about a hundred percent. You've also gotta know that Maureen and I really want to hear some of these stories. In fact, she wanted me to see if you and . . . sorry, I've forgotten your wife's name . . ."

"Erica."

"Erica," Bobby said with a smile. "Would y'all like to come up the hill for dinner? We can grill some burgers outside over a fire. Maybe you guys can provide the entertainment, we can provide the cocktails and with a little luck, those old ghosts may show up to say hello. But, the real entertainment, of course, being those freaking stories, I keep hearing about."

"Oh, that would be great, we'd love to."

"What's your favorite poison?"

"Erica is a Bloody Mary person and I'm happy with just about anything. Just don't try to give me any beer with the word Lite in front of it," Hamp offered.

"10-4, I hear that shit."

They went on to talk about town stuff and, of course, the most popular subject of where exactly in town did Billy-Jack kick the sheriff on the right side of his face with his left foot, and where the ice cream store was located from the old 60s movie "Billy Jack" that was so popular. It was funny as they both admitted that their parents signed them up for Karate almost immediately after leaving the movie theatre. They supposed all teenagers could admit to the same. What a great movie. Both agreed.

Bobby and Hamp would not have denied, if anyone asked them, if there was a kinship between them right from the start. It was as if they had known each other their whole lives. Talk came easy and honest, and Bobby felt more comfortable talking with Hamp than anyone else he could remember in years. In fact, he had forgotten about the Indian. Almost.

CHAPTER SEVEN

It was about 7:00 PM, three days after their lunch on that Friday evening, and there was a light knock on the front door. The voice from inside the house yelled, "I hope somebody's thirsty because I don't know what the hell to do with all this Lite Beer."

There was immediate laughter as Bobby threw open the door and Hamp and Erica came inside.

"You said you were gonna cook burgers, but you never said if we should bring anything so here's a bag of buns and beans! If you can't use them tonight, I don't know, make barbeque tomorrow!" Hamp roared enthusiastically. "Oh, and I'd like you to meet my other half, Erica. She's been dying to meet you both. Spin around darlin. You know, I think she went through about five outfits before she walked out the door."

"Shut up!" Erica whispered. "Oh my god, I can't believe he said that!" She quickly composed herself. "Hi, I am so happy to meet you! Hamp's said so many great things about you—and for the record, it was three outfits, and that's what girls do!"

"Hell, if it were me, I would have gone with the five outfits. I'm not proud! And that's EXACTLY what girls do! Come on in here. Men just don't get it sometimes," Maureen said smiling, and they hugged each other as if they were old friends.

Maureen and Erica almost immediately retreated to another room. Soon there was laughing, and it was obvious that they hit it off just as quickly as their men did.

Bobby felt great love for his wife at seeing the happiness in her eyes upon their meeting. Once again, he felt as if they had found home and moving across the country was a good decision.

The meal was fantastic, and the conversation even better.

Around the fire pit, Bobby had arranged four hammocks suspended in a large circle between large pine trees, with wooden tables to hold drinks, cell phones, or whatever was needed to be easily reachable by the hammock's inhabitants. It was all about comfort and the fire was warm and cozy. Bobby also threw in one of those logs that threw out colors as it burned to add to the fire's ambiance. It was also his way of keeping their guests in a good place, so they didn't feel they needed to drive home if they were too intoxicated.

Earlier that day, Maureen had made a trip to Home Depot and bought a small, outside bar that they placed on the south end of the circle so everything they needed was close and convenient. She had also bought a Dura-Log, actually a few of them, as they didn't pop or spark like natural wood. They were both very cautious and knew of the fire hazards that existed in Prescott's dry climate, so they took every precaution necessary for a safe evening. Maureen was a born hostess, and her parties were always a great success. She was balls out intent on this one being one for the memory books.

Soon the conversation turned to stories.

Soon after, the stories turned into ghost stories.

Hamp began with the tale he had heard most often as a young boy on camping trips. He looked off into the woods as he told it, as if he were looking for someone or something to drift out and kill them all at any moment. Bobby wasn't sure if Hamp was truly a little scared or if he was just giving a good performance for the girls' sake.

As the night drew on, Erica mentioned how interested they both were in the history of Prescott and commented on the devastation that occurred in establishing territory in this region of Arizona. At that point, she looked down into her wine as if she didn't want to have any direct eye contact with anyone.

Maureen asked Hamp about the history of the Yavapai Indians and the unjust killings of the wives and children of the warriors she had heard about from some women she had spoken with in the town's library. She wanted to know if it was true, and if anything had actually happened on this particular parcel of land.

Hamp's mood seemed to turn inward, and Bobby caught it immediately. "These warriors were defending their way of life and their families and were in no way being aggressive towards the white men until they realized they had to fight or be killed," Hamp stated matter-of-factly. "They simply didn't have enough time to prepare for a battle, as history proved that the tribes were caught off guard. It was kill or be killed. Life's a bitch when you don't have any warning." Hamp looked up and stared at Bobby.

Bobby knew Hamp wanted to proceed, but he appeared as if he wasn't sure how, or if he should continue.

Bobby thought to himself, "Ok, this is what I've been waiting for. Let's do this."

Suddenly, as they all seemed to sit in silence for a moment, there was a movement of light on the south end of the circle. It caught them off guard and happened so quickly that no one had time to respond until the moment had passed.

An Indian dressed in full war paint ran toward them and stopped abruptly in the center of the circle. He stood by the fire, completely unaffected by its heat. He was, as the night before, only an apparition. He had no real physical form. Yet, that didn't matter as everyone was still scared out of their minds.

The Indian pointed at the woods. He held up a large cutting tool in his left hand that resembled a knife and a small axe in the other. He walked over towards Maureen and stopped within only a few feet from her.

She whimpered and recoiled into the fabric of the hammock as best she could.

Bobby stood and began to move in her direction, but as he did, the Indian continued to hold up the axe and glare at him as if he dared him to come any further. He stood pointing a finger at the woods with a look of lost abandonment.

Bobby yelled at the Indian, "What do you want?"

At that instant, the Indian picked up Maureen and ran into the woods. Despite having been clearly an apparition, the Indian somehow had the ability to be able to lift Maureen's weight.

Maureen screamed as she looked over the Indian's shoulder as he carried her quickly away. Everyone immediately tried to follow.

Bobby ran as fast as he could for as long as he could, but the effects of the alcohol he had been drinking and the fact that he did not have any shoes on, slowed his progress immensely.

No one had any strength or endurance compared to the Indian nor the willingness to enter the dark woods, except for

Bobby, so they watched with fear and hopelessness as Maureen was carried out of sight and into the night.

Hamp followed briefly, but he was worried about Erica and couldn't leave her behind, alone.

CHAPTER EIGHT

Bobby had been crawling, practically blind in the dark and trying desperately to find Maureen.

As he lay on a hillside, out of breath and panicking at the thought of never seeing his wife again, the Indian appeared.

Again, the Indian pointed at the hillside, and again the Indian's efforts of communication were useless.

A hint of pink touched the sky and Bobby realized that Maureen had been in the woods, alone, all night. These woods stretched forever, the ground was rutty and unstable in a lot of areas, as the terrain was hilly and there were many washes made by monsoons most common in late summer. Despite these issues, Bobby sensed that Maureen was safe. Somehow, he knew wherever she was she was alive. He didn't know how he knew, but he did, and he trusted his gut.

Hamp and Erica had phoned the police immediately. They quickly realized if they told the police how Maureen was taken away, they would be thought of as crazy. No one would believe that an apparition came and carried her away. Instead, their story was she had gone into the woods looking for wood and never returned.

A few officers had started looking for her and now that morning had arrived, they decided to head back to the station and wait out the day. If she didn't come back on her own, they would return with more men and begin a search after twenty-four hours.

Finally, Bobby wandered back to the house, and without a word, he fell on the couch and stared at Hamp. "What the fuck is going on? This is insane! I'm going back out there to look for her."

"The cops just left, but they were looking for her 'til just about sun-up. They'll be back, but they want to talk to you."

"Yeah," Bobby nodded. "I bet they fucking do."

The three of them didn't know what to say. Erica made a little breakfast, which no one ate, only picked at, and then went back into the woods to search for Maureen.

Bobby finally broke the silence that had been lingering. "I know you saw that Indian. I know you saw it and I did, too. Shit, he could have grabbed Erica."

Hamp stopped walking and turned around and met Bobby's eyes with his own. "Yes, I did. Now I have a question for you."

Bobby said nothing and let Hamp continue.

"Have you ever seen him before?"

"I have. Three times in fact. Our first night in the house I went out to take a wiz at the edge of the woods. Something brushed my arm. When I turned around there was an old thin cloth on the ground at my feet. I didn't think anything of it—I thought it came out of one of the packing boxes or something. Looking back, I had a feeling, just a strange feeling, like I wasn't alone anymore."

"Keep talkin'" Hamp said.

"Maureen and I were outside, and he walked right past us. He looked at us for a minute, turned away, and just disappeared. Maureen pretty much freaked out at first. But once we got inside, she calmed down."

Hamp shook his head, held his hands up by his ears and bent over a little feeling both amazement and shock, never realizing this could really be happening.

"The third time I was in the driveway. He walked right up to me. I asked him what he wanted. He only looked at me and pointed to the woods. I didn't feel threatened, it was as if he was trying to tell me something; I didn't tell Maureen about that. I was afraid it would really upset her. It was then I decided to get you over here and listen to your stories and try to get some more history about this place. I was hoping your stories might help me make some sense out of all this."

"So, getting Erica and I to come here was planned."

"Yep, it was." Bobby softly chuckled. "I figured it was inevitable anyway, I thought we hit it off the first time we met. I knew we'd all become friends in time. To be honest, I didn't want you to think I was completely nuts, right off the bat. Otherwise, I would have told it all to you straight."

"I thought so, too," Hamp said. "So now we've got this fucking Indian, and no Maureen. Come on, let's keep walking."

CHAPTER NINE

The sky was slowly darkening, and the air had taken on a dank, organic smell they imagined was similar to when the past battles were fought here.

Erica stayed at the house in case Maureen showed up. Neither Hamp nor Bobby wanted her traipsing through the woods.

As Maureen slowly opened her eyes after her long sleep, she realized she was lying in an indented area of dirt with pine needles underneath her. She knew she was lost, yet she was not afraid. The Indian would be back. He had not hurt her, and when he had looked at her, it was as if he wanted to tell her something. His eyes were full of a story that he had not been able to express. On some strange level, Maureen was looking forward to the Indian's return. She knew she should be scared, but instead felt compassion for him. He seemed so sad and lost. If he wanted to hurt her, he would have already done so. Instead of trying to run, she wanted to stay. The Indian needed her for some reason, and she had decided she wanted to help him. She felt that it was the right thing to do.

The sky was full dark now and there was no moon. The night was full of the sounds of crickets and small creatures scurrying along the forest floor, and the wind was blowing at a good rate. The hair on Maureen's arms stood up as the air chilled with nightfall.

As she drifted in and out of a light sleep, she knew the Indian was nearby. She could feel him. Slowly, he moved out of the shadows, and they stared at each other. He motioned for her to follow him, and she did not hesitate.

They passed a brook where he waited as she bent down and drank some water. She was dying of thirst as she had remained in her little bed of pine needles all day not wanting to risk going further into the woods. Maureen knew if anyone was looking for her, she should stay where she was.

Finally, the Indian stopped walking and pointed to a section of the forest floor. The ground looked as if it was somewhat sunken compared to the surrounding ground and Maureen thought it looked as if it could have been a grave.

Her breath caught in her throat. He wanted her to dig. She was close to tears as she thought of what she might find. If he was strong enough to carry her into the woods, why did he need her now? She pushed back years of old pine needles and brush. The ground was soft, and it wasn't difficult to scoop the dirt up with her hands and move it away.

Within minutes, her hands touched something that was not rock. She looked up at the Indian who had been standing next to her. His face was somber, and she felt herself starting to breathe in short gasps. She heard herself saying "No. No. I can't." The Indian nodded reassuringly and knelt beside her, as if trying to comfort her.

Maureen kept digging. Soon there was a small, native-American doll in her hands. She looked up at the Indian and began to weep. She finally understood why the Indian had brought her to this place and knew what lay beneath this ground.

CHAPTER TEN

Bobby and Hamp had been walking south. Finally, they saw movement in the forest and their worst fear changed to hope as they saw Maureen on the ground. They called to her, and she cried back and waved. She made no attempt to get up and run toward them, however, Bobby and Hamp picked up speed in their effort to get to her.

Upon running up to her and seeing her filthy dirty, they noticed the Indian. On the ground between them were the skeletal remains of a small child in the arms of what they knew must be the child's mother. Maureen held a small doll in her own arms and gently rocked it with great care and cried.

Bobby dropped down on his knees and wrapped Maureen in a blanket he'd brought and held her tight.

The following morning the police and investigators came for the bodies and took them to the morgue for autopsies.

It was confirmed that the two bodies were Indian and that they had been part of the massacre that took place many years ago as the town was established.

Maureen and Bobby submitted requests to the court for the little girl and her mother to remain on the property and be properly buried. This was granted, and they built a small and beautiful resting place for them, surrounded by a white picket fence and two tombstones. A bench was set up and they often placed flowers on the graves.

One year after the burial, Bobby and Maureen visited the graves. It was midnight and the moon was full. It was a beautiful walk, and the night was alive with the soothing sounds of the breeze through the pine trees and the humming of the surrounding wildlife. They placed flowers in the vases at the base of the tombstones and thought of the Indian. They had not seen him at all after his family had been found, and hoped that wherever he was, he was now comforted.

As they sat on the bench and spoke of the sad ending of this family, they saw movement in the trees. As they shifted their gaze, they saw them.

The Indian stood, no longer in war paint or holding his weapons, but instead holding his small daughter in his arms with his wife at his side.

The Indians looked at them and smiled. The woman walked towards Maureen and held out a hand in thanks. Maureen reached out to feel nothing except the comforting breeze. As she brought her hand toward her face, she looked at Bobby who had tears in his eyes. Together they realized how lucky they were to have each other, and they watched as the Indians turned and as a family, disappeared into the night.

THE END

AUTHOR'S NOTES

I believe the "Author's Notes" is the section I like best because it gives the author a chance to say things that are important to them. One being how much we appreciate all of you readers that purchase our books and, most of all enjoyed them. A thumbs up on an Amazon review would be awesome for those that feel the desire to do so, but of course, no pressure from me. However, the reviews help us struggling writers sell more books – just so you know. Then again, as the saying goes if you don't have anything good to say, don't say anything at all. I'm not sure where I heard that, probably from my mom, but it certainly tends to be fitting now. Smile.

This book was a lot of fun to write. I love ghost stories and always have. I'd like to write another volume; we'll see if I have it in me to do it again in the next year or so. I suppose it's a good time for all of us to cross our fingers and pray to whichever God you see fit.

I remember as a child begging my parents to let me stay up and watch Frankenstein with Boris Karloff. Back in those days we only had seven channels and the good movies usually were only shown once or twice a year, so when they aired it was truly a special occasion and viewers had to plan ahead so they wouldn't miss the event. One year just before the end of the movie my brother left the room and said he was going to bed. I think I was in third grade. Looking back, I remember thinking it was weird that he would want to leave just prior to the movie's end, but I was too young and dumb to question it. At the end of the flick, when bedtime was my turn, I laid in my bed scared to death with a nightlight on and my head wrapped under the blankets with only my eyes peering out waiting for the monster who lived in my closet to jump out and grab my foot. I was facing the wall and probably six or eight inches from it when I saw a clawed hand rising from under my bed. I screamed and ran downstairs crying for the comfort of my parents. My brother came running after me laughing. My parents didn't find his actions as amusing as he did, and his karma was sweet. Long story short, I've loved horror ever since. My brother – not so much.

Thanks go to my editor, Jennifer Murgia; critique readers, Samantha-Tyler Sirk, Janet M.; and my beta reader, Kellie Geiger Mora. Your creative instincts helped these stories immensely, your talents to the craft and willingness to continue to work with me have been a huge plus. My cover designer, Brad Peterson whose creativity is spot on, also needs a big shout out. His covers are always amazing, so cheers Brad!

As I sit here at my desk in my most comfortable spot realizing this book is at its completion, I think about the future and what it will bring. I hope everyone's dreams come true.

B.J. Lawyer
Humboldt, Arizona
bjlawyerbooks.com

The Author 2023
Photo by Mallory-Dalton Glenn Sirk

Printed in Great Britain
by Amazon

32817676R00175